PILGRIM'S
Journey

PILGRIM'S *Journey*

JOHN M. BREWER

PILGRIM'S JOURNEY

iUniverse books may be ordered through booksellers or by contacting:

iUniverse
1663 Liberty Drive
Bloomington, IN 47403
www.iuniverse.com
1-800-Authors (1-800-288-4677)

Because of the dynamic nature of the Internet, any web addresses or links contained in this book may have changed since publication and may no longer be valid. The views expressed in this work are solely those of the author and do not necessarily reflect the views of the publisher, and the publisher hereby disclaims any responsibility for them.

Any people depicted in stock imagery provided by Thinkstock are models, and such images are being used for illustrative purposes only.
Certain stock imagery © Thinkstock.

ISBN: 978-1-4917-4518-2 (sc)
ISBN: 978-1-4917-4517-5 (e)

Library of Congress Control Number: 2014916690

Printed in the United States of America.

iUniverse rev. date: 10/2/2014

CONTENTS

I. BRITAIN

II. BETWEEN WORLDS, 1777

III. AMERICA, 1778

IV. IN CYTHEREA, 1779

V. MASSACHUSETTS, 1797

to Mary Sue
my fellow pilgrim

I

Britain

1

A GIANT STEP, 1773

My back to Boston, I stood at the rail of the ship that was to carry me to Britain. Looking at the rail, I saw it was splintery and tarry. Despite being early in summer, the sky and sea were grey, as was my mood. If I was to be a doctor, I would become a doctor with a degree from a well-known place, not pick up the knowledge as an apprentice. To stay this side of the Atlantic risked encounters with Ann or her intended or her family. In addition, I was loath to live in a province increasingly influenced by louts and bullies and demagogues. No: best to break clear, stay away until I could return as a fully qualified practitioner.

I was standing in the bow. We were anchored by the stern, and the tide was ebbing so I was looking toward my destination, my destiny. The wind was from the land and I heard cries and bustle. The anchor was hoisted and top sails set. We began to move to Britain, to a new life, new studies. I continued to stand looking east to my future, feeling some sadness, a little fear, otherwise nothing.

Once on the ship, "on board," I saw how crowded everything was. My chest was stowed in a room which was very small but expected to hold five passengers. The room stank already though was unoccupied, the influence of the "bilge" I understood. Space was precious. Space for cargo, human or goods, was the *sine qua non* of ventures, leaving bits and scraps for crew and wandering passengers, by which I mean un-stowed passengers. On deck, I was always in someone's way, stand where I might. Then I was ordered below to get me out of the way, so the sailors could do their work unimpeded.

Below, I had a level of a stack of places to sleep upon. There were five levels and five of us. Our baggage was set wherever possible, not where it was convenient, adding to my feeling of being cargo. I climbed onto my level—I was not sure how these had been assigned—and found I could not stretch out but had to lie huddled. There was not much space between levels so I had to be careful about raising my head, or I would crack it on something. The levels were wooden, no bedding, so promised discomfort in that direction also.

None of us introduced themselves. Saving one man sitting on a chest, the rest of us crouched on our level. As I lay, I began to smell my companions, who were unwashed, even more unpleasant. The understanding that these experiences were going to continue, probably get worse, over the weeks or months of the voyage made me low. I began to try to withdraw, to think of better times and places, in other words, just about anything and anywhere else.

Ann immediately came to my mind, our happier times together, even our parting. I shook my head, hit it on something, and lay quietly hoping the pain would distract me.

I sighed, stretched cautiously on my level, my shelf, I supposed. I noted a change in the ship's pitching—deeper and slower—and rolling—less of that, thankfully—and guessed we were on our way. I sighed again. I didn't know if we would be offered something to eat or if we would want to eat it. I lay with my head on my crossed arms and tried to feign some interest in where I was going and what I was going to be doing. This was hard.

It occurred to me that it was ironic, that I should be crossing the Atlantic to the British Isles to better myself, for my father's father, my Grandfather Wyeth, had journeyed from England to Massachusetts to the same end.

I remembered my father telling me and my sisters over the dinner table, "Your Grandfather Wyeth was a common carter in Northamptonshire in England. As a young man, he found himself faced with a choice between starvation and emigration and chose the latter. Since he came from a region where the Puritan influence was still strong, he came to Massachusetts. Here he worked for others as lighterman or warehouseman until he was a hand at a farm near Dedham.

"Your Grandfather Wyeth was sober and hardworking, so he was in good repute there as elsewhere, and was able to marry the daughter of the owner of the farm. She was his only surviving child. When his father-in-law died in the scarlet fever epidemic in 1736, Grandfather Wyeth inherited the farm.

"Though he is uneducated—he can barely write his name—your Grandfather Wyeth has wit as well as application. He has prospered, partly by supplying provisions to the Massachusetts militia during our war with the Indians and French. So I, the only child to grow to manhood, had much better prospects than your Grandfather Wyeth."

"Why did you become a lawyer, Father?" I asked.

My elder sister Lizzie added, "And how did you meet Mother?"

Father replied, "Since I was far better educated and wanted a more genteel life, I apprenticed myself to a lawyer in Boston. The daughter of one of his clients, a merchant named Holmes, caught my eye."

Here he smiled at my mother, who smiled back. "We married when my term of apprenticeship was over. Then we came here to Shrewsbury in 1751. Your brother Thomas," nodding at me, "was born the next year. You and your sister Susan came later."

*   *   *   *   *

My thoughts must have wandered. I could not tell if I had been sleeping. Now I remembered something that had happened when I was very young....

I was a quiet child, shrinking from contact from strangers and seeking refuge in books. For I learned to read early, as my mother as well as my father was literate, she having attended dames school in Boston as a child.

Though I early showed signs of scholarly temperament, there were also signs of another sort. While I was usually timid and passive, I could be pushed too far. We had at one point a large tiger-striped cat, a female, and I played with the animal. Though I was as thoughtless of its comfort as most children are, I loved Scheherazade, as our father called her. [My father sometimes named our pets, and he had a somewhat freakish wit; what the animals thought of their names, I can't say.] When I was about four, she was attacked by a neighbor's dog.

The dog was tearing at the cat when I rushed at the dog, screaming and pelting it with clods and rocks (though I think now the cat must have received some share of this), and belaboring the dog with a stick. Confused at first, the dog might have finished me but its owner took it in charge. He was quite angry with me for treating his dog so, an attitude that left me speechless with rage. This to the point of tears, though I think the neighbor, a good enough man in his way, took my tears as penitence.

Scheherazade lay bleeding in the yard, her belly ripped open, but stirred at my touch. I fought down my repugnance at the sight of her internal organs. I gathered Scheherazade in my arms, and ran to the town doctor / apothecary / cow doctor. Reaching his shop, I confronted him with my burden and insisted he treat her. I think now with amazement that, though grumbling somewhat at the task, he got out his instruments and began sewing my pet back together.

He shook his head from time to time, though I do not know whether this was to discourage any hopes on my part for her recovery or whether he was wondering at his own sanity. He made me help, and I, who would not watch her deliver a litter of kittens, found myself assisting a surgery which no one then would have dared perform on a man.

At length, I took her home. I think I too had no expectation of her survival, but was merely bidden to make the patient as comfortable as possible with no hope of recovery. Yet, Scheherazade not only recovered, but produced more kittens and grew enormous. I understood even more sharply now there had been two consequences from this: I was strongly influenced by the power of the medical profession; and the cat adopted me as her protector.

She would sleep in my bed thus sharing her fleas with the bed and with me. I disliked this. Being of a nervous disposition, I found the wanderings of these creatures over-stimulating, so was compelled to bathe and change clothes more frequently than was the custom. Also, my mother, who was a meticulous housekeeper, found the fleas of our pet—for we had no other animals indoors—a trial on her temper. The cat understood and resented this, so that the cat would often hiss and spit at my mother when my mother happened by. This amused my father. Memories that alike brought a smile to my lips and tears to my eyes.

2

RETRACINGS

Inescapably my mind retraced my journey back to where my life's path turned to join Ann's, at least for a while. I saw that my restless nature lay behind everything that had happened....

Since the end of the French and Indian War, the dangers from Indian attack were much reduced in our province, and so I could range farther afield from my home. A few miles away were forests. At the edge of these were bushes, some bearing edible blackberries. I needed no urging to venture there and pick these, in season. But when I went to do this, I found the attentions of the black flies and mosquitoes so bothersome that I could make little headway in my picking. Returning to my home, I complained of this to my mother, and she made me a mask such as beekeepers use, of a sort of porous cloth, so that I could see what I was doing but the biting insects could not reach my face and neck. With some thin gloves and a basket on a lanyard hung about my neck, I was able to pick almost any quantity of berry, provided I was willing to give the matter my attention, for such work quickly became tedious.

Once, when we visited Grandfather Holmes and my mother's

brother, Uncle Thomas, in Boston, we took some of the blackberries I had picked with us.

My uncle remarked, "These would fetch sixpence a gallon, perhaps more, in Boston."

This remark remained dormant in my mind until I neared fifteen. At that time I became possessed of the notion that I would pick several gallons of blackberries and take these to Boston, about thirty-five miles away over roads which were indifferent at best, and sell the berries. That is to say, I would bring them to my Holmes relations and they would sell them, for I could not imagine having the face to actually meet strangers, argue with them and extract money for the berries. However, my head was now full of this scheme. I worked out everything I would do and began making preparations.

Father shook his head, commenting, "Thomas, I must say I think your proposal hare-brained."

Though briefly discouraged, I went ahead and agreed with our wheelwright and blacksmith to take a wheelbarrow of his manufacture to Boston to sell for not less than eight shillings, of which I was to have one, and additionally one half of the excess over eight. My mother and sisters wove baskets of a gallon capacity from local reeds; these would of course be sold with their contents. My mother and sisters would receive a penny for each of the baskets.

My task was first to pick the berries, and since I did not want to be molested by local enemies, I took to carrying a heavy stick. "For protection against animals," I told friends and neutrals. Then I spent several days picking; each day I worked from near dawn to near dark, as the bushes were less than ten miles from our village and I had to walk each way. Full of my scheme as I was, I was nearly immune to fatigue, collecting over twenty-five gallons, for the season was full upon us. Then I retired early and rose before midnight. Having stacked the harvest in the barrow and secured the baskets with cord before retiring, I emerged into the cool night and set out, pushing the barrow. My father watched me go.

After the heat of the day, the night air was delicious. The moon was full—I had planned for this—and my path seemed magical, the earth now a thing of enchantment. Or so it looked at first: the jolting of the barrow, a clumsy thing, and the increasingly burdensome weight on my wrists quickly diminished the romance of the venture. As time passed, my back and arms became painful; not having participated much in the usual boyhood exercises (saving walking and running), my strength was little enough to begin with and vanished utterly before I had trod a mile. My hands had no grasp at all, so I took some extra cord—for I had brought some in case it should be needed—and tied the two ends to the handles, and passed the loop over my head and onto my shoulders. Thereby I was able to reduce the strain on my arms.

I proceeded, using my hands to steer the barrow. This was necessary, the surface of the road being very uneven. As the hours passed, the road gradually became better, and as I approached Boston, I even picked up some speed. By the time it was full dawn, I was well toward my goal, but I was growing exhausted. Yet I would not stop, still less turn back, and as the sun rose higher in my face I saw more and more people, all it seems looking curiously at me. By noon I had reached the hills above Boston. There I rested for a time beside the road, watching passersby watching me. Two women ventured to buy a gallon apiece, and this cheered me enough to finish my journey by four in the afternoon. I had rolled a heavy and heavily-laden (for me) barrow thirty-five miles in seventeen hours.

Grandfather Holmes was astonished at my appearance, but consented readily enough to take my wares, including the barrow, for the price I had expected. Indeed, I got rather more for the berries than I had expected, near twenty shillings, though my grandfather could give me only a note for the bulk of the money. Still, I now had money in my pocket that I had earned, and in consequence was filled with the most extraordinary feeling of independence and freedom.

My Holmes relations had me to dinner with them, and Grandfather Holmes asked me, "What are your plans, Thomas?"

"I am thinking of becoming a surveyor."

My uncle however discountenanced this, "In our province, the office of Surveyor is so very lucrative that it is controlled by the Governor and his people, so that of necessity you would be involved if only indirectly in corruption and knavery."

This impressed me.

I insisted on returning that evening, even though I was tired, essentially because I had said that I would, so compounded a foolish statement with a foolish act. But my grandfather gave me a letter for my mother, and two of their neighbors also had letters for other people in our village. I was given a penny apiece for their delivery, and set out.

Being young, I had recovered somewhat from my earlier fatigues, but these returned in strength, even though I was no longer burdened. The walk back seemed very long. Even so, I returned before dawn the next day, a Sunday. Thus, I missed church, but I delivered the two letters I had been paid to do.

The next two days were times of agony; for I could hardly move, so sore was my entire body, especially my neck rubbed raw by the cord. However, I began picking more berries. This time I would not have a barrow, but proposed carrying them in two bundles, balanced across my shoulders on a yoke, freeing a hand to carry a stick to ward off dogs. I returned again the following week and I also carried letters and two small packages for various people in Boston. Learning from my first journey, I left earlier and actually made better time, reaching my grandfather's store just after noon. The deliveries of the letters took the rest of the afternoon, for the recipients were scattered all across the town, which in addition was unfamiliar to me. I was given a package to deliver on my return journey.

Thus, what began from restlessness became a small enterprise. Since I was conscientious and not prone to linger in taverns, I became the postal service for my village and indeed the farms and inns along the road to Boston. For the man who had performed this task was perhaps excessively convivial, and prone to take more time for his deliveries, despite having a horse. And while I feared his resentment for my encroachment on his livelihood, he appeared to bear me no ill will but shifted his routes to the northwards where there chanced to be more taverns. Consequently, I traveled to and from Boston at least once a week, even when not conveying berries. When I had only enough berries to fill a basket, I could make most of the entire trip in daylight in summer.

In this way, I became more aware of political developments: our Province or Colony, like the others, was considered to exist for the benefit of England, or rather the merchants of that country. So the laws they imposed on us resulted in a steady drain of specie from the Colonies, to the point where a serious shortage of coin interfered with all our commerce. As I charged for my services, I found that people could not pay in coin, but rather in kind. I was obliged to accept produce and firewood. Once, in Boston, a woman of suspicious character offered to pay for my service with one of her own, and I was both shocked and tempted, but she looked somewhat old, and I was afraid.

I remember my father remarking, "Could the image of King George be impressed on a turnip, the Colonies' troubles would be over."

Father did not approve of my activities in terms of a career. Still, I think he was pleased I was doing something. He permitted me to keep my gains, though in truth I suspected what I received for my services was much reduced by the wear on my boots, for example, whose cost he bore. In a sense it might have been more rational for me to have stayed at home, and he to have given me the monies produced by my exertions. But I think he was also pleased by my determination, for he uttered not a word when I would make these journeys in foul weather. Indeed I once nearly froze to death in a sleet storm that winter, but I would not give up my excursions, for the feeling of achievement and independence I prized more than life itself. Or so I fancied at the time.

My activities brought me a knowledge of Boston, and while I was at first timid of the rough-looking men about the docks, I soon found I had nothing to fear. Though I was warned to stay clear of the Royal Navy for they had a name for impressment, I had no trouble. I think this was partly because I took care not to linger about the harbor area, and partly because my travels had strengthened and enlarged me somewhat, so that I no longer appeared so spindly, even while I was growing tall.

My deliveries one day took me to the house of a rich merchant of Boston, a Mr. Crewe. I remember well how this house, all of brick, impressed me. When I knocked, a Negro servant answered. I was to deliver the letter to Mr. Crewe's own hands. This was a frequent injunction and a nuisance since I was rather dusty. However, the gentleman himself, a tall and important-looking man in his prime, came out.

I gave him the letter and then a small blonde girl wearing a blue gown came up the steps and walked into the house, followed by a servant woman. I saw a perfect profile, a glance toward me and my clothes, and I was suddenly overwhelmed by a consciousness of dirt, sweat and insignificance. This was not the intent of these people, I am sure. Mr. Crewe thanked me affably, and paid me tuppence because often postage was paid for by the recipient, another nuisance. Then he went inside. I walked away, despising myself, this from just a glimpse. Since I was too embarrassed to ask who this creature was—I assumed she was his daughter, but for all I knew she could have been anything—I nursed my feelings in silence. Her image became my companion, in my mind my confidante, my Muse.

My schooling had come to an end, as I had exhausted the academic resources of Shrewsbury. Since my delivery service took at first only two or three days a week, I began to frequent the apothecary's shop. I was fascinated by the jars of drugs and chemicals, the counter where he made up his potions and pills, and mostly the air, not of knowledge (for even then I thought of him as an ignorant man), but of discovery of mysteries to explore.

I am still not sure how he regarded me, for then as now the normal relation between such a man and a youth was master and apprentice. I gradually began assisting him about his shop, reading the few books he possessed (which I am not sure he had read), and following him on some of his errands. He served us all as animal doctor, having successfully treated Scheherazade. Otherwise his most successful work was in assisting at deliveries of cattle and horses. Here I was forced to assist him. I had no desire of such labour, so to speak, indeed regarded the entire matter with revulsion.

However, I was constrained to wash well my hands and arms—he insisted on this—and reach inside the birth organs of these animals at times to turn or push or pull the baby calves or horses so they would emerge unharmed. Sometimes I had to help restrain the mothers. This latter task often required more strength than I could supply, in which case I would at his direction do the turning, pushing or pulling. With time I became hardened by repetition to such scenes and activities, and on the way home he would sometimes tell me of other cases he had attended. This was all he ever talked about, never about himself, and little enough ever. Despite my dislike of such tasks and my inexperience, I think I was a help to him for he had no proper apprentice.

My carrying trade kept expanding to the point where I was hard pressed to maintain it as I wished, and at this point I found that I, not yet seventeen, had an apprentice. This was Daniel Mechin, a youth of perhaps fourteen, large for his age, whom I had known in school. When he began accompanying me on my routes, I fancied he was a spy or decoy for some of my enemies at school, set to learn my routine. Hence I took care to carry not only a heavy stick but also insinuated I had a pistol, for sometimes I carried small sums of money on direction. However I misjudged him. Though I found it hard to imagine myself having authority over anyone near my age who had known me at school, he accepted my decisions without comment, even when they chanced to be wrong, and came to act first as assistant then as deputy and finally as partner.

In person he was notably silent even in that region of succinctness. He rarely said anything even (or perhaps especially) when in our kitchen, where my family made him welcome. My elder sister Lizzie would chatter at him throughout his visits while my youngest sister sat quietly, perhaps stirring something or more often merely listening. I fancied some interest between Lizzie and him. Since I had long since found his company very tolerable, saving his lack of conversation, I did not discourage this, nor did my parents, as his family were respectable people, his father a carpenter and joiner of some skill. Why Daniel did not follow his father's trade was something of a mystery to me. I now think that, like me, he was merely restless and fancied life out of doors.

Returning from one of my journeys, I found we had had a great loss in our household: our cat Scheherazade had finally died, being found lying under a bush that was her favourite lurking place, but not moving. This was the occasion for grief, perhaps surprising for she was but a dumb creature, yet a dear one. My older sister was especially distressed, so that Daniel put his arm about her shoulders, which seemed to comfort her.

We had given away nearly all of Scheherazade's kittens, for we children were far too soft-hearted to permit their drowning. We had kept only one, a grey striped tabby cat, a male. He was a most friendly creature, especially to me, who had played with him the most. So Tabby, as we called him, now slept with me. My sisters slept together, and I judged this was too crowded a situation for Tabby.

Daniel's and my activities took us about the countryside in all weathers. I reserved the Boston route to myself, largely in attempts to see the blonde girl who had seized so much of my imagination. By indirection, or so I fancied, I discovered that her name was Ann, that her father was a wealthy man, not a merchant, but whose wealth was in land in and about the City. In fact Grandfather Holmes was his tenant, and I exercised my subtlest wiles to get to take my grandfather's rent to Mr. Crewe, to no avail. She had a younger brother and was herself perhaps two or three years younger than I. The family members were all well spoken of.

Though I naturally managed to pass their house at least once on every visit, I am sure to the complete understanding and probably amusement of the entire area, I never saw her save once. She was attended by several intolerably handsome and fashionable young men as she walked across the street fifty yards or so ahead of me. I was again visited by both ecstasy at seeing her—for she was undoubtedly a very pretty girl—and despair. For how could I compete with or even be admitted to the company of the cream of young Boston?

Indeed, on my peregrinations I found this increasingly on my mind. For what with my reading of cheap books that I purchased in Boston and my delivery business, I was tolerably occupied. Still of necessity I was dusty, often sweaty. Though partly from my attachment to Miss Crewe I kept myself cleaner than most of the citizenry of my province, I could not hope for her, continuing as I was. Setting aside discoveries of buried treasure, Spanish or Indian, or impossible rescues, which consumed a great deal of my conscious thought, I had as much chance of her as of inheriting the moon.

Or so I imagined at the time. This despite the fact that my enterprise was such that had I continued in my course, even venturing into my Grandfather Wyeth's former profession, I dare say I would probably have prospered exceedingly. I could have expanded and hired deliverymen and organized a service over the province, perhaps beyond, and finished my days as a wealthy man of business in Boston, which would have been irony indeed.

Yet though I welcomed the solitude and the opportunity— indeed, necessity—for exertion, I never took any deep interest in what I was doing, but continued in it for the opportunities it afforded for absence of mind, as it were. This sometimes was a trial to me, for I would pass the place I was to attend and have to retrace my steps, so began my habit of using a notebook for writing my errands down to reduce these mistakes. It was also helpful when passing Miss Crewe's house, for I could appear busy and portentous, though I dare not imagine how I actually appeared.

So, turning these matters over and over as I approached eighteen, striding across much of east-central Massachusetts, I finally cleared my thoughts with a resolve: I would attend Harvard College. I hoped this would simultaneously make me a gentleman—though what I would do for a profession still escaped me—, bring me closer to Ann both physically and socially, and round out my education. When I came to this conclusion and saw what I had to do, I began to think of how I would achieve my aim.

3

DANCING STEPS

———◆———

One difficulty might be called political: I had seen men being beaten and abused by the mob in Boston, and while I might be partial to the cause, the conduct of these men seemed too close to bullying and abuse to keep my approval. Indeed on one occasion I was approached by a group of these worthies, and questioned and threatened and had only managed to escape worse by telling them I was carrying communications for Mr. John Hancock, a well known leader of the so called patriot party, and required their names, so that he could express his displeasure at their conduct.

This was not true at the time, though I had carried letters to and from him in the past, but they were taken sufficiently aback to allow me to proceed (though without giving their names), and I went directly to Mr. Hancock's home. He was kind enough to admit me, and after hearing my story and asking me who my father was, readily said that he would see I was not molested again. Nor was I, but though his kindness effaced some of the insult I felt, it did not do so entirely. I noted that he seemed to know my father, and I recalled that some of the letters I carried were between them.

It was at this time also that troops from Britain, perhaps a thousand men, were sent to Boston, supposedly to overawe the people and legislature. However, these soldiers were apparently without permission to take any steps to that end beyond merely existing in the town. Since the soldiers were not permitted to be other than impotent, the opinion of the Province and particularly the town ran very hot, and the officers and men were subjected to constant provocation and abuse. Though I was warned to have no contact with them by Uncle and Grandfather Holmes (and did not), I felt considerable sympathy for them, as suffering under orders, which I thought they did with great constancy. Then the soldiers were attacked by the mob and, evidently through confusion, fired on the mob. I was disgusted by the exaggerations and outright lies spread by the patriot party about this and other matters.

The immediate problem was not money. In the course of these three years I had accumulated above 50 pounds lawful money; that is about £35 sterling. I had not enquired of the expenses of attending, but hoped this would see me through two or three years. This money was the residue after deductions for expenses, viz, boots, the baskets my mother and sisters wove, etc. My father had insisted on these payments being made, and while I readily admitted their justice in the abstract, I relinquished the monies somewhat reluctantly.

No: the difficulty was in convincing my father of the rationality of my course; for I was conscious by now of the unease of mind my conduct had given him, and I regretted this. I realized how this new change of course would affect him, yet I had some merit to my arguments and broached them to him when I returned.

My main point was that I was interested in natural philosophy and scholarly pursuits and hence, lacking a private fortune or a patron, must pursue my education.

My father asked, "To what end should these studies lead you?"

I said, "I might become an instructor, preferably in a college or academy, but I realize such positions are few."

"What about your delivery service? With application you might make a fair living at this."

"With political matters as they are in our Province and to

similar extents in the other Colonies as well, I am entrusted with the delivery of matters of great moment and confidentiality. With the rising antagonism between those who take the part of the Province and those who are for the prerogatives of the Crown, I must become an agent or spy of one and become suspected of both, and have no desire to find myself in such a position."

My father asked me, "How do you feel on this matter?"

"I am torn between both sides, and think there is right and wrong on both, and I simply do not want to be forced to choose a faction to support, for either one would demand a loyalty and adherence I cannot provide. Daniel could take over the whole of the business, so that no one would be inconvenienced, and I imagine that Daniel is a good deal better disposed to the Provincial cause so could work with a clear conscience."

I think Father was pained yet pleased at my frankness. My arguments had some merit, save withholding romantic motives, for everything I had said truly represented my thoughts.

So he said, "I will consult with your mother then talk with you again."

He did so immediately afterward, while I was off to Boston again, this time with another barrow and some eggs as well as the usual letters and packages. For good measure, I crossed the Charles River by the ferry and walked to Cambridge to see the school or seminary as some called it. I later learned the revenues from the ferry went to the college.

I called on the President, Rev. Locke, and after stating my hopes, inquired about fees and admission requirements. He struck me as a rather vague man. He inquired about my studies and asked me some questions about my Latin, which I fear did not impress him. Still, he asked for a letter of recommendation from my teacher in my village and informed me of the costs of tuition and of boarding at the college. I gathered that I would be able to afford two years or rather more. I wrote these particulars down, thanked him and returned home, stopping for my deliveries on the way.

My parents were disposed to permit me this course, though my mother wondered, "Would you not want to apprentice yourself to someone, perhaps the town's apothecary?"

I said, "I feel apprenticeship would probably be as expensive and that I doubt I would learn very much more than I have. While I am not completely averse to medicine, for example, merely being able to practice is not enough: I wish to practice well whatever I do and so want the best instruction available."

At this, Mother said, "I will have some decent clothes ready for you when you matriculate in September."

And that was that, for the teacher readily wrote the required recommendation, and of course I delivered this myself, feeling the novelty of at last carrying letters of my own. A few weeks later, Rev. Locke informed me I could indeed begin my studies as I had hoped.

I found the summer passed very slowly, for I was trying to gain extra money for my education, but at the same time found my duties had lost their savour. The long hours on the road seemed for the first time merely dusty and tedious. So when I reached the college that September, I was heartily ready for the change in occupation as well as the translation closer to the object of many of my thoughts.

4

LEARNING STEPS

◆

I was lodged in the Hollis Hall, the newer of the student residences; some fifty or sixty other freshmen—as we were called—entered with me, many somewhat younger and yet I feared better prepared. We attended a different Tutor the first four days of the week, one instructing us as a class in Latin, another in Greek, a third in Natural Philosophy and Mathematics, and a fourth in Logic, Metaphysics and Ethics. Friday and Saturday, the Tutor in Greek Mr. Ralph instructed us in English Composition and Rhetoric. In addition, we attended lectures, of Mr. Sewell in Greek and Hebrew, Rev. Wigglesworth in Divinity and Ethics, and Mr. Winthrop in Natural Philosophy and Ethics. We were also obliged to attend services Sundays in the First Congregational Church in Cambridge, though some of the students were not of that sect. Indeed, we were charged nine pence a quarter by the college to the support of the ministry there, and seated in the front of the gallery.

Although overwhelmed by the amount and nature of the work required at first, I was able after two months or so to visit my relatives in Boston. I was now reasonably kempt and dressed, but I did not

19

see her. And this pattern continued until we recessed in December, and I had to return home.

I had enjoyed my studies and felt I was making some headway, so had not been troubled by homesickness, as I had feared I might be. My only grievances were, first, that as a freshman I was obliged to run any and every errand desired by the members of the more advanced classes, and while I did not necessarily object to the activity, being occasionally somewhat restless, I did object to the compulsion. In fact in former days, freshmen were often beaten, and subjected to divers indignities, by upperclassmen, merely on account of their status, which of course they could not help, being there precisely to shed it.

Secondly, the amount and quality of the provisions in the Commons were alike insufficient. These deficiencies were generally resented, though not to the extent of former years when actual riots of the students broke out. This was not to say I was a gourmet or unreasonable. At home I had never gone to bed hungry save as punishment, unlike here at the college. Our Commons fare was rather plain involving beans and cabbage a great deal, though my mother prepared these extremely well, and I did miss the food she served. Since our monies for board went to the Steward, it was widely believed that whatever did not appear on our tables would, in different form, do so in his pockets. Consequently there was much discontent on this score.

Still, all in all, I returned home rather pleased with my lot. At home I related my adventures to my family and to Daniel who came over, and we discussed the business. I noted he had made changes and engaged a deputy himself, John Fielding by name, but held my peace, for all was in his hands now. I visited friends, some now married and others with trades, and exchanged news, for all wanted to hear what was happening in Boston.

I ate hugely, I thought, yet my mother complained my appetite seemed gone. She asked was I ill and what were they feeding me at college and said she would make a few things to take back when I returned, which pleased me. I did some reading, less than I had planned, and got my elder sister to teach me something of dancing.

I knew nothing of this art being born clumsy but wanted to be able to perhaps partner Miss Crewe creditably. Daniel accompanied us in this, for Lizzie claimed four were needed for the figure, so he squired Susan. I felt awkward at this, as I did not want to deprive him of the pleasure of dancing with Lizzie. Yet all went well. Though at times I moved badly, I felt that with practice I might do better. My vacation passed and I returned in January.

Some of my colleagues had become friends, and I was invited to the house of one of them in Boston in early February. This was at the home of David Prescott, whose family was influential in Boston and in the Province. We shared a table in Commons, and had waxed somewhat over-inventive concerning the origins of some of the victuals, earning a reprimand and a fine of one shilling sixpence apiece for "tumultuous behavior." This cast me down somewhat and irritated me at the same time. I think David wanted to cheer me. At any event, I met a number of people there, among them Ann Crewe.

As my mind remained somewhat occupied by our reprimand, I was less apprehensive on encountering Society than I might otherwise have been, so entered boldly but also rather sullenly. The introductions took place and of course every other name forthwith fled from my head on encountering the image of earthly grace full face for the first time. To me she was astonishingly pretty, with eyes the clearest, deepest blue I had ever seen, face and figure perfectly formed. She gravely acknowledged my bow and totally destroyed any chance of rational thought or speech.

Yet when I found myself seated next to her, and the conversation being turned (by David, for I could not utter a word) to our disgrace, he applied to me for an account. I told the story, as I am occasionally able to do with some wit exaggerating my own behavior and the rigors of our captivity at college, and was enchanted to hear Ann laugh. Later, tea was served. I had not tasted this beverage before. At home we drank only mint tea.

Ann and I drew into conversation. She asked, "Do you think the rules of the college iniquitous?"

I replied rather loftily, "All rules, especially those externally imposed, are bound to be so regarded. Still I cannot deny that in

21

the main they are necessary for the students being young and full of enthusiasm and free for the first time from parental supervision are bound to act in a heedless fashion on occasion, and cannot reasonably complain in my own case."

To which she observed, "You seem aggrieved on the subject."

I replied, "I did not say I do not complain, but merely that I do not *reasonably* complain."

She laughed again at this. Some of the others applied to her for a performance on the pianoforte. She complied, playing one or two pieces, and then playing while she sang.

I had no acquaintance with either art before, for the singing in the two churches I had attended could hardly be considered in such terms. Of course I was in love with her as well, so I will always hold her voice as the standard of perfection. I do not know whether she could have sung on the stage, whether she could have produced the volume of sound requisite. But in that parlor with its wainscoted walls and dark heavy furniture, I was completely enchanted and marveled at her genius.

David and I had to return by ten and we walked back to Cambridge. At length I forced myself to comment on Miss Crewe's performance.

My friend, who of course had some acquaintance with her, said, "She is indeed reckoned a great proficient."

I commented, "I think—though I admit I am little capable of such judgments—that she could make a living at music."

This was perhaps something of a *faux pas* on my part, but David merely replied, "Her fortune is such that she need not think of it. She is a very serious, religious girl, and I was quite surprised to hear her laugh, not once but twice, at your discourse. I had never known her to do that in my recollection."

I asked—for of course I feared him as a rival—"Is your acquaintance with her extensive?"

"I have known her casually many years, since we were children."

This of course made further conversation on the subject impossible, for loving her myself I could not imaging anyone else not doing so. I feared I might lose his friendship, but comforted myself with the recollection that he had not seemed to seek her company, or she his. So we talked then on more indifferent subjects until we returned.

The weeks passed, and I made good progress with my Latin and was not totally ashamed of my efforts with Greek; Logic and Metaphysics inspired me with little other than a desire to be elsewhere, commenting to David and some others of our friends that if the classes in that subject were imposed on the entire Kingdom, the British navy could forego impressment. Still I was able to avoid disgrace there also. [The major effect of those exercises was to inspire a distrust of overly great facility in argument, the more so as I lacked such abilities.] My compositions in English I found were wonderfully strengthened by Latin, and I won some praise for these.

However, my favourite subject was Natural Philosophy and Mathematics, and here my curiosity was worked upon powerfully. While I was not at the head of my class, I was very near. We studied both plane and spherical trigonometry, some of which I had taught myself years before, and Pneumatics, Optics, Statics and Mechanics. Though I would occasionally fail of comprehension of some point, be balked, fret, eventually I would win through, and by application gained a fairly complete knowledge of the subjects.

At mealtimes, my friends and I would talk about various subjects, usually in a humorous vein, so that conversations at our table often became uproarious. I and some others were again fined, and it could have been worse, for we were mocking some of the customs of the college, such as the seating of the students in class in order of their fathers' position in the Province (which indeed was ended the next year). Also the wooden rooster on the top of the steeple of the First Congregational Church drew our fire, so to speak. Sometimes we would go out into Cambridge, laughing and talking, wonderfully uplifted by a feeling of freedom and fellowship such as I had never known, nor perhaps would again.

With some others of my class (for the regulations of the college acted powerfully to confine our acquaintance to those of similar matriculation), I went to small parties again in Boston, and again sometimes met Ann. I was generally able to speak to her, and it seemed for increasing duration. I lost some of my awe of her and my awkwardness, for she was a sweet, gentle girl and put me at my ease somewhat (for which I loved her the more, if that were possible). We talked of many things: ourselves, and politics and religion.

In our conversations, Ann suggested I become a doctor. I had of course considered this vocation. I had not been attracted by the profession, however. The sight of blood was still quite repugnant to me. My interests in natural philosophy were tending more toward chemistry and those aspects dealing with living creatures and less toward those sciences favouring astronomy, which Mr. Winthrop himself emphasized. To this inclination however slight was added a most powerful one, when directed by Miss Crewe. Then too, the respectability of the profession would aid me in my suit, or so I imagined, and more subtly, so would the world's opinion aid in increasing my self-esteem towards the same end.

Ann had heard of the new medical school in Philadelphia. [The one in New York was not known to her.] She urged me to write to the leading men in that school, Drs. Morgan and Shippen, Jr. I carefully drafted two letters to those gentlemen, briefly setting forth my education and interests and asking what was the course of study, what were the fees, and what did they think was the best preparation for the practice of medicine. This was quite important to me; for having made this decision, I wanted the best possible education.

These being sent, I resumed both my studies and my courtship; my thoughts being so inclined to the latter that I often wondered how I could possibly have any success at the former. Still, I achieved tolerable success academically and some progress romantically, for I was now allowed as a visitor to her home, and as an occasional escort here and there.

It is often said, and truly, that the best cure for infatuations of this sort is not separation of the parties, but rather increasing their proximity, meaning that young people often fall in love, not with human beings, but with images and notions. Being forced to acknowledge the reality of the object of their obsession, they become wearied and disgusted by it.

This was the reverse of my case, for the better acquainted with

Ann I became the more I admired, esteemed and loved her. Though then only perhaps seventeen or so, she was clearly a woman – not a girl – of character and intellect. She was strongly influenced by the writings of Rev. Edwards of our Province, and could give a very exact and detailed account of his reasoning, as I discovered when influenced by her, I read some of them myself. The bleak pessimism of his writings well matched our New England landscape, and evidently struck some deep vein of character in her.

I remember her commenting on the necessity of submission to God's will, and this made me uneasy for some reason. We debated this over most of an afternoon walk.

I maintained, "God's will is often difficult to ascertain, so free will becomes a necessity in human conduct. In acting as a physician, I would be acting counter to this philosophy."

Ann smiled at this and touched my sleeve with her hand, an affectionate gesture and the first contact between us. This greatly moved and pleased me.

We debated this—no one could argue with so sweet a creature—and I forgot what conclusion we reached, for my memory is of the sunlight in her hair and the sparkle of her eyes.

Her interests were not exclusively religious, for she managed to remain *au courant* with political news in all the Colonies as well as Europe. She was also very interested in natural philosophy in all its branches. In fact, I think my learning at Harvard would have been far less complete if I had not had to retail everything I heard in my classes to her and to withstand her gentle interrogation as to its meaning and significance and how it was related to some other things I had told her or she had heard somewhere. I jested with her, saying I should charge her tuition for all the benefits of my tutoring, save that I believed the benefits were more accruing to me, at which she laughed.

Of course I was not her only suitor. At times it seemed as if half the young men in the Province, or at least the half that was richer, better dressed, with more elegant manners and sharper wits, were her infatuated slaves; so that I often despaired of ever succeeding with her. Still, she seemed to favour me, God knows why, and I marveled at this and perhaps will always do so.

The year, my first at Harvard, came to an end, with the usual rowdiness at Commencement. My friends and I were not hostile to rowdiness, provided it was of our own making. So for this reason we disapproved of the spectacle the senior sophisters were making, as the rest of us were kept hard at our studies. However, after my last class, I packed my books and clothes and repaired with the help of a hired handbarrow to my Grandfather and Uncle Holmes, for I was to spend the summer working as a clerk in their counting house.

That evening, I had the joy and honour of attending a party at Miss Crewe's, on the occasion of her birthday, at which she played and sang as before.

However, I was cast into despair anew; for war with Spain being threatened, His Majesty's troops and officers were again in high favour with the Province (and it was much the same, so Ann and others informed me, throughout the Colonies). For this reason the company included a pair of officers of the 14th Foot, of crushing style and manners, very handsome, one of whom sang with a fine tenor voice.

He and Ann sang duets, and my desire to be a physician was shaken somewhat. I was torn between jealousy and the charm of the music, but better feelings permitted me to applaud them as heartily as any. These better feelings were again dashed when I gathered from some of the conversation that officers of His Majesty's armed forces were generally welcome there, for Mr. Crewe was known as a King's man. So from having the Province in competition with my suit, I now had Great Britain as well. Still, Ann made some effort at drawing me into the conversation, at which I was not particularly successful, as I am awkward in large gatherings.

In the week that followed this, I discovered that my success at mathematics in college did not reach to the counting house. Though rapid, my calculations were sometimes in error, and this amused my relations and shamed me, and I had to devote more attention to my duties.

About midsummer, I received a reply to my inquiries about a medical education from Dr. Shippen, Jr. [Dr. Morgan never replied.] On reading his letter, I realized I was asking for the time and attention of very busy and important men, because Dr. Shippen Jr. answered my questions very fully and fairly, even the foolish ones. The course of study was for two years, and applicants had to have some knowledge of Latin, mathematics and Natural Philosophy, which I judged myself to have. To attend lectures, we had to buy tickets of admission much as in some performances on the stage, and the price would consume perhaps fifty pounds, lawful money, at the outside. However, at the end of this time if we satisfied our examiners, we would receive only a Bachelor of Medicine degree. For a Doctorate of Medicine, we had to spend three years in apprenticeship to some physician then return and write a thesis.

Dr. Shippen, Jr. went on to say that he himself had received his degree at the University of Edinburgh, which he praised highly. This was for three years, and living abroad would be more expensive, but while a thesis would have to be written, there was only a requirement for proficiency in Latin for admission. He added that the lectures were in English and one received an M.D. degree. He said that he knew little about the program in New York, that Oxford and Cambridge were both enormously expensive—one hundred pounds to graduate! In his judgment, the education was inferior to that provided by Edinburgh. He thought little of the medical school in Paris, but noted that the one in Leyden was still of great repute. He concluded that I would be welcomed in Philadelphia, but wished me good fortune however I chose.

This gave me much to think about. The education in Philadelphia seemed incomplete, essentially designed to polish and make uniform the education of medical apprentices. I had no wish to be an apprentice, and the time seemed very long. For I not only did not wish to be burdened with another man's ignorance and errors—and I thought of our apothecary—but, like most young men, I put a high value on the theoretical training I would obtain in a regular school. Then, too, the greater prestige of the M.D. degree—here I thought of Ann—appealed strongly to me, as well as the shorter time spent, and on the whole I favoured the idea of Edinburgh. Oxford would have been far more interesting for the prestige, had Dr. Shippen Jr.'s report been otherwise. So, for reasons both foolish and ephemeral,

I took the opportunity of a slack time at my grandfather's store to return to my home and broach this latest project to my father.

He and my mother heard me out quietly and my father read my letter then asked me, "Would you not simply become an apprentice to someone in Boston such as Dr. Warren?"

"No, I want a better education than any one man could give." This indeed was rational, though I did not mention the romantic reasons.

Here, however, my mother threw me into the greatest confusion by asking, "How does Miss Crewe feel about this?"

Eventually I got out, "I have not shown her the letter, but she thinks I should study medicine. But," I went on hastily, "it fits so well with my tastes and such talents as I possess" (I did not then recall my horror of blood and such things) "that I feel it is the best choice. I think I have not the force of character to be a schoolmaster, and have not the fortune to be a philosopher."

My father pointed out, "Fortune is indeed the problem. How much would such a stay abroad cost?"

"I simply do not know. I will be returning to Harvard in the fall anyway, as the year is too far advanced to think of venturing abroad now, and I do not feel my education sufficient to commence these studies anyway."

My parents acceded to this with clear relief.

Later Father got me alone and said, in a surprisingly gentle fashion, "You should not place your hopes too strongly on Miss Crewe, for her family is not merely wealthy but of high Tory persuasion. While such matters as marriage are not treated as rigidly as in England, still her father will certainly attempt to arrange a union with a family of like circumstances and opinions."

This, of course, I knew, but hearing it from so astute a man as my father depressed me.

He asked, "Is this latest bee in your bonnet owing to intellectual or to social aspiring?"

"No doubt it is a mixture. Is it wrong to aspire so?"

"The aspirations should be capable of attainment. I do not object to your becoming a physician, but wonder if you would be persevering enough to complete the study, especially if you should be disappointed in Miss Crewe."

I replied, "I think I have the intellectual capacity for the work and desire to better myself."

"Are you ashamed of your origins?"

I thought about this, about how to phrase my answer, for of course I was, being young and sensitive to the world's opinion—or at least such of it as I had met at school.

Eventually I said, "I feel that my deportment and clothes and manners lack polish. But I could hardly hope for a better family to spring from."

"Does Miss Crewe look down at any of those things?"

I replied, somewhat indignantly, "Certainly not, but her family and some of her acquaintances did, and I would not shame her."

"Your clothes could be bettered by purchase. Your manners and deportment are perfectly adequate. Emulation of fops and so called gentlemen is entirely foolish, and a pursuit of vainglory. There are some things not worth emulating. Your faults lie mostly in your youth and inexperience and will pass with time and judgment, but you should give the matter of apprenticeship another thought, for I doubt I could raise more than £100 toward an education abroad, and this would rob your sisters of their portions."

This made me conscious of my selfishness toward my family, "I beg your pardon, Father."

Still part of me clung to the notion of Edinburgh and a larger part to the image of Ann. I added, "I will try to be a credit to you whatever I do."

So the conversation ended amicably.

As I returned to Boston, I thought about my conduct and was little satisfied. However as I approached the town, my family's influence grew weaker and that of my new life, or what I hoped it would be, correspondingly waxed. I was oddly both comforted and embarrassed by the knowledge that my feelings, that I had imagined such a secret, were apparently universally known. I told myself, that whatever career I chose, that of spy should be avoided.

I returned to my accounts, and on seeing Ann again the next

week showed her the letter. She read it, and asked, "What will you do, Thomas?"

"I prefer to attend the school at Edinburgh, but doubt I can afford it, and will continue at Harvard for the moment."

She pointed out, "A Bachelor of Medicine degree would enable you to practice."

"I could practice as a physician now if I chose to represent myself as such, at least in smaller communities. However I want to practice well—or as well as I can, and if Edinburgh is the best place to go, why go I will somehow."

And on this airy and confident note, our conversation turned to other matters.

Some few weeks later as I was readying myself to return to Harvard, I visited Ann's home and met another officer. I thought this man was from the 64th Foot, a youngish fellow of obviously limited gifts as far as conversation went, yet he managed to convey great style and great knowledge of the world. I was impressed enough by this to ask him how much it would cost to live abroad, adding that I hoped to complete my studies there.

He swelled, sneered, and condescended to opine that 300 guineas per annum was the minimum a gentleman (here he stressed the word) would require.

I perceived he was speaking of London, and though appalled by such a sum and nettled by his manners, I asked about costs in Edinburgh.

This fop replied, "As the Scots are savages and barbarians and live on a handful of oatmeal a day, existence is no doubt cheaper, but" (with a smirk) "no gentleman could endure such conditions, though you would no doubt find it a great improvement."

I stood there, hearing this, not knowing what to do, my mouth hanging open as it does on such occasions, when Ann appeared. She had apparently heard the conversation, and I was even more taken aback at her appearance, for her face was flushed and her eyes flashed. In all the time I had known her, I had never seen her as other than calm and self-possessed. She informed the fellow in a voice of Arctic tone, "My home is reserved to the company of gentlemen, and as gentlemen do not answer civil questions with puerile insults, would you kindly take yourself off?"

Here I had to give the fellow credit: if Ann had spoken to me thus, I would have dissolved in a puddle on the floor, yet though he turned near as red as his coat, and opened his mouth as if to say something, he closed it, bowed and left without another word.

With an effort, I thanked Ann, "for your prompt rescue," adding ruefully, "while I had thought of requesting the honour of wearing your favour at Edinburgh, perhaps you might wear mine in the drawing room, for you seemed better able to defend me than I was myself."

She smiled, but said, "I apologize for your discomfiture, Thomas."

Still trying to be amusing, I said, "I apologize in turn for being the occasion for depriving you of the fellow's company."

This restored her to humour, and she said, "I might bear this loss if you could. I would be a poor hostess if I permitted my friends to be insulted in my own house."

She then went to her other guests leaving me in a state of great confusion, for though her prompt championship both gratified and embarrassed me, her considering me as a friend was also a very mixed matter. I returned to my room very thoughtful and no wiser on how much study abroad would cost.

Just before I was to return to Cambridge, I encountered a Scotch sea captain, a Mr. Fife, in my grandfather's store. Discovering the man knew Edinburgh, I asked him how much living expenses would be for a student in that town.

He considered this to the point where I thought he had forgotten my question, and I began to ask him again, when he opened his mouth to tell me, "For a single laddie, ten pounds English money a year should be more than enough, and perhaps too much, for"—he gathered way here—"there is overmuch carousing and ungodliness and even"—he lowered his voice—"fornication amongst the students at the University there, and I hope you will nae be corrupted."

At this point my uncle appeared with a ledger for me to view, and I went off with it, and not unwillingly. As soon as I had, I realized I should have inquired more closely as to what manner of lodging and diet such a sum would provide, for this was less than a shilling a day. On second thoughts though, I decided I would probably be hard put to get enough grains of information amongst the chaff of his discourse to make the effort worthwhile. I had to admit, however that his descriptions of student life in Edinburgh sounded more interesting than they perhaps should.

The first weeks back at Harvard were as overwhelming as I remembered the same period of my first year being, and the remedy thereof being the same—work—I was unable to make many social visits. My new status as sophomore was little comfort; while I could order freshmen on errands, I forbore, remembering my own resentment at such treatment, and did my own, as did most of my friends.

The meals at the Commons were much the same, as were our opinions of these; and after making some headway in our studies, several of us concocted a scheme which was irreligious, probably blasphemous, childish, and could quite possibly get one or more of us killed and the rest expelled, and we were the more avid for it. This plot involved fabrication of a large egg of paper and paste, gilding it, and climbing the tower of the First Congregational Church and affixing the imitation egg beneath the tail of the large wooden rooster that capped the steeple, quite inappropriately we decided.

The egg was quickly constructed and painted, several of us donating the materials or one or two shillings; and one dark Saturday night, we crept from our rooms, repaired to the church and opened a side door by removal of the pins from the hinges. We climbed the tower stairs and opened a window admitting us to the church roof; then David Prescott, with a line tied round his waist, climbed upon the steeple roof with our assistance. We listened to his progress in great apprehension, which mounted by the moment. He was able to stand on the narrow ledge that ran around the steeple to reach the base of the rooster. He lowered the line. We attached the egg to it. David pulled up the line. When he had the egg, he tied it to the rooster's leg using thin wire from his pocket. He seemed to take a great deal of time, and we were quite anxious until we could help him climb down. Weak with relief, we returned to the side door and restored the pins. We then stole back to our rooms like so many burglars; for if we were caught out after hours that would be the end of us. We went to bed relieved but quite afraid.

The following morning, we cleaned ourselves and dressed for church with eagerness quite contrary to our usual emotions. On greeting David, he told me that his incriminating clothing and gear were safely hidden: I do not know how, but he had managed to stow these in the room of an unpopular senior student.

Arriving at the church taking care to walk separately from each other, we were rewarded by the sight of a crowd of parishioners gazing at our creation. And indeed with the early morning sun on it, I thought it looked quite realistic, for David had taken the trouble to gild even the wire attaching the egg to the spur. As we expected there was grave discussion of this sacrilege, but we detected sternly restrained amusement on nearly all faces. Our classmates were less restrained, and I mainly recall the sermon from the smothered outbursts of amusement punctuating it. I think the egg was taken down the next day by a sailor hired for the purpose. The major difficulty we had over this incident was the continual restraint we had to maintain, even for months, lest we draw undue attention to ourselves.

On our next meeting, Ann asked me about this incident and naturally saw everything in my face. Although I thought she might disapprove, she was instead highly amused, touching my sleeve once more. Despite being of the Church of England, she also had a sense of humour. Aside from this and the magic of some new songs she sang in the course of the evening, my memories of the evening were of a new rival, a Mr. Thorpe of New York, to whom Ann introduced me.

It seemed to me that she was anxious that we be friends. I tried to be civil, and I think succeeded. The fellow was certainly very polished but it was in the sense of being hard and smooth and impenetrable—all surface, and I could make nothing of his character. But perhaps jealousy informed my opinion of him.

As the year wore out, I attended Ann here and there, and this Mr. Thorpe always seemed to be about. For Ann's sake I continued to offer friendship to the fellow; and while he said or did nothing amiss, I could not say at the end of this period that I knew him any better than at the beginning. He was the son of a wealthy merchant of New York, had attended the College of New Jersey, was as well dressed and mannered as these facts would imply, and appeared to be visiting Boston for an indefinite period of time and an equally indefinite reason. He was staying at the home of another merchant, a friend of the Crewes' who had a very plain daughter, and I fancied or rather hoped he was courting this girl.

This minor puzzle in my life was put aside when my father appeared unexpectedly at Cambridge.

"My father, your Grandfather Wyeth, has died, and we must attend the funeral and settle matters."

I was relieved that nothing had happened to my mother or sisters, but grieved at his passing. Though he was an old man being somewhere around seventy, he was a very hearty man and had always been in good health. I received permission to leave at my father's application, and we set out for Dedham. We went in a wagon my father had borrowed and as we rolled down to the Charles River ferry we talked.

"How did it happen and how is Grandmother Wyeth taking it?"

"Grandfather had gone out in the rain to recover some stock that strayed and became ill after; the sickness settling in his chest, pneumonia developed and he died. One of his hired men, who had been out with him, had brought the news yesterday and said Grandmother Wyeth was very grieved, as was natural."

As we made our way to their farm, I reflected on my memories of him. He had visited us a few times when I was a child, a wide, vigorous loud man with grizzled cheeks that tickled me when he held me to him. I remember being startled at first by his accent, and was somewhat afraid of him. But since he seemed pleased with me and played with me in a rough yet affectionate way, I soon got over that. Later, when I was delivering letters and packages, I sometimes would have to go into his neighborhood and would stop at his house when I could. He always seemed glad to see me, as did my grandmother, though she was a placid woman and her enthusiasm at my appearances was less marked.

He sometimes would put me to work cutting wood or some similar task, at which I labored very slowly, not having much skill at such things. This excited some impatience on his part until I learned to tell him I was tired from my deliveries. At which he would insist I spend the night, and fed me like the French feed their geese. He himself was a good eater and drinker, mostly ale, and had a name for hospitality. Though he was a rough, somewhat vulgar man, I came to enjoy his company and was at ease around him.

I remember asking him, "How came you to this province, Grandfather?

He told me, "I wuz takin' a load of flour cross country in a ox cart, since the weather ha' been dry. A big rain hit, turnin' the road ta gruel. The road wuz very bad in wet like all the roads in tha' part of England. An' the cart an' oxen wuz so mired tha' the oxen drowned an' the cart wuz swallert. Tha' ended me livelihood an' disgusted me wi' England. I pulled 'em dead oxen out an' sold 'em an' walked ta Bristol, sleepin' under hedges. I ha' nuff money fer part o' me passage over an' worked the rest."

I asked him, "Have you ever missed the life on the road?"

"Yes, when I'uz younger but am now happy ta stay in one place. My father wuz a farmer, as I'm now and I think most o' me forefathers wuz."

So now he was dead, and what Grandmother was to do we did not know. Father told me, "She is a year or two older than Grandfather himself, and probably cannot manage the farm alone, and neither I nor you ever had much inclination for farming."

We arrived there just before dark and began trying to set matters to rights, for Grandmother Wyeth was too grieved to be able to arrange the funeral and look after matters. This we did and buried Grandfather Wyeth on one of the greyest, most forlorn days I have ever seen, and counted ourselves fortunate it did not snow which would have sent more of us to follow him.

Afterwards, my grandmother announced she would not stay on the farm anymore and wished to move in with Father and Mother after selling or leasing the farm. This occasioned some difficulty, for there was little room in our house unless I moved out or both my sisters married and left. We had four bedrooms in our house, and Lizzie and Susan slept together for the warmth, so Grandmother Wyeth could be given only the fourth, smallest bedroom.

After I returned to Harvard, there were conferences with Grandmother and Mother. I think my mother was not pleased at having Widow Wyeth lodge with us, but yielded, since there was nowhere else for Grandmother to go. Also when the farm sold, it would bring a great deal of money. So it was finally agreed that Grandmother would move in with us, getting the smallest bedroom. According to Lizzie's letters Grandmother did not complain, indeed said almost nothing. Since she had no teeth, Mother had to prepare meals Grandmother Wyeth could eat, which I suspect also did not sit well with Mother, though this was not stated.

According to Grandfather Wyeth's will, I was to have a clear third of the proceeds to further my education abroad. Of course, the rest went to Grandmother Wyeth. This gave me mixed feelings. While I would advance myself, I would also leave Ann for three years, and though I could see she liked me, I could not see more than that. Yet I would have to go.

I begged the favour of an interview with Mr. Winthrop, and asked if he would write me a letter of recommendation to the officials at Edinburgh. He readily agreed to this, which surprised me somewhat.

He asked, "Are you determined to leave Harvard before taking your degree? If you continue as you have begun, you should be able to finish at Harvard next year, which is after three years."

I said, "Family circumstances necessitate my removal to Scotland after two years of study."

He said, "I know no one at Edinburgh, but will write a general letter."

I thanked him and left.

Accordingly, when my grandfather's farm was sold in late January, I was informed by my father that I could take perhaps £85 (lawful money), to pay my way, which seemed a fortune to me. Of course, he had dealt with all the legal matters, though I could have helped him with those. The money was placed with a merchant—not Mr. Crewe—to invest in ventures, perhaps rum or sugar or slaves.

I informed Ann of this news. I hoped to reach some understanding with her, or at least to hint at my feelings. However, we met at an acquaintance's house where there was a large crowd, and the omnipresent Mr. Thorpe effectively forestalled any tête-à-tête between us. A week or so later as I was visiting my grandfather Holmes in Boston on some matter connected with my passage, I saw her walking with Thorpe. I fancied she looked a trifle confused seeing me, but if so, it was for but a moment, and she smiled and waved to me. I smiled back and bowed, but did not venture over, for something told me that I should not. Indeed, I was beginning to feel quite uneasy over my status with Ann, for it seemed that lately she was a trifle abstracted, distant and sad.

5

FIGURE'S END

———◆———

I had little more time to brood over these matters. Before more than a few days had passed, I received a note from her in her own hand that asked me to attend her at her home the following afternoon. As this was a Saturday, I was able to do so. With a hammering heart and a strong feeling of apprehension, I walked to her door and knocked.

As I stood facing the polished door of her house, I urged myself to bear up while marveling at my subservience in these matters. The door opened and there stood Ann herself wearing the blue gown I always thought of her wearing. She seemed serious, as no doubt did I. She bade me enter, and I followed her into their sitting room with its portraits of her father and mother done long ago.

She closed the door, turned to face me, and said, "I shrink from telling you what I know must give you pain, Thomas, but tell you I must. My father wishes me to marry Mr. Thorpe, to ally our families. I have consented, as I would not disoblige him on such a matter. Mr. Thorpe waited on me yesterday and asked me for my hand, and I have accepted him."

I exerted my will to keep my features from collapsing, and for that matter my knees as well. For a long time it seemed, I tried to say something, but what sprang to my lips I would not say, so only bowed acknowledgement. I must have seemed exceedingly wooden, and I think she was somewhat unsettled by my silence.

At length she went on, "I hope, someday, you may forgive me, someday when we are both old and married, so that I might retain your friendship which I value."

At this point I spoke and found my voice hoarse and strained, so that I had to clear my throat once or twice before attaining any semblance of human speech, let alone elegance. I said, "Ann, there is no rancour on my part, not towards you, or really towards anyone. I knew my chances were poor. I"—here I cleared my throat again—"count myself fortunate to have had your society." I went on after a moment: "I have never wished for wealth, but that your family might have viewed me with more favour." Here I stopped, conscious that I had blundered, and saw Ann frown.

But her face cleared again and she said, in her gentle voice, "I don't think you will ever be rich, Thomas." Then she added, looking at me, "Yet I think you will have everything you want else."

There was silence again, and I finally said, "I shall not wish Mr. Thorpe luck, for he has already had far more than any man deserves, but I wish you good fortune, and God's blessing." At this, she gave me her hand, and I kissed it—the first such intimacy between us— and, straightening, said, "Goodbye, Ann."

"Goodbye, Thomas," was her reply.

Without seeing her for my eyes would not focus, I turned and somehow made my way outside.

I began walking blindly back towards the ferry, trying to maintain an indifferent exterior, yet hardly capable of purposeful movement. I was conscious of near collisions with people or walls or animals, and nearly ran headforemost into a tree on nearing the ferry landing. I have no idea what people thought, who saw me; my only conscious aim was to hide, to indulge my grief. Finding the ferry on the opposite shore, and at length perceiving its stay there likely to be prolonged, as some loading was going on, I turned and began walking rapidly up the course of the Charles River.

Slowly, coherent thought returned. I was conscious of resentment, as well as pain. I wondered (and was ashamed of myself for the thoughts), how many other suitors were awaiting their dismissal and whether they were scheduled in order of their fathers' positions as we were seated in classes, or whether it was done in order of the alphabet. At length, I began to see matters more charitably, realizing that Ann had been actually at considerable trouble and pain to tell me what nine girls out of ten would have allowed me to discover for myself from gossip or in newspapers.

Nor could there be any cavil at her father's judgment, for what could I offer, save a two- or three-years' engagement, followed by a further period while I established myself in a practice. Even then, it might be years or it might be never—for I had no confidence in my ability to fashion a popular practice—before I could support her in any way similar to her present condition. I was happy I had attempted to be gracious and ashamed at implying her father had effectively sold her much as my grandfather disposed of, say, cheeses, even though the implication was in a sense true. I understood that the match was intended as a way to perpetuate their attitudes and habits of living rather than amalgamate banker's accounts.

Yet it still seemed rather cold. I could not imagine Thorpe as her lover, for he seemed all surface to me. But since I really couldn't say anything bad about the fellow, I supposed her father's judgement had to be superior to my own and certainly was superior in effect.

At length, I noticed it was beginning to grow dark. Spying a ford ahead, mainly a scattering of rocks (for the river was low), I crossed and reached the far bank safely, having done this now and again in years past. I then extended myself and hurried back, not wishing another fine.

I was unwontedly silent at supper, not even joining in the transport of comment, all adverse, about the meal. I attempted to be pleasant, and smiled, but wished only for an end to it. After we had retired, I sought out David Prescott, for my feelings were threatening to burst from me. I told him of my day, all in a rush, like beer from a broken barrel. I paused, emptied of speech.

David stirred, having made no comment during my recital, "I

am not surprised, for her match with Thorpe was so commented upon that even I had noticed it, the match being considered a very good one. The difference in her circumstances and yours must always act, first to prevent your union and after to strain it."

I sighed, and said, "I am aware of all this, and have always been so, but suppose I am too great a fool to conduct myself accordingly."

"We are all fools in such matters. I am sorry you have received such a disappointment, but you will recover, given another girl."

I had no enthusiasm for such, and said so, "I should not find her like again."

He demurred, "There are plenty such, as you will find when you are through school, and a professional man." He reminded me with a gentle push to my shoulder, "We have a Latin recitation Monday, and must prepare."

So I reluctantly turned to my studies, and though I made heavy going of it, I performed passably that day and continued working, though with much less spirit than before, or so I fancied.

On returning home later that spring, I was still sore enough over the matter to wish for silence concerning it, and imagined I need only hold my tongue to obtain this, but was mortified to discover my entire family in full possession of all the details. Mother and Father were sympathetic and my sisters indignant against Ann. Even the apothecary, my near master, made some remark about aspiring above my station. My chief bully at school, Robbie McDowell, made a sneering remark, at which I looked about for a weapon to secure a cadaver to practice upon. Evidently my romance had furnished my entire village with much food for discussion this past year.

At length, as I prepared to return for my last months at Harvard, I began to see some humour in the matter. I even asked Father, "I wonder if I can copyright my adventures, for if I am to entertain half the Province, at least I should profit thereby."

He laughed, and clapped me round the shoulders, and I returned in better spirit.

6

LAST RITES

———◆———

I was within some weeks of finishing my last term when I received a letter. At first I thought it might be from Ann, but the hand was my older sister's. I opened the letter and read:

Dear Brother

I have the most dreadful news. Mother had been feeling a pain in her lower right side. Her appetite was less because of this, but four days ago, she broke her fast and ate well. That night she felt a terrible sharp pain in the same place and cried out, waking us all. From then she went into a high fever. The doctor said he had seen patients with these symptoms and could do nothing. He warned us that Mother would die, probably in a day or two, and indeed she did. Her funeral is Saturday.

I am very very sorry to be the conveyor of such news. Father told us not to warn you earlier as it would do no good to you or to Mother, who was delirious before she died, to have you here for her last hours. This was

his judgment, and we could not gainsay him of course.
So please come.

Lizzie

This news shocked and stunned me. Mother was never one to complain of her health, but then she had little cause to complain. I readily obtained permission to go attend her funeral, and almost ran the distance, not that greater speed would make any difference.

I tried to comfort my father and sisters. Father sat motionless at the table at which we all ate staring at nothing. My sisters were in tears. Grandmother Wyeth seemed bewildered; now she would be in mourning even longer. Mother lay in her coffin, eyes closed but I could see signs on her face of the agony she must have felt before her end. A chin strap was tied in place to keep her mouth closed. She was so silent, so still. My eyes filled with tears and I bent to kiss her forehead. I had expected her corpse to be ice-cold but instead was the temperature of the surroundings. She was buried the next day. Everyone was sympathetic. Father, Grandfather Holmes and Uncle Thomas, I and two other men carried her to her grave, the last service we could perform for her. Then I returned to Harvard.

After my return, I struggled to direct my thoughts to my assigned tasks. When I thought of my failed suit, I grew unhappy, but in addition I now felt such thoughts were a reproach. My mother's death should, I told myself over and over, have been uppermost in my mind. Yet I was confused: Mother had always been healthy, and as children will, I had simply accepted her presence and her love, assuming these would persist forever. Was her sudden loss a rebuke to my ambition to become a doctor? To frustrate God's will? This brought my conversation with Ann to mind, and I sternly told myself once again not to think of Ann.

Was God warning me I must become a minister or simply a much more religious man? I could not accept that my beliefs or lack of piety provoked God to end Mother's life in such a way, to force or inspire me to follow the True Path. So I found my scattered, interrupted musings had instead confirmed my earlier decision to study medicine. The pains my mother had felt meant something and should have elicited advice from the doctor, advice or perhaps drugs that would have kept Mother alive, perhaps even cured her.

Would I have enough money to study medicine? Becoming an apprentice to one of the doctors in Boston would cost money. I did not know how much, but I did not want to stay in Boston, as I would be continually reminded of my failed suit. Going to another province to study was of no greater merit in terms of what I would learn and would cost more money. I realized that, having some money, I must go abroad, and I would inquire further as to where I could receive the best training possible.

End of term should have been a joyful occasion. Despite the distress from the recent death of Mother, I had finished with considerable credit, which made me feel oddly guilty. The rest of my family was there, my sisters attracting considerable attention from my fellow classmates, which pleased my sisters notwithstanding their mourning. Father reminded me about the money Grandfather Wyeth's will had left me, some 85 pounds lawful money, which was about £60 English money, so I could indeed pursue my education.

I had also asked several doctors in Boston as to where I should go. I was told the same things Dr. Shippen had told me, viz., Leyden, Paris, London or Edinburgh, with Edinburgh the favourite. And of course I wouldn't have to learn Dutch or French first, which would speed matters. I told my father and sisters this. After we all returned home carrying my things, my father and I returned to Boston to the merchant who had my grandfather's money.

Here the fellow wanted to give me a letter of credit, which he assured us was just as good and far more convenient to carry about. But my father surprised me and vexed the merchant by insisting on specie.

The merchant protested, "Our province has little specie and £60 would take much time to gather."

But Father continued to insist. "The money in specie, if Thomas wishes it, is lawfully Thomas's."

The merchant, growling, agreed but told us, "You have to give me a week to gather the coins."

So we left. On our way back home, my father told me, "Despite the weight and danger of carrying that much coin about, sending you across the Atlantic with a piece of paper that might be honoured or might not, perhaps leaving you stranded and penniless, was not something you should or should have to risk."

So we returned. I was quite impressed by Father's knowledge and force of character.

Father also told me, "The times lately have been much better, so there is much more specie in the provinces than two or three years ago."

Though £60 seemed a great deal, I would have to live some three years upon it. I had no notion of the scale of prices in Edinburgh, still less how much the University of Edinburgh charged, for it must have fees.

A week after we met the merchant, we returned and outfaced the man again, so he sullenly produced the specie. Father and I counted it, rejecting some pieces as foreign, so of doubtful value, or else counterfeit. This provoked another argument, which Father won. The merchant had to produce coin from his own pockets to make up the shortfall, but we left with £60 in English money carried in a cloth sack brought for the purpose.

At home, my sisters had sewn a belt with pockets for the coin, a money belt, which we loaded with the specie. I had obtained a stout wooden chest with a lock and a leather strap attached to carry it. So I packed my things for my next journey. Our cat Tabby rubbed against me as though he knew we would be separated for years or perhaps for all earthly time.

At length, all was ready. I shook hands with my father, embraced and kissed my grandmother and sisters and lifted and caressed our cat. Then I walked away, my chest in a hand cart pushed by my eldest sister's suitor Daniel Mechin. I turned and waved then went on toward Boston where my ship awaited, feeling a mixture of excitement and apprehension.

Just before I climbed into the boat to take me to the ship, I had posted a letter I had written Ann, a letter I had laboured over many hours in the composition.

My dear Miss Crewe

I board today on a voyage to Scotland to obtain, I hope, my qualifications as a doctor. We may or may not meet again. Please be assured that if it ever is within my power to assist you in any way, you may rely on such assistance being given by

Your firm friend
Thomas Wyeth

A very short letter, considering the time and thought—and tears—that were expended in its preparation. The several longer versions were burned. But all were heart-meant....

ON BOARD

A thumping on the door of our cabin awakened us or at least bestirred us. One by one, we and the other passengers used the "heads," projecting shelves for emptying ourselves down the side of the ship. This was cold, so we were not tempted to prolong the experience. It was morning, a grey, cold, windy morning.

We were fed in shifts, six of us at a time at a heavy, scarred, wooden table. Breakfast was beer to wash down "ship biscuit" (very hard baked pieces of bread) and slices of very salty pork. I could see the white bits of salt sprinkled thickly over the meat. Again, another experience we didn't want to linger over.

I decided to return to the deck and just try harder to stay out of the sailors' way. I could not imagine remaining day after day in the fetid hole of a cabin even alone, still less with four others. So I stood away from where the ropes were secured, trying not to hinder the sailors from getting to these, and looked about me.

A grey sky merged with a grey sea. The sailors were attending to their own duties as the ship moved with the waves, rattling and creaking, all very busy. Otherwise it was cold despite being midsummer and I began to move about, trying to stay warm as well as not underfoot.

There were groups of ropes supporting the masts, arranged so it was possible to climb up them to a platform about halfway to the top. I decided to climb up these, as I was feeling incredibly restless.

Climbing the ropes was surprisingly hard. I had to hold hard to the ropes and cross ropes so I did not lose my grip. The ropes were tarry and my hands became tarry. Still I persevered, eventually getting to the platform. I was not used to this manner of exercise, so had to rest. There wasn't much to see, just a much greater expanse of grey ocean. At length I went back down the other side. At times, I was more afraid I would lose my grip, as my hands and wrists were fatigued, but finally got to the deck feeling relieved.

No one had paid much attention to me when I did this. As I again stood out of the way flexing my hands and wrists, I wondered how I would get the tar out of my palms and fingers. Of course I had aspirations to be judged a gentleman and I understood that tarry hands signified the reverse. But my accursed restless nature impelled me up and down the rope ladder again and again, at first on the upper side of the rope ladder then on the lower side until my arms were simply too weak to sustain my climbing.

It being near noon when the ship's position was determined, I closely watched the ship's captain "shoot the sun" as it was termed. I was able to get them to allow me to try to do this and see how the calculations were done as well. I had expected the process to be mysterious, even magical, but instead it was all quite mechanical: obtain the reading then look up our position in some tables.

This gave us our latitude; longitude was obtained from a clock, apparently a very accurate one, and the time it gave when the sun was at its zenith. Again a very simple calculation. I felt a sense of disillusion but of course said nothing.

I was allowed to see the chart on which the ship's progress was plotted. We seemed to be making a good passage but I was discouraged from commenting on this. It was an understood thing not to make such comments, lest this cause the winds to shift or some other stroke of bad luck to occur. Sailors were a notably superstitions lot, I began to understand. I supposed this was the result of being at the mercy of the winds and weather.

After the midday meal, much the same as the morning meal, I again climbed up and down the "rat-lines" as they were termed until I again had no strength left in my arms. At this point I sat at the table where we dined, resting and occasionally flexing my arms and hands.

This was repeated the next day and the next and next. We had no rain, good in one way since I wasn't penned up in our cabin and could move about. My arms and shoulders became quite sore and stayed in that condition. On the other hand, I noticed the climbing up and down was easier and realized I was becoming stronger.

I was pleased at this, remembering my humiliation when the second year students challenged us neophytes to a wrestling match. This was the first Monday at the start of term, and was the custom. Some of my classmates won their matches, so would have to face the third year students, then the fourth year students if they continued victorious. But I was easily vanquished, having little strength in my arms, it seemed. I was unable to do any better my second year either, deepening my shame. This was very foolish of me, yet the feelings were acute. But perhaps by the end of the voyage I would be as strong as the sailors who went up and down the lines easily and quickly.

8

CONTINUANCE

I noticed now that some of the sailors were able to climb down single ropes, hand over hand, or even climb up single ropes without using their feet at all. This was discouraging, yet gave me something to strive for. I began by trying to climb down a single rope. Here I nearly miscarried for the strength in my arms gave out before I reached the deck and I almost fell the last few feet. This made me more cautious, but the weather continuing good, I had to continue. So continue I did.

My activities drew some comments, though those were good-natured and I did not take offense. [Not that I was in any position to do so.]

"Lad, we shall make a sailor of thee yet."

"If y'are gonna monkey around in the riggin', do it proper like. Free yer toes ta grip the rope."

The sailors thought I should doff my shoes, as they went about their duties bare-footed, but I felt my feet were not hardened enough to the ropes and the deck, and I was, after all, preparing to study to be a doctor, not a sailor, so continued dressed as I was. My coat seemed to fit more ill as the voyage proceeded, but I wanted to keep wearing it to conceal the money belt with the specie that was my inheritance. This added to my weight, of course.

Little by little, I became able to climb down a single rope without touching it with my feet. The soreness in my arms and shoulders eased as well, and I began to essay climbing up a rope using my hands and arms alone. This was much harder; still I was able to do more and more each day.

I greatly envied the sailors their strength of arms and hands. At times, they exhibited the grace and sureness of acrobats. But occasionally they were led to acts of hubris in their self-esteem, and falls or other injuries resulted. One morning I was resting my arms and hands when I saw a sailor lose his balance, miss his grip and fall to the deck.

He landed on one leg, the leg visibly broke and the sailor screamed. He lay on the deck, his right upper leg bent sideways and a blood stain growing about the break. Several of us went to his aid. I could see a bloody white projection out of his skin, through a tear in his trousers. I realized this was his broken thigh bone.

Two of the other sailors went to get the ship's carpenter, who apparently doubled as a surgeon. He appeared, got several bystanders to hold the injured man's arms and his uninjured leg, and with his bare hands the carpenter forced the broken end of bone back to near its proper position, all while the injured sailor shrieked. The carpenter went below then returned with some barrel staves and cordage. The carpenter used the staves and ropes to enclose the injured leg and keep it straight. Then several sailors lifted the injured man and carried him below.

I watched all this with a feeling of complete helplessness. Here I was going to study to be a doctor yet had no idea about how to treat an injured man. I followed to the forecastle where the injured man was laid, still in intense pain. The captain appeared and administered what I took to be tincture of laudanum. The injured sailor took this and gradually quieted. At this point, the rest of us returned to our business, or in my case, my vocation.

Several times that day and the following days, I went to inspect the man's broken leg. The carpenter had no idea whether the man would recover or not, merely shrugging when I asked him. But I could see the leg becoming swollen with reddish streaks appearing where the broken end of the bone had come through the skin. The sailor became feverish, delirious, the laudanum only partially successful in reducing the man's pain. To me, he was not recovering but getting worse. The carpenter loosened the cords holding the staves, yet that helped but little.

The sailor died a week later. There was a service conducted by the captain. The sailor's body had been wrapped in a hammock and weighted down with a stone from the ballast and laid out on a plank. At the bosun's signal the plank was raised and he was slid over the side of the ship and into the sea. In a way, I think all of us were glad his suffering was at an end. But I remembered the man who had sewn up my cat and my cat had lived. That was a much more severe injury, but my cat's recovery had been swift and uneventful. There was one thing that had been done differently: the man who had cured my cat had washed his hands and forearms before the stitching; I remembered the strong smell of the soap. In fact, I think the thread used was washed as well. The ship's carpenter may have washed himself at some point in his life, but clearly not recently. Was there a connection?

That night, trying to ease sore shoulders and arms, my thoughts turned again to the town apothecary-cow doctor who had saved Scheherazade. I remembered his insistence on both of us washing our hands and forearms to assist deliveries of dumb beasts. Could such a practice have any utility with deliveries of women?

I continued my climbs and descents. By now I could climb down a rope and was beginning to be able to pull myself up one, all without using my feet. But now there was another problem: my coat was coming apart at the seams. I decided I would take instruction in sewing from some of the sailors. I had grown into manhood, thinking sewing was women's work, but the sailors repaired their own clothes and made nothing of it. I began to wonder if I might have to sew up injuries to patients. This was, strictly speaking, work for surgeons, but such might not be available. I wanted to be able to help, to treat patients, I hoped successfully.

So I had to find thread of the right colour, so my efforts would not be obvious; I did very much want to appear the gentleman. This was difficult. Then the sewing: there were several stitches employed, a number of knots as well, all which I had to learn. The sailors instructing me were somewhat amused at my struggles but for the most part were sympathetic and patient. At length I finished my repairs, though my repaired coat felt very tight about my shoulders. My second coat did as well. I would have to be measured for two new coats, and this would cost money. Had they shrunk during the voyage?

The only recourse I had was to doff my coat prior to my climbing, lest the seams pull free again. I pulled my shirt out to cover my money belt. As long as the day was not too cold, I could bear this. By the time we were nearing Glasgow, I was finally able to climb a rope using hands and arms alone, and I gloried in this accomplishment. I was following our course on the chart and knew our voyage was nearly over. Now perhaps I could allow my hands to lose their calluses and perhaps the ingrained tar as well.

We saw land the next day and were able to check our position. The captain now felt free to comment on how good a passage we had made; steady winds in the right direction, not too strong, no calms throughout. Our luck held: we entered the estuary where Glasgow lay, launched a longboat and were able to tie up at an actual quay, no having to be rowed to shore. Our voyage was done.

I went below and got my chest. I was very surprised at how light it seemed. Had it been opened and robbed? However, when I opened it and looked through my belongings, everything was there. I carried my chest onto the quay and realized my rope climbing had made me much stronger. That probably was why my coats now fit so ill as well.

For a few minutes I fancied I would walk to Edinburgh, but good sense prevailed and I went to obtain a seat on a coach. Walking to the inn I would depart from, I looked about me. Glasgow was stone-built and crowded: narrow streets, buildings right together, people everywhere. I had some specie in my coat pockets so I would not have to delve into my money belt to pay my passage in the coach.

Because I was delayed by looking into my chest, I had to ride atop, beside the coachman. Since the day was fair, I did not object but looked about me as we left Glasgow and drove east. The land was hilly. The farms looked poor as did the soil. Sheep grazed in some places. A close land, I thought: hard to travel within Scotland, which was probably why so many Scots had emigrated: to England, to America.

The road was well traveled, but it was a shaking, lurching journey. We stopped twice at inns, which I thought remarkable for wretchedness, but no one else had any comment. The meals were similar to those aboard ship, but again, no one else commented.

It was well past dark when we reached signs a city was near. There was a three-quarter moon, so all was well lit. Buildings became more numerous, taller, then in the distance what was clearly Edinburgh. By now it was well past one. As we entered the city, we encountered a fulsome stench: a midden, a privy, human excrement, far worse than the confines of the ship, though no one remarked on this. We reached the inn that was our destination, fully presaged by the inns we had already seen, so I decided to curl up on my chest, with my shoes as a pillow, rather than sleep several abed. Still, here I was at my destination, where I would spend perhaps three years attempting to qualify as a doctor.

9

EDINBURGH

◆

I slept but ill. Not because of having to be curled up, I had to do that all through the weeks of the voyage. And the smells inside the inn were not much worse than aboard ship. But several thunderstorms came through and wakened me again and again. By morning, very early morning to me, I rose still tired. The breakfast served was of a piece with the accommodations, so I left that place as soon as I could, carrying my chest.

Edinburgh was high, blackened stone buildings, close together. The buildings were barely separated by narrow, twisting streets, more like what I thought of as alleys, cobblestoned, rising and falling with the hills the city was built upon. The classical term "labyrinth" sprang into my head. I saw only thin strips of sky as the upper floors of the buildings approached each other more and more closely. Since there were many people in these streets, they were crowded, which made walking with my chest a trial to myself and everyone I encountered. Even Boston which I had thought was populous was vastly more open.

By asking any respectably dressed men I saw, I obtained directions to the Medical School. More questions gave me the locations of several lodging houses frequented by medical students. I thought it useful to enable me to talk to fellow students about costs, courses, the professors, etc. On the way, I noted the rains had washed much of the filth from the streets, so my journey was better in that respect.

The lodging house I chose had only about a dozen students, all much senior to me, and all busy writing. For the quarter, I had to pay £10. This gave me two meals, dinner and supper, tea as I wished, and candles. All very well, but this was for but one quarter, and I had only £50 or a little less now. This dismayed me: costs were much greater than I had been told. How was I going to continue three full years? Of course there was washing, I would need new coats and I supposed I would have to pay something for my instruction. I set my chest in my room, extracted £10 from my belt and took this to the landlord. Then I went to the great table we were all to eat at and sat down to take tea. Due to continual exposure to this drink, I had acquired not merely a tolerance but a taste.

Several other students appeared for the same purpose. I introduced myself, the others did likewise. Some were Scots of course but several were from various shires in England, one was from America, the colony of Virginia. I learned that Americans were often to be encountered, though no one had heard of any from Massachusetts. Most of the other students were taking the Botany course given summer term, also Clinical Lectures. Two were writing their theses. These two remained after the other students left. I gathered they wished to talk to me for some reason.

The two students looked at each other, and then one told me, "Our theses must be in Latin. Unfortunately, we have forgotten most of the Latin we had in school."

A pause, then the second asked, "If we give you our theses written in English, could you translate them into Latin? We can pay five guineas."

"Apiece," said the other.

This caught my attention: ten guineas would pay the quarter's board and lodging. And of course, there were almost certainly more students desiring the same service. So I said, "Give me your manuscripts and I will do it."

However, the first student told me, "They must be done soon, by the first of August. And we must copy your Latin so the theses are in our own hands."

I replied, "Then I must start at once."

I went to my room, extracted my Latin Lexicon and went to the room where we dined. One student gave me his manuscript, about forty pages, and I began work. The first of August was ten days away, and the medical words would be unfamiliar. But I was determined to do it. Aside from the money, I would be learning something of medicine and also some day I would be writing a thesis myself.

Some parts I was able to do quickly, others I needed to look at medical books in Latin. But I worked hard the rest of the day, the next day, the next day and the next. Latin is shorter than English for the same meaning, so the forty pages of the English manuscript were reduced to twenty-five in Latin. When I had completed half, I gave that to the student so he could begin copying my translation in his own hand.

The second student had not finished his but did so as I neared the end of the first student's thesis. I think that my willingness to do the translation encouraged him to finish. So I continued. The second thesis was longer, about forty-five pages, but by now I was better at the translation. So I finished the second in about the same time. I pocketed ten guineas, a great relief to me and I suppose to them.

The students were questioned on what they had learned, also in Latin. Here my two colleagues hired tutors called "grinders" to enable them to be able to understand and answer the questions of the professors. I understood this was often done.

My work completed, I remembered I should write to my family, informing them of my safe arrival. I did this, writing to my older sister. Then I went to be measured for two new coats, another unexpected expense but one which had to be bourne. I felt badly about abandoning my old coats, as they had been lovingly cut and sewn by my mother and sisters, so I decided to keep them, neatly folded, in my chest.

Being now at leisure, I consulted with my fellows about the courses I would take. Everyone agreed on three: Anatomy and Surgery,

Chemistry, and Medical Practice. Several of my fellows thought Mr. Cullen's Medical Theory much better, but that may have been because of Mr. Cullen's popularity. I thought I might take all four but I was advised against this, as the three everyone recommended, together with Clinical Lectures, in which one saw actual patients and actual diseases discussed, would keep me very busy.

I was of two minds about this, for having money for barely one year in my pocket, taking as many courses as possible made a sort of sense. However, I decided I would take the three, along with Clinical Lectures, given by various professors, out of prudence. For each I would have to buy a ticket to attend the lectures, each ticket costing three guineas. A man checked at the door to be sure everyone coming in had their ticket. Clinical Lectures cost only two guineas, making eleven in all. However, I was warned the Clinical Lectures, given Tuesday and Friday, were very crowded.

There were notes taken by various students for all these courses and I read these with great attention. Also some disappointment, for the notes often consisted of barely intelligible fragments, some quite obscure, all scattered and haphazard. Still, by comparing notes from the same lecture taken by different students, I could make a sort of sense of what I was reading. Since I had been able to take very complete notes from the courses I had at Harvard College, using abbreviations in English and Latin, I was confident I could do a better job. And the thought occurred to me that some fellow students might pay me for copies of my notes, if these were good enough. So there was another possible way of supporting myself. As a consequence, I inquired about the cost of paper, ink, quills, to try to gauge how much I should charge.

My restless nature began to reassert itself, but here I was thwarted again, warned not to venture onto the streets of Edinburgh evenings, as the inhabitants made a custom of emptying contents of chamber pots and such out their windows. Sometimes they would warn passersby but sometimes not. It being still summer, with few rains and often no wind I now understood the reason for the stench that greeted me when I first arrived. At times, indeed, the smell in the streets was almost unendurable.

The meals served at my lodging house were much better than I had encountered for months, since leaving my home in fact. We had soup, as much as we wished, often roasted or broiled meat, beef or mutton, fish and eggs as well. Our £10 was well spent in terms of our fare. Provided I could pay for it, I would live very well.

However, the meals were a trial in another respect. My fellow students fancied themselves as "gentlemen" and were quick to despise anyone who seemed of the "lower orders." This of course included surgeons and apothecaries, so I kept to myself my desires to learn something of both professions so I might be a more efficacious doctor. As an American, I was at once suspect in this way though my father's profession should have averted such aspersions. So I was at pains to imitate what I took to be the behavior of a gentleman and also to keep my calloused, tar-stained hands as much out of sight as possible.

Once the summer term ended, many of my fellow students left, so I could pursue my studies unworried. The two students whose theses I had Latinized remained. They were being "ground" so they could answer the questions the faculty would ask. I gathered that these were known or could be guessed in advance so the two students' task was not at all an impossible one. On a few occasions, I was pressed into service to help make their responses more correct or hopefully more elegant. I asked no money for this, first because it might be thought inconsistent with the status of a gentleman, second, because I was learning something about how the examinations were conducted, and third, because I was feeling some stirrings of friendship toward them. I much desired them to succeed.

There were two examinations: the first private, the second in the University Library. These were both *viva voce* and both in Latin. After that the students had to write commentaries on several topics. These were also to be done in Latin and again my friends were assisted by grinders. Since I lacked the medical knowledge to help, I simply read what the two students were going to submit and suggested corrections if I saw any mistakes in the Latin. I saw none.

Finally the students had to defend their theses in the Public Hall of the University. I waited at the lodging house. At length my two friends appeared, dressed in black Doctor's gowns. They were ecstatic; they had passed. We spent the rest of the day and much of the night, laughing, talking, and, I fear, not a little drinking. One would have his thesis bound, to present to his family. The other just wanted to return to his home, in Dorset I think, and take up his practice with his uncle, who had supported him. We parted, shaking hands and extending invitations.

I had perhaps a month and a half before Matriculation. Unusually, I was approached by a student who wanted his thesis Latinized. It was over sixty pages, consisted of discussions of a disease or group of possibly related diseases. He had read about these in various books, much like most theses, or so I had heard. His request was unusual because the first deadline for submitting theses was perhaps eight or more months away.

However, he told me, "Since I've finished the d...mned thing and since it is on the long side, I want to get it done when a Latiner has time."

I did, so set to work. It was half again as long as the other two that I had done, but I now knew the terms much better, so completed it in eight days, not working at full press. I gave him the entire thesis and he gave me five guineas.

The notes other students had left concerning Chemistry, these from lectures of Mr. Black, were most interesting, though annoyingly fragmentary, the words he employed occasionally unfamiliar to the students so they were sometimes misspelled. Also the ideas were clearly unfamiliar to the takers of the notes. I knew I could prepare much better notes so might derive more income just from that course alone.

My first two "customers" having graduated, this left very few others about as nearly all left for the rest of the summer, that is, August to October. As the first of November, the time for Matriculation, drew closer, more and more of my fellow students appeared. We talked about our courses. Nearly all the first year students, including, I decided, myself, were taking Medical Practice, given this term by Mr. Cullen at 9-10 AM. Then we would take Chemistry, given at 10-11 by the celebrated Mr. Black. Anatomy and Surgery was from 1-3, afternoons, given by Mr. Munro, called *Secundus* as his father had given the same course. Mr. Munro *Secundus* was highly praised. Clinical Lectures were at 4-5, afternoons, Tuesday and Thursdays.

Some of my fellows said they would only attend these lectures through winter term then pursue their education in London or even in Paris for a few. At these places, particularly Paris, opportunities for anatomical studies on human corpses and vastly greater opportunities for treatment of patients existed. This gave me pause, but not for long. I did want the MD if I could qualify and, more to the point, moving to London after six months instruction would leave me with no money and no opportunity for earning any. Here I was beginning to see how I might support myself.

Matriculation took place in the library. We signed the Matriculation book, paid half a crown, told the clerk what courses we proposed to take and bought the tickets for these. We were told the half crown matriculation fee was to buy medical books for the library. So I began my studies.

I transcribed the lectures using abbreviations and Latin words and phrases. I was not put off by the Scots' accents, though some of the words were unfamiliar. After classes I would write out the lectures, producing verbatim transcripts. This greatly helped me to remember what was said.

Some of my fellow students were indeed impressed by this achievement, so I began as a copyist—a sort of medical monk. I sold my copies of the lectures at two shillings a week, each was five lectures and about six pages a lecture. I sold these to three fellow students who as a result stopped taking notes themselves, merely listened. Of course I paid for the paper, quills and ink, but I calculated I should have a £10 profit over winter term, though at the additional cost of being busier than ever.

I perceived some shortcomings with the instruction, however. Anatomy and Surgery was conveyed entirely by watching (at a considerable distance) dissections and listening to the lectures. We all decided that this was only useful as an introduction to the subject. Mr. Black taught us the principles of Chemistry, not so much its applications to medicine, but still we all found the subject fascinating. Clinical Lectures cost only two guineas though was not worth its cost, as there was such a crowd of students that we could hear what was said only with difficulty as some of the other students about the edges of the crowd were talking to each other. Of course, we were too far away from the patients to observe much of what was being talked about. Nonetheless, I felt I had to persevere.

One of my "customers," a fellow from Cheshire named David Withrow, became friends with me. At one point I confessed my embarrassment about my hands, which still retained bits of tar and memories of calluses, but David told me, "A gentleman may do anything, no matter how menial, that he chooses. But as long as he isn't paid for doing it, as long as it is his voluntary choice, he remains a gentleman."

I was greatly comforted by this, even more so by his remarking, "Your note preparation and Latinizing were of course paid but might be considered learned professions so were still consistent with gentle status, even if on the edge."

Unhappily, David was one of the "occasional auditors" who would go to London to continue his education, after winter term ended.

Through the holidays, I began to become impatient for a letter from my sister. Of course, there was not much traffic across the Atlantic in winter. And of course my letter might have miscarried. So I wrote another.

As winter term continued, we began to hear rumours of an outrage: a mob of disguised colonists boarded a ship of the East India Company and threw chests of tea into Boston Harbour. This was because the Crown was offering the tea at a lower price than our merchants could charge. My fellow students were loud in their criticisms, which at times seemed directed at me since I was from that Province. This even though I was much of their opinion; destroying the property of others was simply wrong, indefensible, and I condemned the men who did this deed. But I was also apprehensive that my own family might be caught in the middle of this clash. So I wished even more for a letter.

I began to fear my sister's suitors were among the perpetrators. I commenced following the printed accounts with greater attention, without relief of my worries. Rather the contrary: affairs at home seemed to become more conflicted and more dangerous.

It was early spring, near the end of winter term that I got a letter from my elder sister:

> *My dear brother*
>
> *Grandmother Wyeth died in her sleep, as quietly as she had lived with us. Father said her candle just went out. So he has lost his father, mother, and wife in little more than a year. We try to comfort him.*
>
> *Otherwise, we are well and rejoiced to hear of your safe arrival. Matters have become very troubled here. Both factions seem to be pushing matters to a clash of arms, with what result only God can forsee.*
>
> *Your father's practice has fallen off, as few cases are brought to the courts. All await resolutions of the dispute between this province and the Crown. Still we manage to stay afloat.*
>
> *I continue to be courted by Daniel Mechin. If it weren't for these conflicts, I would have set a date for our marriage. As it is, all is unresolved save for our esteem for each other.*
>
> *Susan has been enjoying the attentions of John Fielding. I suspect that if matters are resolved peacefully, there will be two weddings. Of course, without your presence, our nuptials would not be as joyous. Three years is such a long time under certain circumstances.*
>
> *Tabby is well, though become too lazy to mouse the garden as heretofore. At night, he climbs up onto your bed, circles several times then lies down on your old pillow and sleeps, sometimes crying. He misses you as do the rest of us. There is a kitten, what we call an Occasional Kitten, who might help in the garden, but he or she is too shy.*
>
> *We hope these matters are not causing you too much distress. Write us when you find the time.*
>
> *Lizzie*

I wondered how careful my sister felt she had to be writing this, for letters could be opened. I saw no signs this had happened, but her letter might have been resealed very skillfully.

Aside from that, I was deeply moved by what I read. Such a longing to see my family, even just to see our cat, came over me that I feared I would burst into tears. Though my studies required my close and immediate attention, I had to go out and walk for some time before I could venture again into the company of my fellows. Though very uncertain of its delivery, I composed a reply at my first opportunity.

David Withrow was sympathetic, particularly about Tabby. He told me, "I too had a cat I was very fond of that had died when I was at school. I did not dare venture to ask for leave to return home to bury the creature, as it would just invite ridicule from the masters."

The end of winter term was almost immediately followed by the beginning of summer term, actually at the beginning of May. Many of my fellow students left Edinburgh for the summer. Some of us stayed, for in my case, where was I to go?

David Withrow took his leave of me, a sad occasion, as I would miss him. He invited me on completion of my studies to venture to London, to "perfect my knowledge" of my profession. Though I feigned skepticism of this last, I of course agreed.

In summer term, only Botany and Clinical Lectures were offered which was as well, as I would be hard pressed to afford another term's fee of eleven guineas. Fortunately three students required Latinizing of their theses, which would at least pay for my lodging next quarter. Though I had been most careful of my expenses, I had but £15 left even with what I had earned as a scribe and Latinist. So I was again very busy indeed, as were most of my fellows, and I was not conspicuous in my industry. At least the crowds in Clinical Lectures were much smaller, so I was able to hear the professor and to see the patients better. In fact, I decided I would not take Clinical Lectures in winter term again, as it was wasted money, and especially time as well.

Toward end of summer term, two more students solicited my much improved skills at converting their English theses to Latin. Only one student wanted my Botany notes, so I made less than £1 therein. Withall, paying for even the rest of my second year would be a near thing.

Beyond that, I now knew a great deal more about the subjects I had taken. I had watched many surgeries with a great crowd of fellow students. But I had no real experience actually dealing with patients. Though my knowledge was growing more extensive and detailed, it was all from books, and I owned that having to practice by myself daunted me. The only answer for this was more courses, more lectures, more gazing at patients and surgeries, assuming I could pay for these.

August brought no custom, so I went for walks, read some of the medical books in the library, and fretted. News from Massachusetts, when there was any, added to my fears. No letters from my family appeared. None of my friends were about; in fact, hardly anyone I knew was present. I began haunting the Infirmary, trying to pick up any bits of knowledge I could, assisting physicians and even surgeons whenever I could do so without having to pay.

My fellow students who were Scots had told me that wandering about on Sundays was forbidden in most of Scotland. Everyone was expected to be in church or "kirk" as they called it. In fact, this was compulsory. Edinburgh was uniquely liberal in this respect, but they warned me that I shouldn't venture farther. So I confined my "rambles" to the city. I had thought Massachusetts was severe in terms of church going but I was assured I was mistaken. I did as I was bidden but was left feeling somewhat confined.

It was in a way curious; in Massachusetts I attended church regularly. Here, not at all. Was I becoming a heathen, as some would say?

I attempted to become a "grinder," for I had learned from conversations with fellow students that it was possible to determine what questions were likely to be asked. These were in Latin, of course. So I became a schoolmaster of a sort, with three pupils. I asked them the questions likely to be asked and instructed them on their answers. I did get them all through their examinations and thereby earned a few more guineas. At this point I began to think I might be able to support myself beyond my second year in this fashion.

For my second year courses, I took Materica Medica (at 8 AM unfortunately), Medical Theory (11-12), the Royal Infirmary (open to students 12-1) and Clinical Surgery, at 5-6, Monday and Thursday. Overall, this was only ten guineas, a slight easing of cost. On the other hand, my notes for Medical Practice, Chemistry and Anatomy and Surgery were bringing in less than last year. Still I had to make additional copies for those who asked, though I couldn't be certain the lectures remained unaltered.

The holidays were approaching when I received another letter. I felt a mixture of fear, disappointment and relief when I saw it was from David Withrow, now in London. It said:

> *Dear Thomas of Wyeth*
>
> *(I would have styl'd you by your province but cannot spell it.) I am well lodged in Covent Garden, at No. 12, King Street, which I send you so that when you propose to come to London, you may as well stay with me. I attend Anatomical Lectures and demonstrations under Dr. Wm. Hunter. I have my own corpse to dissect, imagine that if you dare. And I walk the wards at St. Barthomews (call it St. Bart's), so hope to obtain my degree in two years or so.*
>
> *St. Bart's is quite different from Edinburgh. No peering over countless shoulders, straining to hear what the professor is saying. I learned a great deal at Edinburgh but London is the place to learn to practice medicine. But I think you know this. So come here when you finish there.*
>
> *Soon I must visit my family, also my intended. I told you about Dora. She writes often, having little else to do. But perhaps I am being unjust. I am sure she will be a good wife. She is fond of me, faux de mieux, no doubt.*
>
> *I must off to the school as my cadaver waits, but not forever.*
> 　　　　　　　　　　　　　　　　　　*Yours*
> 　　　　　　　　　　　　　　　　*David of Withrow*

I smiled, or as he would write it "smil'd". As soon as the holidays began and I had more time (another thesis to be Latinized), I replied:

> *Dear David of Cheshire*
>
> *I thank you for your letter, which has given me much occupation in ascertaining the meaning thereof. I continue here, my attendance fueled by fees from my lecture transcriptions, from acting as "grinder" to a few luckless souls and from Latinizing theses. I am certainly learning a great deal, such as, viz., it is far better to take Clinical Lectures in summer term than winter.*
>
> *For the nonce, I have enough (just) to complete my second year and by the same means, God or the Devil willing, the third as well. I haven't yet begun thinking of what I shall write my thesis about, but sufficient to the day...*
>
> *I have received but one letter from my family, but matters are so troubled in my home province (it is Massachusetts, please to note) that I count myself lucky to have that. My family misses me as does my cat, and I miss them as well.*
>
> *Pray give my regards and profoundest sympathies to your intended. Should we meet, be assured of my discretion, even though it will probably require a vow of utter silence.*
>
> *Yours in turn*
Thomas of Wyeth

The new year 1775 began and proceeded as the previous year had. Finally in March, I had a second letter from my family, this time written by my younger sister:

> *Dear Thomas*
>
> *We have received three letters so far from you, all very welcome. We had no idea Edinburgh would prove*

so expensive but you have supported your aims very well. We are proud of you.

We are all well, still, but Tabby is dead. He began to require assistance climbing onto your bed where he would sleep after crying some, looking for you, we believed. One morning we found he had died during the night. We buried him near the spot where he liked to lie, in the sun. The Occasional Kitten remains that, though he has condescended to take bits of meat we leave for him.

Matters remain distressed here. Boston is under military rule, which is much resented. Any dispute between soldiers and townspeople causes a great outcry and increases resentment on both sides. Talk, and I hope and pray it remains that, is of a clash of arms.

Father carries on but remains distressed by Mother's passing. Neighbors are beginning to suggest matches, but Lizzie and I wish they would leave matters as they are for a while. Business has increased some, which helps keep Father busy.

We all, including Lizzie's and my swains, think of you and pray for you and wish you well. Pray continue to write.

All our love
Susan

Reading this, I did indeed burst into tears, evoking concern from my fellow students and causing me to retire. For how could I explain that my tears were for a mere cat, a dumb creature? Yet so it was. After composing myself, I wrote another letter to them and posted it.

I had heard of the measures taken by the Crown. My feelings were mixed. It was hard on the province though some had provoked the measures. I could only shake my head, guiltily glad I was away, yet sorry matters seemed to be getting worse and worse. My sister's hint about "arms" was especially worrisome.

Three days later, I received a second letter from David Withrow. I opened this with much less trepidation, though my fellow students were looking askance at me. In David's letter, he again gave me the number of his lodging, again inviting me to stay with him. He told me his marriage was to be upon his qualifying at St. Bart's. He had completed Dr. Hunter's course and told me of a dissection of a man with the "sugar disease," diabetes. He and the other students were curious to see if there was any anatomical reason for the disease, but could find none. Dr. Hunter's brother John was considered a rising anatomist and surgeon. He came over to examine the corpse as well. David closed by saying he would attempt to find me a match, asking if I preferred an elderly wife with money or a young woman with very bad eyesight.

I smiled and replied in the same vein, but by now I had several theses to translate in addition to all my other tasks so was made very busy indeed. Still, David's comments about diabetes stuck in my mind and I began to read about the disease whenever I had a moment. I thought about it: people with diabetes ate sugar yet it passed through them so they derived no benefit thereby. Why was this?

Two more theses to convert to Latin, one of these not well "Englished" to begin with, so I had to ask the student what this or that passage was supposed to mean. I did not charge for the extra work, though I felt the fellow was going to have to be exceedingly finely "ground" to have a chance at passing. This term I had eight theses, giving me a total of forty guineas and I was now very hopeful I could pay for my last year.

But first I had to survive this term. I worked and studied very long hours, scanting my sleep, my leisure nonexistent, happily too busy to worry. In lectures and conversations I was now much more alert to anything about diabetes. I looked intently at patients with the disease, crowding other students to get closer to the patients. Asking questions of the doctors gave scattered bits of what I hoped was enlightenment. I began to ask myself, should patients with diabetes be fed only fats and meats? This would be an expensive diet to be sure, if it was helpful.

My second summer term I took Clinical Lectures again and also Clinical Surgery, only four guineas, but now I had still more theses to do and some "grinding" as well. This was very welcome but distracting. My readings about diabetes suffered, though again I was arrested by scattered comments, such as that the urine of diabetics, being sweet, attracted ants. I wondered how one might measure the sugar in piss. I began to long for August to have leisure to work on this problem.

However, now reports came from Massachusetts that the feared armed clashes had begun. An Army detachment had seized some stored arms and powder in Lexington but after shooting some of my fellow colonists. During the entire return march, the soldiers were shot at with many losses. A sort of siege of Boston appeared about to begin. I realized I would hear no more from my family for a considerable time.

I used my tasks to distract me from worries about my family. I was not worried about my father and sisters falling victim to violence, but my sisters' swains' fortunes were of course of great concern to them and perforce to me. Since I had so many tasks, these should keep me from such worries, yet it seemed the opposite was the case. So I spent summer term being very busy but much distressed.

After the first of August when theses had to be turned in, I had only my "grinding" but I had eleven pupils. Since I wanted to instruct only one at a time, again my accursed conscientious nature ensured I would have little time for my thesis.

Still, after much thought, continually interrupted as it was, I purchased two pounds of sugar and was allowed to use some apothecary's scales for weighing such. I also obtained a yardstick, a clean pail, a teaspoon, a tablespoon and some clean, well-corked, glass bottles.

At the first decent rain, I collected some rainwater in the pail, used this to rinse out the pail, collected more rainwater and poured this into the stoppered bottles after first rinsing them with the water as well. I thought rainwater the purest water I could find, so proposed using that for my experiments. I also collected two or three bottles of my piss after drinking two quarts of the rainwater.

By now seven of my "grinded" ("ground"?) students passed their examinations so with only four left, I had time for my trials. On a sunny Sunday, I looked for ant-hills outside, away from dwellings. One field had three, well separated. I chose one, measured two yards' distance from the hill and selected a dozen spots, each about a yard from the others, all two yards from the ant hill in the centre.

I had brought the apothecary's scale, carrying it very carefully of course, also some of the sugar, the spoons and two bottles of piss. I poured a tablespoon of my piss into three of my dozen spots then prepared tablespoons of piss to which I added weighed amounts of sugar. I let these dissolve, then poured the samples with sugar onto some of my other spots. I made a careful record of what was poured onto each spot.

When all twelve spots had sugared or pure piss added, I took my watch and waited, moving cautiously around the circle, looking for interest from ants. Within half an hour, they began exploring the spots I had poured the samples on. I counted the ants at each spot at the half hour after I finished adding the samples, after another hour, then after two more hours. To my delight, the number of ants clustered on each spot was greater, the more sugar in the tablespoon of piss. I could measure the sugar in piss. I brought everything back, feeling triumphant. My method worked, but I would test it further when I had leisure. Still I was happier than I could ever recall being.

This feeling was immediately scotched by the news that reached my lodging. Some armed colonists seized a neck of land north of Boston Harbour and were attacked by regular soldiers of the Crown. Our soldiers prevailed, driving the colonists away, but evidently at heavy cost. Boston was in fact now besieged. War had begun. I felt sick and angry at those colonists who were fomenting this. But I wondered uneasily if the Crown by its actions might have contributed to the situation.

I was more surprised to find the few fellow lodgers present sharply divided in their opinions, some of course supporting the Crown, others actually sympathetic to the colonists. I could only shake my head and try to retreat into working with my remaining pupils and thinking about my experiments.

By September, I was able to return to what I hoped would be the basis of a thesis. Having to prepare the sugar solutions one at a time was awkward, so I purchased some one- and two-dram bottles to prepare all the solutions I was going to test before going to an anthill. I remembered from somewhere that ants and other insects were much more sluggish in cold weather, so I needed to note the temperature. For this I purchased a thermometer. Then I went to the Infirmary to get some piss from a diagnosed diabetic. Finally, I performed an experiment on myself. I ate a half a pound of sugar, washing it down with two quarts of rainwater. I collected my own piss at half an hour after, an hour after that and one and a half hours after that. By now it was late in the afternoon, so I used the rest of the day preparing my sugared piss samples, using what I had produced that morning. I hoped and prayed for good, warm, dry weather on the morrow as I thought all my samples should be used while fresh.

Blessedly, the next day was dry, warm (61 degrees Fahrenheit), and I carried out my measurements using two anthills, essentially repeating what I had done with the first anthill. I used only one of each sample with each anthill this time, since I had so many samples.

Once more, with the sugared piss samples, the number of ants found about each sample increased with the amount of sugar. So far, so good. My own piss samples showed a small amount of sugar after half an hour but nothing in the two later samples. I gathered that the sugar I had eaten was in my tissues (or else in my bowels). The diabetic piss had too much sugar, more than in any of my sugared piss samples. I would have to mix it with my own morning piss to lower the amount.

The next day also being dry, though cooler (55 degrees Fahrenheit), I made up more sugared piss samples and several mixtures of diabetic piss with my own. I used the anthill I employed originally. Once more, my own showed no sugar, and I was able to add enough of my own piss to that of the diabetic's to make two measurements of the sugar in the piss of the patient with diabetes. Happily, no ecstatically, the two measurements were close to each other. My method worked and might even be useable to diagnose mild cases of the disease. I now had material for my own thesis, which I began to write without delay.

Having read many theses by now, I knew what to say. I described all the printed accounts of the disease, in my best Latin of course, then went on to say that a method to measure sugar in piss—urine, rather—would help diagnose mild cases, which probably were forerunners of more severe disease. This might make possible changes in the patient's regimen which would forestall the disease.

That written, I began to write about my experiments. Here I ran into difficulties. I had to describe, precisely and accurately and above all clearly in Latin: what I had done, how I had done it, why I had done it the way I chose and what I found. These requirements made heavy going and many sheets of paper. Eventually, I was forced to write everything of an experimental character out in English, work on the English until I thought it was clear then translate the English into Latin. Finally, I described what I thought my results meant in terms of Natural Philosophy and in terms of Medicine. All this took nearly a month, and Matriculation was approaching. Still, it was done, though I knew I would almost certainly rewrite parts of it.

For my third and I hoped final year, I decided to take Royal Infirmary at 12-1, Military Surgery at 2-3, Midwifery at 3-4, and Clinical Surgery again at 5-6. This was even cheaper and left my mornings free, allowing me to see more of patients and their treatments. I was hoping my free mornings might provide greater income over winter term, for if I was going to London upon graduation, I needed money.

Though my courses were less in expense and required less time, I tried to do justice to all of them. I found Midwifery unusual for two reasons. There were many women in the class taking the course for the certificate enabling them to practice their profession perhaps better but certainly more profitably. These were women of mature years, so not as distracting as younger women. For eleven shillings sixpence more, we were allowed to attend women in their lying-in. I paid this for I wanted the experience. Since we consequently saw the private parts of these women, this was disturbing to me and I thought to the other men present. I kept reminding myself that I might be called upon to attend my sisters in labour, so must look on the patients as my own sisters. Still, I did get experience attending actual patients, so the course was very worthwhile for that reason. Remembering my assistance to the cow doctor at home, I washed my hands before attending women in labour, without understanding why. However, I saw this was not the custom of the doctor in attendance, certainly not the students, at least beforehand.

Military Surgery was lectures since there was no war at hand. I was intrigued by the mention, several times, of a surgeon practicing in London named John Hunter. On asking the professor, I was told he was "another Scot" and the younger brother of Dr. William Hunter, both of whom I had heard of in one of David Withrow's letters. John Hunter was considered a very capable anatomist and surgeon. I resolved to ask about John Hunter in my next letter to my friend in London. Both Hunters almost certainly gave private classes and I still grievously felt my lack of practical experience.

One part of a lecture concerned John Hunter's discovery that the practice of enlarging wounds, supposedly to promote healing, had the opposite effect and should be stopped. I gathered that John Hunter was a man of keen observation who thought for himself. I wanted to meet this man.

Many of the other students were surgical apprentices, hoping to qualify to become assistant surgeons in the Army. We were told in one lecture that while assistant surgeons were forbidden to wear uniforms, we were strongly advised to obtain an officer's red coat, though without regimental facings. This would greatly ease our way among officers and men, giving us an official position among H. M.'s troops while in garrison or on the march.

I again read my thesis during the holidays. I decided not to change anything. The obvious objection would be raised that the method was unworkable since it required an anthill, but I had an answer to that. In fact, I decided I would submit it for the early examinations, that is, by March 1 instead of September 1. I felt the other demands on my time allowed me to do this.

On inquiry, I was told the examinations for the MD began with going to the Dean of the Faculty in March with certificates of attendance for my classes. Then I was to go in the evening to the home of one of the professors to be questioned by the professors present. This was to see if I would be allowed to continue with the examinations. I was told by my fellow students that the questions would be on subjects covered in lectures. Since I had prepared verbatim transcripts of all the lectures and moreover had copied them many times for other students, I was confident of this part of the examinations.

Since my thesis was done, or so I fancied, I could then pass to the second examination in the University Library by two of the professors. Next I was required to write commentaries on an aphorism of Hippocrates, a general medical question and two case histories, all in Latin. This was to be done in my lodgings and I could use any books or notes I could find. Again, this should be within my powers.

Finally, I would have to defend my thesis, once more in Latin. While I did not imagine any reasonable objection being made to my work, the imagined possibility of other kinds made me apprehensive. After all, my thesis was unusual. Instead of a compilation of others' work or opinions on a disease, it was new, experimental work at which some professors might look askance.

Fortunately I was getting more requests for my notes, even from two years ago, some requests for grinding, and translating two theses. During summer, I hoped I would have much more custom to divert me. I needed the income to enable me to graduate, since the cost of the examinations was £10 to be divided between the six professors.

The only letters I wrote and received were to and from David Withrow. He confirmed that though Dr. William Hunter had a fashionable practice—he was Male Midwife to the Queen—his younger brother was rising in esteem among those interested in Natural Philosophy. David also told me that John Hunter was highly respected as a surgeon and anatomist.

David himself was hoping to qualify for the MD at St. Bart's this coming summer, after which he was obliged, as he put it, to marry his Dora. As a younger son, he had to set up in practice to support himself, his wife and any children. He was kind enough to suggest we practice together.

This took me by surprise. I had been intending to go to London to study, to gain more experience, more practical experience, but my plans beyond that were vague. I had so much to do here. I would need money. I didn't have any experience of London…. But joining with David in practice seemed a solution to these difficulties. So, after thought, I wrote back saying I was happy to give the arrangement a trial and that I would probably be on his doorstep the end of September.

Over the end of winter, aside from informing the Dean of my plans, I kept busy with my courses and my commercial pursuits. A few more theses requiring my translation were given me. I was beginning to feel I would have some money in my pocket when I went to London, a great relief to me.

May arrived and my examinations began. I was invited to the home of one of the professors, Mr. Cullen, to be questioned, in Latin of course, about my knowledge of medicine. I had reread all the notes for all my courses, so should have felt confident but was instead very nervous. Mr. Cullen must have noticed this and asked me a few simple questions to set me at ease. I was able to answer these and the subsequent ones of increasing difficulty to be sure, and at the end of the evening was told I could continue. I had given my thesis to Mr. Cullen, so this meant I would now be questioned by two of the other faculty in the Library. Since winter term was over, most of the faculty were at leisure to examine candidates.

This *viva voce* examination went on about two hours and differed little from the first. I was somewhat more confident, so less nervous. At the end, I was told I had passed and could now proceed to the written parts of the examination. I thanked the men and left, too tired and sweaty to feel like celebrating.

The aphorism and general medical question had been given some other students so were not surprises. The two case histories were also familiar. Still, I daren't take these lightly, so bent to work on them, with occasional interruptions from customers. This was vexing, yet probably helpful, as I seemed to progress faster with the interruptions than without.

It was early in June when I heard that Crown forces had left

Boston and removed to Canada. I hoped for news from my family, though we would probably maintain a blockade on the port. I also wondered about the Loyalists, as they were now called, in Boston. Would they leave? Where would they go? Ann and her family would be among them, though Ann by now might be long married and a mother, perhaps laughing with her husband about the countrified swain who aspired to court her.

At this point I had completed my answers to the questions and given them to the faculty. Assuming they were acceptable, only the defense of my thesis remained. I was taking no courses this summer term. Aside from the examinations, I had six theses to translate and some grinding to do.

I was walking to the Medical Library, anxious about some point in Celsius, when I encountered an acquaintance, a surgeon's apprentice who was in Clinical Surgery with me. We exchanged greetings and told each other what we were doing.

He first asked, "Are ye not taking Clinical Surgery this summer term?"

"Or anything else," I informed him. "I am preparing to defend my thesis."

"Once I hae completed Clinical Surgery, I will obtain a licentiate in surgery, so I can practice as a surgeon."

So I rejoined, "We are both on our way to punish the afflicted."

He laughed at this. We shook hands, clapped each other on the shoulders, and proceeded on our individual ways, both cheered.

As I entered the Library, I began reflecting on the differences between the education of surgeons and physicians. It struck me for the first time that an essential difference was that the examinations for a physician were conducted in Latin. The lectures, which were attended by aspirant physicians and surgeons alike, were in English. One of David Withrow's comments came to mind about the differences between gentle and "simple," as he put it. That was the reason for employment of Latin in our examinations: gentlemen were supposed to know Latin. Latin then made the gentlemen and physicians were supposed to be gentlemen... no, physicians wanted to be regarded as gentlemen. This was why they were paid in guineas, not pounds. This division could certainly be found in the colonies, but it was much less absolute, much more easily bridged there than here in Britain. Aspirations and merit and work alone could be sufficient where I came from, not here. Was that what some of the fighting was about?

About the middle of June, I and the other aspiring graduates assembled in the Public Hall of the University. We were told the Oath we were to swear to and were questioned about our theses, one at a time. Once more I was nervous at first, for two of the candidates were given a very hard time. I was indeed asked about the practical value of my discovery. I suggested several modifications by which measurements of sugar in urine could be made in a hospital, which of course prompted one professor to ask why I hadn't tried my suggestions. I pointed out I hadn't a hospital position or the wherewithal to do this. My reply was somewhat evasive but the professors seemed satisfied and turned to the next candidate.

I was a little shaken. Should I have done more? I waited until we had all been examined and were told to leave the room. Outside, we all put on black Doctor's gowns, somewhat presumptuously in my case I thought. We were readmitted, permitted to swear the Oath, and told we had all received the degree of Doctor of Medicine. Then we could leave, our efforts rewarded.

I think most of my fellow doctors celebrated, probably in taverns. I had never been in a tavern in Edinburgh. Perhaps I should have celebrated with them, but for two reasons. First, I had five theses to translate and two pupils for grinding to begin tomorrow. But most of all, I felt oddly low. My separation from my family and the circumstances producing this, my future being uncertain in many ways, and the criticism of my work all made me feel that if I went to a tavern and imbibed, I would begin crying again. So, after staring at the work I was to do, I retired early and slept late as my own celebration.

Until August 1, I continued translations, netting fifty guineas. My grinding efforts produced twenty guineas more. I still had to pay for my lodging, for washing, etc., nonetheless was able to take above £50 to London, about what I had brought to Edinburgh three years previously.

News of General Howe's victory, sending the rebels fleeing and capturing New York City, cheered some here. My feelings were tempered by wondering if any of my friends from Harvard or the province were among the rebels. My sisters' suitors, I suspected more and more strongly, had been in the fighting but I had no definite information. The outcome I most devoutly wished for was peace, a peace of reconciliation, of forgiveness, between Crown and colonists. Then I could go home once more, there to live and practice my profession.

On the day of the graduation examinations of my students in September, my grinding done, I hoped successfully, I hired a man to carry my chest through the city in which I had spent three years. I saw many things I had not paid any attention to before such as the Castle and Arthur's Seat, finally reaching the quays at Leith where a ship for London was waiting. With all my lecture transcripts, I had to reorder the contents of my chest several times, finally forcing the chest closed and locked. The weather was dry, with some sun, and the wind was from the west. So I began the next stage of my journey.

10

LONDON, 1776

◆

My voyage south down the east coast of Scotland and England was uncomfortable. Not just because of my fellow passengers, all Scots insofar as I could tell. They were a silent lot—"dour" I think the Scots' expression is—keeping apart from me and each other. But the movement of the ship was different from that of the one I crossed the Atlantic in. At first I thought it was because of the smaller size of the one I was on. Whatever the reason, I often felt sickish, wanting to vomit.

As we rounded eastern England, preparing to sail into the Channel, I told the captain about this, "Your ship's motion is very different from that of the ship I was in crossing the Atlantic."

"Ah, aye," he said, "North Sea be shallow, Atlantic is deep. So waves be different." He seemed happy to converse with a passenger; I supposed the sour visages of the other passengers discomfited him as well.

The winds were less favourable in the Channel than for sailing south, so we tacked often. However, the distance to the Thames estuary was but small and as the following evening neared, we could see innumerable buildings and a thicket of masts of a great crowd of ships, so closely moored it seemed possible to step from one to the next and thus attain the shore. We dropped our anchor and passengers now had to be ferried upriver, in my case through an opening under London Bridge, then to shore.

I had managed to claim a seat with my chest in the first passage. As evening advanced, I stood on the quayside looking about. Several men approached, wanting to carry my chest. I decided on this course as I needed guidance to King Street. So I told one of them, "King Street, number 12, just off Covent Garden."

The fellow nodded, took up my chest, a little surprised at its weight, for I had lifted it from the rowboat without much effort. Off we went. "Wot's so 'evy?" the fellow asked, asked twice in fact for at first I didn't understand him.

"Papers," I told the man.

I thought that he had spoken overloudly. But I realized everyone in earshot was doing the same thing to make themselves heard over the sound of vehicles of all sorts, horses' hooves on cobblestones, boots and shoes on pavements, cries of costermongers, and bells large and small, all joining into a turbulence of sound. This added to the excitement of being in the capitol, of being seized by the energy of the city.

Despite the advancing evening, there were many people about, people of all descriptions, all classes and all conditions. This was very unlike Edinburgh. Some of the women I saw gazed boldly at me. This at first was flattering. I saw some of them make what I took to be obscene gestures and I suddenly realized these women were prostitutes, whores, and the first clearly of that occupation I had ever seen. I tore my gaze away, not wanting to suggest I was for buying the services they sold. I kept close to the fellow carrying my chest, not difficult as he was clearly tiring, shifting his grip on the strap from one hand to the other.

The streets were of different widths set at various angles to each other, most straight or nearly so, some curved. Then we came to a large square, a great market for flowers and vegetables and fruits surrounded by some buildings. To one side I thought might be a public house from the sign. To my left was a building that I recognized was a church. My guide told me it was St. Paul's church. King Street formed the north east side of the great square, and there we directed our steps.

No. 12 was marked and here we stopped, the fellow clearly glad to set his burden down while I used the knocker. I was thinking I had no idea how much to pay, when the door opened and David himself stood there, looking at me.

"Thomas, come in, come in," he said, grinning at me.

I grinned back; I was so happy to see a friendly face, then remembered and turned to the bearer of my chest. I extracted a crown from my pocket and offered it. He was delighted, and I guessed I had overpaid, but I didn't care. The fellow walked away rapidly, I suppose to forestall my asking him for something back. I picked up my chest and carried it in past my host.

David showed me where I was to sleep, a small but comfortable-looking cell, much like the one I had inhabited for three years in Edinburgh. There was a curtained window looking out on the square. I set my chest down.

David asked me, "Did you take Midwifery?"

I said, "Yes, but only winter term."

"Did you attend any lyings in?"

I replied, "Yes. I paid the extra eleven shillings or so. I assisted in above a dozen deliveries and was present at about another thirty. So I actually have experience for that."

David was pleased, and told me, "I have several women nearing their term, so your arrival is opportune. Did you bring your Midwifery notes?"

In answer, I opened my chest and went through the packets of notes, each tied with string, until I found the Midwifery packet.

I handed this to David, who said, "I will look these over from this evening. Come and have a cup of saloop."

"What is that?" I asked.

David replied, "Milk sweetened with sugar and flavoured with sassafras, from the southern colonies, I think."

I shook my head, "I think I have heard of it, but have never tasted it."

David raised his eyebrows. "But it is from the provinces."

I affected humility. "I am a very provincial provincial."

David laughed and poured some "saloop" from a pitcher into a pannikin, which I took and drank from. It was very tasty, the smell rich. I realized I was thirsty and hungry as well. I had a refill and some fire-browned bread I recognized as "toast", spread with butter and jam.

David accompanied me, saying, "My servants, a manservant and a housekeeper-cook, are away. I give them holiday every so often. You just happened on my doorstep when that was the situation. They will return tomorrow."

I asked, "Much custom so far?"

David nodded, told me, "I am well pleased with the numbers. Not so few that I would worry, not so many I would be hard-pressed to keep up. But numbers are increasing and so I am glad you are here."

I said, "I hoped to take a dissection class."

David replied, "There are several given. A corpse costs about £3. The classes are given in winter, naturally. I understand John Hunter is to give lectures on surgery over fall and winter."

I was pleased, and told David, "Just what I think I need. Aside from work with actual patients, of course. I suppose I should buy surgical instruments. At present I have nothing of the sort at all."

David said, "I can tell you where to get those."

We sipped more saloop then David asked, "What did you think of London?"

I considered then replied, "Very populous, very large, very smoky, very noisy, very busy. Everyone scurrying about. Except for some ladies who seemed in no hurry to go anywhere. But perhaps they weren't ladies after all. When I looked at some of them, I thought they were making gestures at me that seemed lewd."

David again grinned and asked, "And how would a provincial provincial be able to tell such?"

I protested, "I'm not that provincial. Such things go on even in the provinces." Silence ensued, then I continued, "Or so I have heard."

David and I both laughed. He seemed about to say something when there was a knock at the door.

"Custom?" I asked.

David nodded, got to his feet and went to the door. I decided to go too, as I might as well start my prenticeship now.

There was a boy on David's doorstep. He said, "Please, doctor, me mum's pains are startin'."

David came back, took a stout walking stick, more properly termed a cudgel, from a large vase in the corner. Then he got a black bag I took to be a medical bag from a side table and went out, I following. We walked together, following the boy after David carefully locked the door of No. 12.

As we walked, I nodded at the stick and raised my eyebrows. David told me, "Very necessary in London, Thomas. You should get one yourself and never go about without it."

I asked, "Is there no watch?"

David shrugged, "There is but that is useless. A small sword and pistol in addition would not be amiss."

I said, "Let me carry your bag, then," and he relinquished the bag to me.

I looked about, now seeing sinister purpose in every lounging knot of men and even women moving slowly along. When we reached the boy's dwelling, we followed him up two flights of somewhat uncertain stairs, turned and encountered an open door. In the room were several women standing about, two or three other children and a bed on which lay a woman obviously in labour.

David told the women, "This is my colleague, Dr. Thomas Wyeth, to assist me."

I went to the woman, noting the timing of the spasms, guessed the delivery was some hours yet, and began talking to the woman. I asked her, "How many does this make?"

One of the women wiped sweat from the patient's face, and between gasps and grunts the patient said, "This is sixth. Me 'usband's at sea, again. These alus 'appen then."

"He will return to another happy event, then, with money in his pocket."

The patient replied, " 'E's Royal Navy, so mebbe some prize money."

Since she had been through labour five times before and apparently considered this one unexceptional, I was reassured. I turned to the three women in attendance, asked if they had all had children, and hearing they all had, asked if any were midwives. None were. However, they were friends, so I did not ask them to leave. Having friends about during such an ordeal could only comfort the patient and care for the three children I saw, also helpful.

There was a box nearby on which sat a basin and ewer. I decided to wash my hands before examining the patient, a practice that with me had approached the status of a religious rite. So I did. This elicited comments from the three women, comments I ignored. David was sitting on the only chair and opened his medical bag in case I needed forceps or anything else he carried.

Everything did indeed seem unexceptionable, and noting the intervals between spasms using David's watch, I saw they were becoming more frequent. From time to time, I talked to the patient, who assured me matters were proceeding normally. One of the women offered the patient a cup of gin, which I quietly but firmly forbade, saying, "Not until after."

Annoyed at my exercise of authority, the woman asked me, "'Ave ye 'tended many women, in childbirth, I mean?"

I said, "Yes, above a dozen."

If not impressed, she was at least silenced. As the evening proceeded into night, the intervals between spasms shortened and the patient's delivery approached.

As delivery seemed imminent, I examined the patient again, once again after washing my hands. All appeared well, no sign of a breech delivery. Blessedly, all did indeed go well, an infant boy making his entrance onto the world's stage—I was feeling so relieved that I became very slightly poetic. The time was 1:57 AM, which I noted, grinning at the patient, all of us delighted, the patient's children asleep. The boy began to suckle almost immediately, so after clearing away the afterbirth, David and I took our leave, saying one of us, probably me, would call tomorrow. The great fear, of course, was childbirth fever. All we could do now was hope.

As David and I walked back, I told him, "The fellow carrying my chest asked me if I didn't mean 'King Place,' not King Street. I told him 'No, Number 12, King Street.' But I thought he was smirking at me."

David laughed aloud then said, "King Place consists of five houses on one side of the road. All are brothels."

I could see women, individuals and small knots of them. As it now approached three in the morning, their occupations were obvious even to a naïve colonial.

David continued, "There are half a dozen other brothels about Covent Garden, such as the Bedford Head, Tom's and King's coffee houses, Hummum's Hotel and a few others that burned down a few years ago. And there are two or three bagnios."

"Bagnios?" I asked, shaking my head politely at two women who were looking for custom.

"Bathhouses or hummums" said my companion, "though other services are provided."

I thought a moment, said, "At least the participants are clean." David laughed.

I went on, "So Covent Garden is a nest of vice?"

David was gazing at three mean-looking men loitering near two women. He shifted his stick so the men would be certain to see it, but replied to my question: "Covent Garden is perhaps central, but such establishments are scattered from the Royal exchange to Charing Cross. So you see people, men looking to satisfy their lusts, women prepared to sell themselves, at all hours. However, Thomas," here we were at No. 12, and David, after carefully looking about, unlocked the door, "most of the people living about are honest folk, living here because rents are cheap."

Now we separated to our beds, not before time as I was wavering on my feet from fatigue.

Unhappily, David's patients began appearing early that morning, about eight by David's clock and I was pressed into service, sleepy as I was. There were two rooms that could serve to meet patients and I was allotted one. I was able to deal with these: put a name to what the patient suffered from, remembered the treatment I was taught, offered words of encouragement and advice and collected the fees.

David's servants returned about ten and so David and I had at last a proper meal, downed between patients. I deposited the monies I had collected in a shiny black vase with a neck two inches or so in diameter. This graced the side table behind David's medical bag. So our day proceeded by fits and starts until about three, when things became quiet. At this time, I was released to purchase a cudgel, a medical bag and my medical instruments, a list of which David had prepared. He had also given me the names and directions of the shops.

My purchases took above two hours, so it was nearing six when I returned. I had also stopped to examine the woman whose labour I had attended early that same morning. She and her new son were well: the son suckling lustily, the mother with no sign of fever. Still all well, as I would report to David.

Over dinner that evening, I said to David, "As I told you, I want to buy surgical instruments also. I am beginning to feel that the division between medicine, as it is defined, and surgery, is artificial. If I am to be of the greatest benefit to patients, I must be prepared to do both. And aside from the instruments, I really need to practice at surgery and that means dissection of a human body."

David listened to this, and told me, "I think the division between medicine and surgery is basically to allocate profitable fiefdoms to doctors and surgeons, nothing more than that. So perhaps tomorrow you can get those. I still have the instruments I did my dissections with. Magnus Falconer has a school where dissections are done, in winter, naturally. And John Hunter is giving a course of lectures starting October and continuing until March."

I again said, "That is what I want."

The next day I added to my collection: scalpels, tweezers, forceps, two catheters, needles, silk thread, a tin wash basin and a wooden box containing a bar of soap. I decided I also needed some drugs and one or two bottles of spirits of wine, as some of the drugs were administered in that solvent. But that was for the morrow or rather the day after, for the morrow was a Sunday. Not that the day made a great difference to our custom, as patients would appear without warning at nearly any time. This was aside from men injured by thieves in nearby streets who were brought to our door as we were prepared to treat the injured or sick at any hour of any day. We assured each other the experience was valuable, as robbed men of course could not pay us.

11

CAROLINE

◆

I had gone to inquire as to Falconer's and John Hunter's courses, fees and times and locations. Returning to King Street, I remembered I needed to purchase opium and a few specifics as well as spirits of wine, so began looking for an apothecary's shop. There was one near the middle of one set of houses: Avebury Apothecary. I went in. There was a woman behind the counter, a little surprising as apothecaries were licensed and that meant were men.

"Yes, sir?" asked the woman.

As my eyes adjusted to relative darkness—it was a bright day outside—I saw a tall woman with flaxen hair, a willowy figure and grey eyes. I could not guess her age. I took out my list, and showed this to the woman. At this point a man appeared, greying hair but also tall with an athletic figure. I couldn't tell if he was the woman's husband but then I noticed his resemblance to the woman including the same grey eyes and realized he was her father.

The woman went to fill the order. She seemed to require no instruction, and the father asked me my name.

"Thomas Wyeth, sir. I am a doctor, in practice on King Street with Dr. David Withrow. I take it you are Mr. Avebury?"

The proprietor, as I took him to be, smiled and replied, "No, I am Roger Vandelys. I inherited the shop when my wife died."

This was a trifle confusing, but here was the daughter with what I had requested and the charge which I paid. I left thinking the daughter was a comely lass and telling myself not to be entertaining such thoughts. I didn't even know her name.

Still, she must have remained in my mind. Over dinner, David told me, "Thomas, your notes from the midwifery lectures are most instructive. I thank you." I nodded with my mouth full of beef. David continued, "But I am afraid I must leave you here to deal with patients. I am to marry my Dora in eleven days. Then we will return to a house I have taken on Selwyn Street to begin life together. The lease on this house runs several more months, so you may stay here."

I cleared my palate with ale and replied, "I will leave all the hard cases for you when you return." David smiled, and I asked or rather commented, "Dora is a somewhat unusual name, is it not?"

"'Dora' is the familiar form for 'Theodora', which is a Greek name," David informed me. "My Dora is supposedly descended from a Byzantine princess of that name brought here after the Fourth Crusade, I think it was the Fourth, and female descendants are always named 'Theodora' in honour of their ancestor."

I absorbed this. I then asked David, "Have you ever had carnal knowledge of a woman? I have not: with lust pushing me to do so and fear of the possible consequences, the pox I mean, pushing me back, perhaps some hard cases may divert me."

David looked away, smiled and answered my question: "As I told you once, Dora and I grew up together and have been intended for each other since childhood. Once when I was thirteen or fourteen, I and a scullery maid began fondling each other and I am certain we would have satisfied our lusts in some bushes except Dora came upon us."

"What did she do?" I asked.

David said, "She began to cry. This made me ashamed of myself, quite unmanned me. The scullery-maid took herself off. I was so remorseful that I knelt before Dora and made a pledge of celibacy until we married, and one of monogamy after." David sipped his wine, looked at me and assured me, "A pledge I have kept, though it has been hard, but I would not see her in tears from my behavior again for a kingdom. And you? Is there a sweetheart, perhaps back in America?"

I shook my head. "There was a girl I was in love with, but she was intended for someone else. I met a girl today in a pothecary shop, Avebury's. She is a daughter of the owner I believe, and works there. I have been wondering how often I can plausibly find excuses to go there."

David smiled and said, "I am certain you will come up with some. What is her name?"

I again shook my head, confessed, "I don't know. I fear I exhibit lack of enterprise as a lover."

It was two days in fact before an excuse presented itself—several dropsical patients required diuretics so I went to obtain such. The girl or rather woman was with her father, each dealing with a customer, so I waited. To my silent relief, the woman dealt with her customer first, looked at me, recognized me and smiled. I smiled back, then told her what I came to get. She obtained all the items save one, told me how much these cost, which I paid, and then said, "I know where you may get this one. It is not far. I can show you the way." This offer was very acceptable to me and after a word with her father, we set forth together.

As we walked, I struggled with shyness but finally managed to tell her, "I don't know your name."

The woman said, "I am Caroline Vandelys. As he told you, my father inherited the shop when my mother died."

I was conscious of my companion's womanly shape, the movement of her hips as she walked, not like the way whores walked, but straightforward yet most intriguing. But there we were at our journey's destination. The woman stayed with me while I purchased the remaining drug, then we walked together back to Avebury's.

I really couldn't think of anything else to say. Finally I remembered what had mystified me and I remarked, "So Avebury was your mother's first husband?"

Caroline nodded. I noticed our pace had slowed. She told me, "Mother had no surviving children by Avebury, and I was the only survivor of Mother's second marriage. Then Father remarried and he and my stepmother have two children alive. I suppose my half-brother will inherit the shop, for it is hard for a woman to get a license as an apothecary."

This was said in a matter-of-fact tone, yet of course I was interested, certainly in continuing the conversation. I said, "Then otherwise you are fully conversant with drugs and pills and could carry on the business yourself."

Caroline replied, "Oh yes, I daresay I could if I had to. I have had a long enough apprenticeship." Turning to me, Caroline asked, "You do not speak like an Englishman. Are you from one of the American colonies?"

We were standing before Avebury's. I said, "I am from the province of Massachusetts, from a small town west of Boston. I studied at Edinburgh before the war started. Now I am cut off from contact with my family."

"Have you a wife?" Caroline asked.

"No wife nor child," I replied, "just my father and two younger sisters. And possibly a cat." This last was said smiling and Caroline smiled too.

She said, "I daresay you miss the cat most of all."

I acknowledged this, "We miss each other greatly." At this we separated.

Returning, I forced my attention on my path, as my way went past two or three brothels at the windows of which stood whores, some naked and some as near as might be, gesticulating and exhibiting their private parts or caressing these. A few of the passers-by stopped to watch and some of these might enter, but I hurried on. It was something of a relief to return to No. 12 where patients awaited.

With two of us, they did not wait long, perhaps one of the reasons their numbers seemed to have increased almost magically. An elderly man was having trouble pissing; so I oiled one of my new catheters. After explaining what I was going to do, I pushed this gently into his penis. There was some obstruction behind the sphincter so his prostate was grown, partly blocking the passage. I emptied him, explained that he could buy a catheter and do what I did when he chose, and for nothing, but he gave me the crown and said he would return when he felt he needed it.

A stoutish man told me of pain in his lower right abdomen. On finding the area to be tender and his other symptoms like my mother had, I told him, "Sir, you have what is called an inflamed appendix. For the time being, you should eat no solids. Take only liquids, milk and broth, until the pain goes away. After, reduce your eating, especially of solids. If the appendix bursts from your intestine being overly full, you will die from internal sepsis."

He seemed disappointed I would not prescribe a cathartic or purgative but I assured him those would probably kill him faster. I added, "Please take my warnings seriously as we are new practitioners and do not want to waste patients." I smiled as I said this and hoped he would do as bidden.

David and I worked through the day's customers by late afternoon, so retired to talk over the day. Once professional matters were dealt with, I asked him, "There is a woman I wish to see more of. What places or events are available to accompany a respectable young woman to?"

David frowned, shook his head and replied, "There are plays, but be warned: brawls frequently erupt, especially in the cheaper locations. You will needs take your cudgel. There are also concerts, but you and the lady must be dressed fashionably, that is expensively. Even on walks in parks like Hyde or St. James Parks, one can be accosted by so-called gentlemen who object to your dress or to anything they choose. Then there are tea shops. That is about the lot."

This was discouraging. Thinking matters over, I decided to call on Caroline, solicit her company and ask her to choose the venue. Since I was a stranger in London, asking her advice was reasonable. What I really wanted to do was take her to bed, but I realized that would take time and probably marriage. I would have to come up with some reason for going to Avebury's.

However as it happened, we met in the street the following day. I had just returned from a newly-delivered patient and saw her ahead of me. She was carrying a basket and was clearly going to buy something in Covent Garden. She was attended by a manservant. I increased my pace, as she was no sluggard, yet I think she heard my step, for she turned, saw me and stopped. She did not so much smile as her entire face lit up, as I daresay did mine. For she was a most attractive woman, tall, lissome, her grey eyes sparkled.

I raised my tricorn and said, "Good day, Miss Vandelys."

She curtsied, replying, "Indeed, Dr. Wyeth." Looking at her basket, I raised my eyebrows. Caroline raised the basket and told me, "My father and half-brother are very fond of pines, so I am to buy two and bring them home for our dinner."

"Pines?" I asked.

"Pineapples," she amended, "I am sure you have heard of them."

"Yes," I said, "but I confess I have never eaten any."

David Withrow emerged from No. 12, saw us and came over. I said, "David, this is Miss Caroline Vandelys. Miss Vandelys, this is my associate in keeping the population of London under some measure of control, Dr. David Withrow. Of Cheshire," I added, as if it were highly prestigious.

His mettle up, David spoke, "Thomas of Somewhere Unspellable, as I call him, resides here, since he made the most pitiable whimpering sounds when outside. I am endeavouring to instruct him in some of the elements of physic, though I must say, he is but an indifferent pupil."

I responded, "My abilities will adjust with my wages."

David was laughing, as were Caroline and I, and informed us, "I am bidden by my fiancée to have my locks shorn, as she wishes to be certain of whom she is marrying. Thomas, no dinner for you. Again."

I turned to Caroline, "It appears I will have to rehearse whimpering and scratching at his door."

Caroline told us, "Since the subject has been raised and reiterated, I feel I must invite you, Thomas, to dine with us this evening."

David gave me a broad wink and walked on to have his task accomplished and I bowed my acceptance of Caroline's invitation.

She selected two pineapples and two lemons and we walked back to Avebury's together. She asked me, "And when is your associate to marry?"

I thought and replied, "The Saturday next. He is a younger son, hence his profession."

Caroline wondered, "How long has he known the bride?"

I told her, "All their lives. They grew up together and have been intended for each other probably as long."

Caroline commented, "That doesn't sound very romantic."

I said, "I agree, but I daresay the result—the marriage—is the important thing."

Caroline's family graciously allowed me to share their evening meal, the pineapples not excepted, though I partook only cautiously of that viand. This was partly out of courtesy, as Mr. Vandelys and his son Richard ate most of them, and partly out of caution, as I had noticed that unaccustomed food or water sometimes produced cases of the flux, brief but awkward. However, the meal dispatched, and the questions of Caroline's family answered, she and I were allowed to sit together on a sofa before a good coal fire without obvious chaperonage. Mrs. Vandelys, a plump, dark woman of middle height, asked most of the questions, I assumed to see if I was potentially suitable to take Caroline away. I sensed some interest in both father and stepmother for that result.

The fire was surprisingly welcome for the evening had turned cool, and Caroline and I basked in the warmth. I noticed that she looked positively beautiful by firelight. We sipped from cups of ale. Caroline commented on some remarks made by a vicar who visited the Vandelys's several times. Caroline's family thought he was going to make Caroline an offer of marriage, but Caroline thought otherwise.

She said, "He drank whiskey and water and tried to get me to do the same. He said the whiskey protected against bad water, but I think he was trying to get me drunk enough to take liberties with me."

I leaned back, stretched out my legs, and commented, "I applaud his good taste and eyesight though I deplore his morals." Then what she said made me alert. "He said the whisky *protected* against bad water?"

Caroline was trying to recall the conversation. Finally, she replied, "He said it was in a biography of Alexander the Great. When he and his soldiers were marching through a land with bad water, they would not dilute the wine with as much water."

I vaguely recalled reading or hearing some such, but now I was wondering if this was of medical relevance. I turned to Caroline and, half musing, said, "Then the alcohol is providing the protection against the agents of sickness in bad water. So spirits of wine, which is concentrated alcohol, should be more effective, effective perhaps against sepsis."

Caroline was caught by what I had said, understood it, though she reminded me, "But soaking a patient in a vat of whiskey is hardly practicable."

I said, "I certainly have to think this matter out, but spirits of wine could be employed in soaking one's hands and one's surgical instruments before surgery. When I was young, my cat was torn open by a dog, and a man who treated animals sewed her back up, and I remember that he washed his hands and soaked the needle and thread he used in soapy water before he did the sewing. When I treat patients, I make it a practice to wash my hands in soapy water before and after treatment. And I have been successful with deliveries, no cases of childbirth fever so far."

I had Caroline's full attention. But I remembered I was not on a professional visit, turned to her and apologized: "This is not the sort of topic a man should be discussing with a beautiful woman before a fire. But you have gotten me thinking about this. I will discuss it with David tomorrow."

Caroline responded, "I thank you for the compliment. You look at things differently from most doctors and most men. Sometimes that can be helpful."

I returned, "And sometimes it can get one burned at the stake."

We sat silently for some time, continuing to enjoy the fire. But seeds had been planted in my mind that I realized would probably preoccupy and bedevil me. At length, I remembered my conversation with David, so asked Caroline, "If I might, I would like to escort you to some event, perhaps a play."

Caroline softly clapped her hands together and told me, "I would so like to attend a play, perhaps one of Shakespeare's. And I have heard 'The Beggar's Opera' is quite good."

I told her, "David warned me I should take a cudgel, as brawls sometimes occurred. So, in addition, we will take more expensive seats. If you will consult a newspaper and decide what you want to see, we can settle on a time."

Caroline was delighted, and said, "Come around, let us say two days hence and I will have a choice."

"As my lady wishes," I replied, smiling, so the thing was fixed.

12

COURT YOUR PARTNER

—◆—

At this point, another direction was added to my life. I was courting Caroline in addition to seeing patients and I was continually surprised at how easy everything was. No parental opposition, quite the contrary, no rivals to contend with, and no reluctance on the lady's part to being courted. We attended several plays. I purchased clothes that while not making me a dandy, at least did not produce the impression I was a clergyman, and a Scots clergyman at that. Caroline attracted attention from other men, which I could see flattered her, but she remained steadfast by my side.

David married his Dora, and after a few days of becoming accustomed to each other as spouses, I was invited to dine with them. Seeing them together, I was struck again and again by how easy they were in each other's company. Despite Dora's supposed exotic origins, she was very English-looking, fresh-faced, rosy cheeked and fair. Despite David's casual comments about her, I could see real affection between them. They were very interested in Caroline, and I gathered wanted to meet her. Caroline was nothing loath, and we began dining at David and Dora's Selwyn Street house at least once a month. I would probably have been visiting or going somewhere with Caroline every day but for my practice and certain other activities.

I was listening to John Hunter's lectures on anatomy three evenings a week. Of course I took nearly verbatim notes. John Hunter was not eloquent, but very straight-forward in his lectures. David was at the King Street house during my absences, read my notes with interest, and we had some most interesting conversations. This was yet another direction to my life, and as fall became winter and the temperature became cold enough to allow dissections of human bodies, still one direction more became part of my days.

We students each had to purchase our body and at that point work feverishly at the dissection before the corpse became too foul. Of course, the provenances of the bodies were almost certainly illegal, which made me uneasy, yet if I was going to perform surgery, there was no alternative.

Some of the corpses were old people but some died in gaol of sickness (a few were hanged felons). But one corpse, from Bridewell, particularly captured my attention. We were told that this was a man who had contracted the Great Pox and had died insane from its effects, chained to a wall. But his face was the food for nightmares: his nose and ears rotted away from the disease, several other places eroded, leaving bone exposed, it seemed a living death, rotting alive, shunned by all. I heard many with the Great Pox became insane, that was one of its eventual effects, that and deafness. I thought knowing what it did to the appearance would have promoted insanity because of the isolation it imposed.

Seeing this and observing less advanced cases had two effects. If I was scrupulous about washing my hands before, I now became excessively so, washing hands and forearms before and especially after treating anyone for anything. My clothes as well: I had a suit for dissections, frequently washed. So I was a paragon of cleanliness. Whatever my patients thought of this, at least few of them contracted sepsis. David noted this and adopted my hand-washing habit.

The other effect was that what I had seen of Pox cases produced nightmares. So my sleep was now a troubled one. I hoped and prayed this would not cause me to make mistakes with my patients from sleepiness. David suggested I nap when I could, and this appeared to help.

Conversations with Caroline about this and, indeed, about almost every conceivable topic also helped. She was a woman of considerable intelligence. While my lusts were quite independent of my respect for her mind and quite rampant, I began to regard her as a confidante. She began to look at me in the same way. She was probably older than I, and her family very much wanted her married and gone. I gathered she had suitors but she also had an independent spirit, so was not disposed to accept any offer. Still, despite all the distractions, our intimacy advanced.

John Hunter's lectures were not merely informative; they were stimulative of thought. I was able to talk to him after several of the lectures. He asked me about my dissertation and I told him what I had done. He was quite interested, asked several questions, I understood not for the purpose of embarrassing me, but because he wanted to know, to understand. I told him about my half-formed ideas about spirits of wine and their use in preventing sepsis, and he was intrigued. Several of his comments stuck in my mind, possibly to bear fruit later.

Aside from the dissections over the winter and John Hunter's lectures, the major hindrance to my courtship was our practice. I had feared that with two of us the income therefrom would be reduced, yet the reverse seemed the case. Rare was the night I could sleep through, we were both seeing patients often well into the evenings, Sundays not excepted, and it was hard to find a time when I could take Caroline anywhere. Part of my purpose was to ensure David could go to his home and be with his wife, and now David was required to perform the same service for me, but he made no complaint, rather the reverse: he and Dora were promoting the match, or so I gathered.

The spring had advanced then passed into summer, when I contracted with Caroline to walk about St. James Park. No respectable woman would walk unescorted about a public place, and Caroline had never been there. I was flush with funds: two evenings previously I had been summoned by a loutish man, I guessed he was a hired bully for a whore or brothel, perhaps one of the establishments on King Place. Since I often had to attend cases in the night, I slept in shirt, breeches and stockings.

I quickly finished dressing after I had answered the hammering on the door, took my cudgel and medical bag and locked the door of No. 12 after stepping out. The fellow led me to King Place in fact, to one of the whorehouses there. Inside, all was ornate, perfumed, and a little garish. The woman who seemed in charge took me to one of the rooms. I could hear a woman sobbing and shortly saw why: the left side of her face had been slashed. Two other young women were attempting to comfort the injured girl, for she seemed young, and to stanch the blood which stained sheets, the girl's dress and the floor alike.

"Can you fix her face, Doctor? It is her livelihood."

I looked at the wound: long and fairly deep, but hadn't penetrated the girl's mouth. All I could do was sew the skin back together. If I used many stitches, silk thread, close together, there should be a less visible scar. But that would take time, so I decided to give the girl some opium. I had gotten Caroline to make opium into pills, and since the girl was rather slight, I reckoned one pill might do. So I answered the proprietress, "I will sew the edges together, trying to leave as slight a scar as possible. But I will need more light."

Several candles in ornate holders were brought. I persuaded the girl to swallow one opium pill with wine. While waiting for the opium to work, I took out my gear, basin, soap, a tin dish for spirits of wine, and silk thread and a needle I had bent into a semicircle. I also told her what I would do as I washed my hands and the girl's face, threaded the needle with the silk, and waited.

At length I decided to begin. On the voyage from Boston, I had learned to tie knots and to sew, and had learned in Falconer's class how to repair incisions and tie the knots, so I proceeded, keeping the stitches close together. The girl bore this without much flinching or weeping. I took great care with the stitches, so the edges of skin would lie together, hopefully heal together and hence appear as natural as possible. I told no one that this was my first essay at such a venture.

The stitching took nearly an hour. I told the proprietress, "I will return tomorrow to see if there is sepsis. I should be able to remove the stitches in perhaps a week or ten days. In the meantime, let her rest."

The proprietress nodded, handed me five guineas, a substantial sum, and told me, "Doctor, don't talk about this or inform the magistrates. I want no scandal."

I replied, "I will talk about this case to my partner, as he must substitute for me if I am away, but to no one else."

Except for Caroline and Dora, I mentally amended, but the proprietress or madam nodded again and I returned to No. 12. What had happened, I really did not want to know, nor, I was certain, would David.

I called on Caroline at the agreed time wearing a new suit of clothes, quickly made to be sure, but I was assured that it was appropriate for walking about with a young lady. It being summer I looked at the offerings in Covent Garden for a suitable bouquet. I bought some lavender, for Caroline often wore a lavender-coloured dress.

By fortunate chance, she was wearing that dress. I presented the bouquet with an exaggerated flourish like some we had seen on the stage, whereat she laughed and went to get a pin to secure one sprig to her dress. Then I gave her my arm and we walked to St. James Park.

A most pleasant day, a pretty woman on my arm, the park now fully green, unalloyed pleasure save for some fops who seemed to be taking exception to our dress. To be sure, our garb was somewhat on the sober side, but what of that? I was angered, Caroline was annoyed, but she urged me to pay no heed.

I heard one of the fops refer to me as an "industrious 'prentice out with his gel."

They had swords, supposedly one of the marks of a gentleman, but I still naively imagined behavior was part of such status or so I told Caroline.

She told me, "You are the gentleman here, Thomas. I never go out unescorted, especially evenings, lest I be attacked and molested or worse, perhaps by some rowdies called 'Mohawks'. These count themselves as gentlemen because of their income and dress, but their behavior marks them as the reverse."

I shook my head as we walked on, and I told Caroline, "My profession is to be a healer, a man of peace, not a brawler, so you are right to remind me of this."

I was carrying my cudgel, I did this without thought now, yet why was I obliged to do so, in the midst of a great city, the land itself at peace within? Because I carried it, I doubted I would be assaulted as there were but four of them.

I tried to make light of the matter, telling Caroline, "I suppose they are correct in a sense. I think I am tolerably industrious, and I endeavour to learn more of my profession from every new patient. So I daresay I will always be a 'prentice."

Caroline smiled and we walked round the park without further incident. There was a tea-garden on our way back, and I turned to Caroline with my eyebrows upraised, which she correctly interpreted, saying, "Yes, I should like to try some, Thomas."

So we indulged in a cup apiece, eyeing the other patrons. Some of them, groups of bold-faced, rather expensively-dressed, young women, I took to be whores trolling for custom. Caroline's and my eyes met and I remarked on this to her and she agreed. She did not seem offended at my choice of topic of conversation, and my feeling she was a woman I could confide in deepened. At this, I told her of my professional visit to a bawdy-house and my reward, which David had generously remitted to me in full because I was roused from my bed to treat the girl.

Caroline was concerned about the injury, asking me, "But will she recover fully?"

I replied, "No tendons were severed. The muscles should reconnect and heal. So far, there is no sepsis."

We each sipped then Caroline asked, "How old is this girl, do you think?"

I shook my head and told her, "She may be sixteen or even younger. I did not ask."

Caroline shook her head in turn, remarking, "What an awful

life. In a sense, she is a prisoner of her profession; I mean more than most people."

I agreed, saying, "The furniture, dress and, I daresay, everything about her life is gentle save one thing."

Caroline nodded, wondering, "And how long will such good fortune, if that is the right word, last?"

Sobered, we walked back together. I was invited to dine at her family's dwelling. As we walked, I noticed we were now hand in hand. I could not recall when this began but of course was content with the arrangement. At Avebury's, we paused on the doorstep while a short procession of costermongers passed, each calling out their wares, often almost unintelligibly. When they had passed, on an impulse, I lifted Caroline's hand that was in one of mine and kissed it. She curtsied in acknowledgement and our eyes met.

Our smiles faded, transformed to looks of wonder, of awe. Again on an impulse, I leant forward, as did she. Our lips met and we kissed. Drawing back, I saw and felt smiles returning, shy smiles to be sure, shy and wistful. I put my hands on her waist, she put her hands on my shoulders and we kissed again, several times.

Finally she told me, in a voice that sounded a bit out of breath, "Let us go in, Thomas. It is time for dinner."

As we entered Avebury's I saw a small crowd disperse that had gathered to watch us. Unusually, there were no comments or noises.

Returning to No. 12, I was conscious some sort of Rubicon had been crossed. This was unsettling, yet still I felt happy. The scattered bits that were my life were assembling, with Caroline as its centre. I began to think about marriage to her, what it would be like, this for the first time since Ann. But there were patients waiting even at this hour, despite David's best efforts. David had sent a note round to Avebury's, asking for my assistance, so there was no opportunity for an intimate conversation with Caroline after the meal, but I think we both felt there was time enough.

II

Between Worlds, 1777

1

A LETTER

Two days after these events, a morning in late August, a miracle occurred: a letter written by my older sister was presented me. With equally strong feelings of relief and dread, I stared at the thing. It had been sent to Edinburgh from Le Havre in France, judging by markings on the envelope, then sent here as I had reminded the Medical School at Edinburgh of my London address on at least two occasions. Finally I broke the seal and forced myself to read:

Dear brother

Three copies of this letter are being sent by three different privateer captains to France, to be sent thence to Edinburgh, your last address known to us.

Father is well. Several widows or their agents have made their availability and willingness known to become Mother's replacement, but Father has evinced no interest. Susan and I keep his house and I think our presence comforts him. He still mourns Mother and perhaps will do so until his own end. The death of his mother, Grandmother Wyeth, I think also continues to sadden him.

Susan and I are well, but I am anxious and Susan, though apparently composed, is most distressed. My fiancé—we are betrothed—is serving in Gen'l Washington's army. He was in good health at last writing.

Susan's sweetheart was wounded at the battle now being called Bunker Hill and taken prisoner. He and the other prisoners were removed to Halifax. We have heard nothing of his condition. We did hear he and the other prisoners were taken to New York and have we suppose been there since that city was captured. Please, please try to find how he is.

A number of Loyalists removed from Boston with Gen'l Gage's army. We heard that many if not all are now in New York. We understand the Crewes are among them. Their holdings in Massachusetts were confiscated. Ann Crewe's fiancé, we were told, went to England in '75 as he has business connections there. Their marriage never took place, we don't know why.

Occasional Kitten turned out to be female, as she has produced two litters of kittens, three and four, so far that we know of. We have been able to play with them so they have become quite domestic. All were given to other families save one. It is a tabby, the image of our Tabby so it now lives with us with the title Tabby Too. We think Tabby Too is a he but he is very friendly to us, yet a terror to mice.

We have received just four letters from you. If you wrote more, they have miscarried. We do not criticize you. Sending letters is nearly impossible and we can only pray that one of our copies is able to take advantage of the "nearly".

Your sister
Lizzie

I read this letter standing. David was sitting eating but stopped when he saw my face. "Bad news, I suppose. I hope not your family."

I was silent, then looked at him and spoke, "My family is well, though anxious. My younger sister's sweetheart is a prisoner, probably held in New York. She very much wants me to determine his condition." More silence before I could continue, "There was a girl in Boston—Ann Crewe—that I wanted to marry, but she was intended for someone else. Before I left for Edinburgh, I told her if she ever needed my assistance, I would give it. I know this sounds quixotic, but I gave my word."

David said, softly, "What about Caroline?"

Now I walked about the room, thinking.

Finally I forced myself to reply. "I have never asked for her hand. We are on good terms… dammit, I wish this cup away, I do indeed, but I will, I must go to New York. I will have to tell her, and I would rather drink melted lead."

I made several more circuits of the room, sat down, looked at David, and told him, "This means I will have to join the Army, probably as a doctor or surgeon. This will allow me to get there and give me some status, some protection, as I could not find either of them as easily or perhaps at all as a civilian."

I got up again then sat down again. "I will ask John Hunter for his help obtaining a commission, probably as Assistant Surgeon." I was silent again, thinking. "I suppose he is at St. George's. I will go now."

We had no patients waiting, so I arose and went out walking rapidly in the direction of Hyde Park. All around me was the life and movement of London. Inside me was a concoction of determination, some excitement, but mostly despair. I was comfortable here, no, I was becoming happy here. Now I was leaving my new life here in London—and Caroline, more than all. Yet what else could I do?

John Hunter was on rounds, not unreasonable given the hour, and I soon located him, a cluster of acolytes about him. I waited what seemed a considerable time until I could speak to him privilly.

"Sir," I said, "I have received news from my family that requires my presence in New York, just captured. For this, I must obtain a commission as Assistant Surgeon. You know my qualifications. Can you write to someone in the War Office to affect this?"

Hunter looked at me, nodded and replied, "Aye, I will write to My Lord Germain directly. It may take two weeks or more. Where do you lodge?"

I said, "Number 12, King Street."

He nodded again and I went on my way. One hurdle crossed, but now I had to see Caroline and tell her I would be leaving and why.

With David newly married and visiting his family, I had done a great deal of the work these summer weeks, seriously limiting the time I could spend with Caroline. Scattered brief visits and conversations, precious I think to both of us were all the press of patients usually allowed. Of course, during the winter, when I was dissecting and attending John Hunter's lectures, David had taken my place even at the cost of time with his Dora.

Avebury's hove into sight all too quickly. I slowed my steps, finally deciding to show Caroline the letter, then explain its significance as to what I felt I must do. I entered the shop. There was a new prentice there, an older boy or younger man, I realized probably because Caroline's father thought she would be leaving soon. I was going to ask for Miss Vandelys, when she appeared with a filled order.

Her face lit up on seeing me then this faded, seeing my solemn expression. Without a word I gave her the letter. She read this then looked up at me.

"Who are the Crewes?" she asked.

Right to the rub, I thought, but I told her, "They are, or were, wealthy people in Boston. I was in love with their daughter, Ann, but her family intended her for someone else. Before I sailed I wrote her a letter, pledging to give any assistance in my power. I know this sounds strange but I feel I gave my word. And I must find my younger sister's sweetheart and help him in any fashion I might. So I am trying to get a commission as Assistant Surgeon in the Army. I cannot get to New York otherwise."

As I talked, I could see her eyes, which had sparkled at the sight of me, lose their sparkle and fill with sadness, becoming remote. This tormented me, but I had no choice.

Caroline handed me the letter, not looking at me, and said, "If you feel you must go then I suppose this is our last meeting."

I swallowed, shook my head and managed to utter, "I would it were otherwise, I do indeed."

But she was walking away. I thought I could see her shoulders shaking.

I left, feeling desolate, near tears myself. But what else could I do? David saw in my face how distressed I was, shook his head, but offered no comment, just more patients. Indeed, my work was now all I had.

2

ALL ASEA

Over the next ten days or so, I ventured out as little as possible and then only at night to visit patients having critical—or so they imagined—need of my presence. This was to avoid seeing Caroline, as I feared sight of her would unman me. The girl whose face I had sewn back together healed well. I removed the threads from her face, no sepsis and the scar was hard to see, probably impossible to see, given powder. The brothel-keeper was pleased at the result as was the girl. I think that the girl would cheerfully have rewarded me further but I did not hang about, as I was feeling low.

On one such night, I was accosted by three men accompanied by what I took to be a body servant, a large one carrying a big stick. The three men were well-dressed, so it was easy to guess their errand.

"I say, fellow, can you recommend a good place? You seem at home hereabouts." The speaker appeared a little drunk, in fact all save the body servant were in that state, yet something in the speaker's accent and form seemed familiar. Not his face, for the three were wearing masks.

I was about to tell them "No" when I remembered who the speaker was.

"Thorpe," I said.

The speaker stepped back, startled, and said, "How do you know my name, sir?"

I replied, "We met in Boston, sir. You were supposed to marry Miss Ann Crewe. Did you? Is she now in England?"

He looked as though he was going to bid me go to the Devil, but for some reason he decided to answer my questions, perhaps because he didn't really know who I was or what harm I might be able to cause him.

"No, I didn't marry Miss Crewe. Too pious for my tastes. And I heard her family is now penniless. No, I married an Englishwoman, not that that is any of your business, hey?"

He resented me, yet I stood foursquare before him. I was sober, he was not, and still he couldn't place me. So I decided to enlighten him, saying, "Doctor Thomas Wyeth, at your services, should you require them. No, I have no recommendations as to particular whores or whorehouses, only that you needs best use cundums, for the sake of yourselves, your wives and any children you may have by them. Gentlemen," I said, bowing, "a good evening to you all." And I walked away to No. 12.

So my sister's intelligence was correct. Ann, unless she had married someone else and I found myself hoping she had, almost certainly required my protection in the form of money and possibly marriage. And I had given my word… and wished I hadn't. But there was John Fielding. Prisoners were supposed to be treated decently and exchanged as soon as possible, but I feared captured rebels were being treated as, as rebels, with no rights soever. I had to go see.

My commission arrived. I saw it as a sentence of captivity, but had to bestir myself. I required a uniform, including a heavy and rather hot red wool coat. I also went roundabout to avoid Caroline to buy more surgical instruments, needles and very fine small scissors among them. I decided to buy an apothecary's balance, one that could be disassembled and packed to withstand a rough journey.

Now a letter appeared, telling me to board a ship leaving two days hence. This laid off Gravesend, so I had to leave tomorrow morning. David and Dora invited me to dine with them, most kindly, yet the meal was shadowed by an absent guest: Caroline.

David saw me off early the following morning, shaking my hand. I tried to smile, not very successfully, before turning to follow a man carrying my chest and medical bag in a hand-barrow. I reached Gravesend that evening and boarded my ship. It was clearly meant for cargo as she was short and stubby, and I fancied would pitch and roll most abominably.

We set sail the next morning after three newly-commissioned lieutenants with their servants boarded. We were carrying round shot: three pounder iron balls. I thought our ship wallowed. We were sailing alone, though I had read that rebel privateers were pouncing on unescorted ships.

We dined together in the wardroom, very crowded indeed. One of our number was a regimental paymaster. His talk added to my low spirits: I was supposed to get ten shillings a day, about £180 per annum, surely enough to perform my tasks, but the fellow informed us of a mort of "stoppages", reductions in our pay for uniforms, food, a hospital in London for sick soldiers, etc., etc. until I guessed I would actually have perhaps half that in hand. This was very vexing, though the fellow treated it all as a great joke.

Even being able to divert myself by climbing to the "crows nest" then climbing down again was little help. I was oppressed by sadness. I had disappointed Caroline grieveously, and indeed myself. Thoughts of a reunion with Ann, could I find her, helped not at all. Grey skies, grey seas, grey eyes…. The officers mostly sat about in the wardroom talking and drinking. I didn't know where their servants bedded.

3

NEW YORK

———◆———

We anchored in New York Harbour and waited, our ship gently wallowing. I stared at the city. To my right, a fort occupied the southern tip of the island. To the north of the fort were a great many tents, and at first I thought our Army was encamped there. Then I recognized many ruins of houses, destroyed by fire. Had the rebels tried to burn the city when they were retreating?

Otherwise, New York City was mainly buildings of two or three storeys, many brick built, some wooden, occupying some of the lower or seaward end of the island. Near the middle of the island, the land rose sharply so that reaching the upper part could be done only through a narrow pass. I assumed that was garrisoned.

A small boat was rowed out to us. A portly man in the uniform of a captain in the Royal Navy boarded, and gave our captain his orders. At least so I gathered, because we hoisted our anchor after the naval officer left, set our sails and made our way to a dock. The last few hundred yards our sailors towed our ship to this. Once we were tied up, the passengers could leave.

I was happy to leave, even carrying my chest and bag, even

without knowing where I was supposed to go. Just being on dry land was a relief. Perhaps as a result of my unhappiness, I fancied this voyage was by far the worst of the three I had undertaken.

By asking anyone in a red coat I encountered, I discovered where the regiment I was assigned to was quartered. So sweating and cursing, I struggled for what seemed miles until I found a large stone building. I was permitted to enter, was assigned a room—the place was actually a hotel—and immediately lay down on a protesting bed and, thinking I was hungry and thirsty, opened my eyes to the next morning.

My life as a soldier slowly became a routine. I dined on indifferent fare in the officers' mess, found I had a servant, and visited all the men of the regiment who were sick or claimed to be. There were but few cases of illness, casualties being light in Gen'l Howe's capture of the city. I did what I could for each and finding my work done by noon, ate and then began asking about the rebel prisoners, where they were kept.

I asked several officers, or so I guessed them to be, where prisoners were kept. I was told that depended on whether they were privateer crews, officers or men of the rebel army and when they were taken prisoner. Rebel officers were on parole but rebel soldiers were housed in sugar houses and a few churches. Rebel privateer crews were kept on a prison ship, called a "hulk," the *Jersey*. Men taken in battles about Boston were in another hulk, opinions differed as to which.

So I was obliged to go to the wharves to hire a crew to take me to the other hulks. The crew consisted of four oarsmen and a steersman. I got into their boat and we set forth. Our way lay past the *Jersey*, which was pointed out to me: a ship of the line, two rows of gun ports boarded shut, two or three flimsy-looking wooden dwellings on top of the upper deck, only one lower mast, and no spars, anchored fore and aft near the shore.

The shore had a quantity of what I took to be driftwood upon it, but as we approached, I saw sailors throw naked bodies overboard, heard the splashes then realized the "driftwood" was corpses. Perhaps the high tide would wash some of these away, but from the smell, had failed this office many times. I was appalled, staring open-mouthed at this vile spectacle. My crew had no comment.

We reached one of the other hulks. I climbed on board, saw men I took to be prisoners appearing, two by two, on the deck to use the heads. Only two were allowed on deck at a time, so they could be guarded effectively. If more required the use of the heads, all save two had to wait their turn, whether they could remain continent or not. And some clearly could not, as they had a dysentery.

I explained my errand to a bored lieutenant who was in charge. He shrugged and pointed to a set of stairs, guarded by two marines carrying muskets with fixed bayonets. I was dismayed by the steepness of the stairs and feared falling headforemost down them. There were no hand rails, of course.

I had to descend another set of stairs to get to the deck where the prisoners were kept, the "orlop." At this point, the smell or rather stench became absolutely vile, almost corporeal, and I feared becoming sick or fainting in that place. By attempting not to breathe at all, I managed to stay on my feet, but as my eyes became adjusted to the dark, what I saw made me think unconsciousness was perhaps, by comparison, a blessing.

There was a square hatch or hole in the deck. This opened into the "bilge." The men themselves were so wasted, so feeble that I feared that some would fall or throw themselves into the "bilge," certainly to drown, as there seemed no possibility of rescue.

I began asking the men for John Fielding, but no one answered to that name. I could see all the men had the appearance of scurvy, despite being in harbour. Then one prisoner told me that Fielding was in one of the other hulks, if he were still alive. Indeed, I could see two or three prisoners lying motionless on the deck. They had no shoes. I realized these men were dead, because among the stink of faeces, piss and unwashed men I could smell decomposition, the dead men were rotting.

I had to get out of this place. I had heard descriptions of how prisoners in Newgate Gaol were kept but conditions here beggared description and even imagination. I ascended the stair faster than prudence called for, but I reached the upper deck and stood, breathing in the blessed sea air.

It was dark before I got to our billet. I managed to secure some bread and cheese and ale, though I was thinking my visiting place was obvious to everyone near me. As a result, I bathed as best I could, hung my garb near an opened window though the night was a cool one, and retired, hoping to be spared nightmares from what I had seen and smelled.

This hope was dashed repeatedly, as I awoke from dreadful dreams several times, so my rest was not so much refreshing as endured. I dined with the other officers of the regiment the next morning, beginning to recognize faces I had seen yesterday. No one made any comment about how I smelled, so what I had done had worked. However, there were two more hulks to visit. I would try to do that this afternoon, but I realized I had best take something to eat, something that a man whose teeth were falling out could chew. The best I could find in that direction was some soft ration cheese.

The second hulk seemed worse than the first, which was most hard to believe. But worst of all, John Fielding was not on the second ship either, though again one or two men said he was on one of the prison ships or had been. So after some delay, I managed to be rowed to the third hulk. There seemed no reason why the third should be worse than the first two, but indeed it was: I truly thought I was going to faint, the smell of rotting flesh was much stronger, yet smells from faeces and piss were as strong, though I couldn't essay a precise comparison.

By calling John Fielding's name when I wasn't gagging, I heard several of the prisoners say he was on board, and the voices directed me toward a bulkhead.

Then one of the other prisoners said, "John's gone."

"Gone?" I asked, "What do you mean, gone, gone where?"

"Dead," said the voice, "died mebbe a week past."

It was true: he was lying at the base of the bulkhead. I saw his shoes were also gone, presumably stolen to trade for food. He was starting to stink, though his body was so wasted, his flesh couldn't produce much stink. I managed to bend down to examine him. His left arm had apparently been broken, perhaps by a musket ball, and badly set so that it had healed crooked. Despite his beard, I could still recognize his features, so there was little doubt.

Then I saw a string around his neck. I forced myself to pull it away from his flesh. There was a miniature on the string. I pulled the string over his head and walked to the hatch where there was more light. Again I feared I would fall into the hatch, shook my head and opened the miniature. The face inside was recognizably Susan's. Now there was no doubt at all.

I said, "I'm sorry, John." I said it aloud. I was just too late, too damned late. I cursed, tears in my eyes. I had to get the news to Susan somehow. And perhaps the miniature, that now pathetic relic of affection. My poor, poor sister. And John of course.

Some of the other prisoners recognized me or my voice or both and called to me. I remembered the cheese in my pocket and drew it out, moving toward them. One was the bully of Shrewsbury, Robbie McDowell, so wasted, so weak. I gave him one of the pieces of cheese, telling him, "I believe I could thrash you now, Robbie."

He ate the cheese, and said in a soft voice, "Ay, that you could. But thankee, Thomas."

I said to them all, "I will try to get some fresh food to you. I don't know what I can buy now, but I will do it if I can."

By now I was in tears again and left, I could not bear another moment in that place, muted cries of appreciation and gratitude following me. I wanted to be worthy of such before lingering to accept them.

My return this time was early enough, but I was very conscious of how foul I must smell. So once again I tried to wash but had only the one red coat so hung that up once more before the open window, donned my Caroline-courting wear, which made me feel worse if that were possible, and dined in a tavern, alone. Tomorrow I would try to find Ann.

No: just before essaying sleep, I remembered that I had made yet another promise, to bring some sort of fresh food to those surviving prisoners. It had to be soft, because ship biscuits and salted pork were difficult enough to eat by men with a whole set of teeth. I had to see what was being sold.

After performing what duties I had, I asked where food was sold, and set out to see what was on offer. It was fall; perhaps some late apples could be purchased. But today all I found were potatoes from Long Island to our east. So I bought a bushel of these, washed the dirt or most of it off using a town pump, then picked the dripping basket up and carried it to the docks. Prices of food were very high.

I again had to pay a crew to row me to the prison ship that John had died on. As we approached, I wondered how long his corpse would lie in the hold before…burial? Being tossed over the side in a hammock with a six pounder shot sewn inside his shroud? Or simply tossed over the side? I did not want to find out; his spirit, his soul was free, free to wait for Susan's.

Climbing down those steep steps with a bushel basket of potatoes was undertaken very cautiously. I was thankful we were in harbor, anchored and not at sea. With the stench I was climbing into, I counted it as miraculous that I reached the deck the prisoners were on without spills or falls. I handed out the potatoes to the living, with apologies for them being all I could buy, but I think the fact that I had brought something, that someone, anyone, was prepared to help them, cheered them more than a Parisian gourmet banquet. More tears were shed, and I realized I had given these men, some of whom I had grown up with, hope. I told them before I left that I would return when I could and when I had fresh food to distribute.

Back on the land, smelling as I did, I tried to keep to "leeward" or downwind as I began asking people if they knew where the Crewes were staying. After I realized how large a city New York was, I changed my approach and began going up and down streets in what I hoped was a systematic fashion, knocking on doors, first at every third house, then every other. As I canvassed street after street, I began to notice that some houses were in receipt of a steady traffic of soldiers, all in good humour. I began to suspect what was going on was prostitution. A few questions of the soldiers confirmed this, and the occupants of houses not involved in this trade were unfriendly to me until I explained myself.

As I talked to more people, a most distressing picture began to form in my mind: families forced to flee with little more than the clothing on their backs but with young women, were supporting themselves by selling the bodies of their daughters, sisters, aunts or sometimes wives to soldiers. Ann was a very pretty woman. Of course, the prettier ones might become mistresses of the higher ranks, perhaps guaranteeing better treatment but a most bitter comedown for their families and of course themselves.

This traffic continued past dark. Indeed it seemed to increase then. I once more elected to dine at a tavern, the smells of the other patrons differing only in origin, and then retired once more after bathing. I was beginning to realize my bed had a very active population of fleas, and while I had slept for many years with a cat, sharing its fleas, that was an intimate connection. This was somehow very different.

4

A MEETING

It was on a fine, dry day in late fall that I continued my daily search. Aside from nominal medical duties, usually quickly dispatched, and deliveries of whatever fresh food I found (apples or potatoes largely), to the prisoners of the hulk John Fielding had died in, I traversed the streets of the city searching for Ann every afternoon.

New York was laid out in a much more regular fashion than London: wider streets, set usually at right angles to each other, cross streets producing "blocks" of fairly uniform length. This made my task somewhat easier. Also, there had been a fire in the southern end of the city, leaving hundreds to live in tents in an extraordinarily foul-smelling quarter of the town. I decided I needn't inquire there, though perhaps I was simply being cowardly in this decision. There was no sign of any assistance being offered by the Crown to the people huddled in the burned areas.

Many buildings had been taken by the Crown for billeting, especially since the fire had reduced their number. King's College was used as the hospital for Crown forces—I did not care to think about medical care provided to rebels. Many churches had been marked "G. R." and used for barracks, stores or even stables. But in my search I noticed the churches so taken by the Crown were those of dissenting sects, Presbyterians, Methodists, Baptists, etc. Anglican churches were left untouched. I could hardly imagine greater insult to probably the majority of citizens there in the City. Many might sympathize with the rebels but by no means all: I was one of them, and those of undecided loyalty were not going to be favourably impressed by the Crown's actions in this respect.

A heavily veiled woman was approaching. Young women were much more likely to be about the streets unescorted even at night, as the Army kept far better order than was to be found in London. The veil was odd. Was the girl disfigured by smallpox? She had a basket, so had bought something. I thought I recognized her and her steps toward me now slowed. A few feet from her, I raised my tricorne. She stood rigid then raised her veil. It was Ann.

It was not the smallpox that disfigured her. She had contracted the Great Pox. The greater part of her nose had gone, exposing the bone and part of her upper lips as well, so I could see some of her upper front teeth. I had the impression of a chancre elsewhere as well but could not bring myself to a closer and more extensive examination. This sight left me rooted to the ground. The enormity of what had befallen her made me incapable of speech.

Finally Ann broke the silence between us saying, "Wouldst lie with me, Thomas? Only a shilling."

There was a mockery in her voice, also a lisp from the loss of part of her upper lip, yet I saw tears in her eyes. This so horrified me that I turned from her, and I ran away. I heard her laughing, but it was a sobbing kind of laugh. I ran faster and faster trying to escape that sound, running, running from her, running from my pledges, my honour, my word. Atop of what I had seen and smelled in the hulks, it was too much: I vomited into an alley, retching and coughing until I was quite empty, empty of lofty intentions, of decency, of compassion, of illusions.

At length I had recovered sufficiently to continue to my quarters. There I sat, my head in my hands, ignoring the fleas, ignoring the evening meal in the regimental mess, alone, fallen, forsworn, failed.

Night found me in the same posture. Lacking anything at all better to do, I lay down on the bed, not daring to close my eyes for fear of what my memory of this day would resurrect.

I daresay I must have slept but by God's uncovenanted mercy I did not recall any dreams. I washed after emptying my bladder, shaved and presented myself for breakfast. I was expecting questions, but no one paid me much attention, just as well. Then with relief this time, I turned to my duties.

Today, there was work. Skirmishes, some heavy, between the rebels and our Army occurred occasionally. We were trying to drive the rebels away. I thought we were trying to get them to make peace, but I did not sense any purposeful movement in that direction. Even so, men of our Army and some rebels were brought in with bullet wounds and I and others were summoned to treat these.

My habits of cleaning about the wounds, frequent washing of my hands and soaking lancets and forceps in spirits of wine drew attention, at first in the shape of looks, later questions, and then comments. The other surgeons were not pleased with me, but I had managed to deal with all the wounded brought to my care. I suspected the men I had treated would fare better in terms of avoiding sepsis, but was prepared to let the outcome prove the merit of the method.

The recent skirmish must have been a large one, as more men were brought the next day, the next, and some the day following. I insisted on keeping to my customs, and was seeing that men I had treated were indeed recovering faster and I thought better, though I heard complaints of my patients' wounds not producing "laudable pus." This caused me to venture further into heresy and begin to question whether any pus could be considered "laudable."

Now having leisure once more, I sat down and tried to think what I should do about Ann. I couldn't simply avoid her as I had done with Caroline. [Ah! Caroline! Here I felt such a pang!] Over ale in a tavern, I finally forced myself to a conclusion: I would have to go to her and offer her marriage if she wanted it or at least money, so she didn't have to whore to keep her family. If marriage was her wish, I would not lie with her but would provide what treatments I could. That was a compromise in a sense but the best I could offer.

So I returned to where we had met, again knocking on doors, but this time with greater assurance of success. Three places knew nothing of any Crewes, but the door to the fourth was opened by Mr. Crewe himself. I recognized him though he had grown much thinner; I doubt he remembered me. I raised my hat and said, "I beg your pardon, Mr. Crewe. I would like to speak with your daughter, Ann."

He stared at me, swayed slightly, I smelled alcohol on his breath as he told me, "Ann's dead."

I could not believe what he had said, just repeated, "Dead?"

"Yes. Yesterday. Threw her body in the pit myself. You will have to find someone else." I tried to say something, something of consolation but he closed his door in my face.

Burials in the city at that time for those without money were in a great pit dug at the south end of the city. I had heard that bodies were simply pitched into the hole onto previous dead, no rites or ceremony whatever. No covering of dirt either. All simply left to rot together, a community of corruption. I bent my steps in that direction, not from any purpose, for what could I do now?

When I reached the place, there was a gentle wind at my back, keeping the worst of the stench and the flies away. Some great birds and half-starved dogs were down in the pit worrying the bodies, some bodies clothed in shrouds or nightshirts, some naked. One of the bodies on the top was a small naked woman with yellow hair, lying on her face. Then the wind shifted, and I had to retreat, pursued by the stink and the flies. So, I thought, I had at last visually possessed my lost love.

It was all so hard to believe, yet all too real, too grotesque, a girl so sweet, so favoured, brought up so gently, to meet such an end. Instead of offering to sweeten her last days, I had abandoned her as Fortune had, leaving that grisly pit as her final resting place. Fate? My own failure of resolve, my own cowardice.

I thought of returning to where her family lived and offering money, so crass, so inadequate, though I suspected quite acceptable to her father, judging from the colour of his nose and cheeks. But I could not bring myself to do it. I cravenly flinched from having perhaps to hear more of her last days. My imagination would supply such and in great detail, I thought grimly.

As a student, I had never patronized taverns as I felt I hadn't the money. Even now, my attendance in those was largely for meals. I was in no wise a toper. Now I felt so desolate, so lost, so miserable and worthless that, after wandering through the streets some hours, I went to a tavern where other surgeons gathered.

There I found the talk was of the rebels' alliance with France and what it would mean to our prospects of eventual victory. I thought the answer to the last obvious, but merely nodded, said as little as possible, and began to drink as much as possible. I wanted to forget, to forget what I had seen, what I had done, what I had failed to do. I now understood why some threw themselves in the Thames; I was beyond despair.

5

A DUEL

The tavern was much frequented by surgeons, though my relations with these were not convivial. I had set myself apart through my methods of procedure, especially as these appeared to be more successful. However, most were courteous and I tried to be likewise. There was one exception, a Scot, who seemed personally insulted by my methods, indeed by my existence.

He began loudly insulting the rebels, calling them degenerate, cowardly spawn of the dregs of the population of Europe. When I said nothing, he extended his criticisms to all provincials, loyalists and rebels alike. I began to understand he was referring specifically to me. I also noticed the others in the tavern had quieted, which made his voice the louder.

For reasons I did not understand, I became intensely angry. "Was that characterization directed specifically at me, sir?" I asked. The room became utterly silent save for the two of us.

"Aye, yare one of them bastards," was his response.

I told him, "I know who my mother was and who my father is,

I strongly suspect unlike you, sir." I said this with as much edge as I could; I wanted to insult him in return and I succeeded.

His face turned a dusky, mottled red. He swore and told me, "By God you'll die for that, laddie."

"When and where, sir?" was my reply.

At this point, cooler heads interceded, asking us both to reconsider, to apologize, and indeed I was aware I had pushed the matter across the edge of argument into something else.

But the Scot was beyond conciliating, instead shouted at me, "I'll see ye on yer knees, begging for mercy, at the southern point, tomorrow at six."

I replied, "That is indeed a vain hope, as you will discover when we meet tomorrow, sir."

Now one of the older surgeons proceeded to take charge, asking the rest of the company for seconds for the two of us, who sat in our chairs glaring at each other. Volunteers were obtained, and the senior surgeon told them to escort us to our quarters. In the end, it took two to shift the Scot. I was able to walk unassisted to my billet. It was a silent journey. I was not regretting anything I had said, I was merely numb, feeling nothing in particular.

My second awakened me at five. I rose, pissed, washed, shaved and dressed. It suddenly occurred to me I should have written letters, to my family, though without knowing how they could be delivered, to David and Dora, and above all to Caroline. But there I came to a full stop, for what could I say to her, except that I loved her and hoped we might meet in spirit someday.

Aside from that, I hadn't drunk enough to have much of a headache, seemed steady on my feet, and felt no fear, indeed still felt little beyond the cold. My second seemed impatient, was I too slow? But I looked at my watch, shrugged and turned to accompany him to the rendezvous. We walked briskly, so were feeling warmer by the time we got there. We were in good time, in fact, for only the senior surgeon was there. He was carrying a case of pistols. Another surgeon appeared, and they began to load the things. I stood watching, detached. The two men loading the pistols had lanterns, for it was not yet sunrise.

Three men emerged from the darkness. I saw one was the Scot—I didn't know his name. Perhaps he didn't know mine. He stood alone as did I, while the five men who accompanied us discussed where we were to stand and how far apart. We were moved so the lightening sky was to my right. We were perhaps twenty feet apart. I couldn't see the Scot's expression.

Now I began to shiver. It was cold, and these might be my last minutes of existence. I forced myself to be rigid.

The loading was complete, and the senior surgeon said, "It is impossible to say who offered the insult, so I will choose the pistol for each of you. But I ask, can you not each apologize, shake hands so your services may continue to be of use to His Majesty?"

Neither of us said anything.

My second took one of the pistols and brought it to me. The thing was heavy. I realized I had never fired a musket or pistol before. I heard somewhere that one pulled back on the lock on top of the pistol. This held a piece of flint between metal jaws. When I pulled the trigger on the underside, the flint, driven by a spring, would strike a piece of steel which would produce sparks which would ignite the priming powder...for the first time, I felt, not thought, but felt, understood in my bones, that I might die here, in the cold semi-dawn.

The senior surgeon was speaking: "When I say 'One', you cock your pieces. On 'Two', you raise your pieces. On 'Three', you may fire. Am I plain?"

No one said anything. The seconds were standing well clear. I decided to turn as the Scots surgeon was doing, I guessed to present as small a target as possible. I shivered; I thought I saw my opponent sway. Though dawn was minutes away, I could see him clearly enough.

"One!"

I was startled, reached for my pistol with my left hand and pulled back on the lock, just remembering not to turn the pistol upside-down to avoid losing the priming powder. The lock was stiff, but I pulled until I heard the thing click and guessed the pistol was now "cocked," and I prayed not "half-cocked" but I couldn't pull it back any further....

"Two!"

I raised the pistol so it was pointing at my opponent. I could just see notches which I took to be sights and adjusted my aim. The Scots surgeon's hand was not steady; either he was afraid—shouldn't I be afraid?—or had continued drinking through the night. My hand was reasonably steady, but I suddenly asked myself if I shouldn't point the pistol to miss the fellow...

"Three!"

I pulled the trigger without further reflection. There were flashes from both pistols, I felt my pistol thrust itself back into my hand as a long spout of flame and smoke stabbed the half-light toward him and his pistol did the same toward me. Something whipped across my chest, tearing at my uniform red coat, turning me slightly. I looked down at my coat, could see torn cloth with a flash of white inside.

My second now came up, inspected the tear, and told me, "Nae blood, just a torn coat," and I realized he was a Scot as well.

We both turned toward my opponent. He was lying on the ground, his pistol a few feet to his side. Two of the seconds were bending over him, but even in the half-light I could see he was not moving. The two men inspecting him turned to the rest of us and shook their heads. The fellow was dead. I had killed a man. If I had just fired into the ground or the air, "honour" as it was termed would be satisfied. Instead, I had taken life.

What of the Oath of Hippocrates that we were all supposed to adhere to? Now my detachment, my lack of emotion, vanished. Instead I was so desperately sorry. The man I had quarreled with may have been an ill-mannered lout, but I had myself pushed the quarrel, no doubt because I was upset over Ann's fate. Perhaps I couldn't have helped her. No, of course I could have helped her, by following my training, my profession...

I was too ashamed to throw myself on the ground and weep. I turned toward the City, allowing my second to take the damned pistol from me. I began to walk back to my billet, walking mechanically, trying not to think of how deeply I had failed as a doctor, as a man, trying but not succeeding. There was a cart nearby, I guessed for taking any victims back. I didn't even know the fellow's name or anything about him. Did he have a wife, children? What would happen to them?

My second was again at my side. I think he realized I needed to be accompanied by someone. We had walked in silence some hundreds of yards when I turned to my companion and asked him these questions.

He did not seem disposed to be critical of me, merely said, "Nae wife or bairns I ever heard of. Not surprising, for he was nae blithe when he 'uz sober, but when he had the drop in him, he'd have quarreled with the sun for not bein' the moon. Nae friends either."

This should have comforted me, but at the moment I was beyond comforting. So we continued our walk to our billets, in silence.

There was breakfast but I was unable to eat it. I had committed not murder, but homicide, and felt myself a pariah. However, my companions in the mess seemed to regard me with something perversely resembling...respect, there was no more apt description. I went to my duties as quickly as I could. There at least I had to perform my sworn, proper function.

My work done, I walked the streets, finally becoming aware that my torn uniform coat was attracting attention. Several officers told me to have it repaired, as it was unseemly for an officer to be walking about with disordered dress. It was cold, so I turned my steps to the house where lived the sempstress we all employed. She had me sit by the fire after taking my coat off. She then sewed the bullet tear closed, and very skillfully too. I paid her, put the thing back on and wandered some more.

By nightfall my appetite had returned, though not my self-esteem, so I dined in my customary silence in the officer's mess. Now there was no doubt: the other officers were looking admiringly at me, which was a little flattering but made me quite uncomfortable, as I felt I had done a shameful thing, no—two most shameful things.

6

SIDE STEP

———————— ◆ ————————

Day by day, I continued my work. Over time, I felt my despair lifting, to be replaced by sadness. Aside from some of my medical efforts, the only thing I was doing that was of benefit to my fellow men was my presents of fresh provisions to the prisoners in the hulk where John had died. I took his death as a personal failure, foolishly to be sure, yet the feeling persisted. My provisions couldn't last. The winter had descended, almost emptying the markets of anything fresh other than fish, shellfish and such. Of course the rebel prisoners couldn't cook anything.

Robbie McDowell had recovered enough to take charge of the survivors so that the corpses were taken away. I did not know where and did not ask. The dysentery that had plagued them all seemed in abeyance, so I fancied the place even smelled less toxic, but that may have been the cold. Potatoes and apples were all I had been able to bring but these were welcomed. I talked with Robbie and two other prisoners about fish, but they agreed that, without being able to cook these, there was no point to bringing them. Beyond that, they seemed quite friendly, which I savoured as their survival was my sole success, except for some of my patients.

There was something also I must needs attend to, and that was to notify Susan of what had befallen her John. Yet how to get word to her baffled me, ask whom I would. None of the British officers or men was able to help, and I knew no Loyalists in New York, saving Mr. Crewe. Still I persisted, without success.

On a bitter day in January I was summoned to General Clinton's Headquarters. An aide to the General told me, "Wyeth, General Howe asked us to send more surgeons to Philadelphia. So we are sending you. There is a dispatch boat, the *Paris*, awaiting our dispatches. It will sail with tomorrow's tide. Be on board. That is all."

I walked out, very surprised. Indeed, we had no great amount of work, but surely once spring campaigning began, there would be more…. I realized I had not spoken at all, merely listened. Then I remembered those men in the hulk. I would be leaving them to King George's rations, for how long I could not say. I flattered myself my leaving would distress them, certainly it unsettled me. So I gathered my cloak about my body and went to the harbour to be rowed to the hulk.

The men were disappointed that I hadn't brought anything, not that there was anything to bring, not for that number. But they were disposed to be philosophical about my transfer, regarding it as one more display of His Majesty's malevolence. I shook hands with them all, telling them that if I returned I would again bring what I could buy. I had to wait on deck until near dark before being rowed back to the City.

After dining in the mess, I assembled my medical and personal belongings and put them in my chest and medical bag. I left instructions for one of the servants, "mess-men," to waken me before dawn and retired early. My sleep was troubled but no more than usual.

The *Paris* left midmorning because of the wind and tide. As a dispatch-boat, it was fast of course, armed with only one six-pounder and that, I guessed, was for salutes. I discovered I was the only passenger and began to think I was being sent into exile. I suppose that should have distressed me, but I remained numb, without feelings save regrets.

The captain of our ship was very proud of his ship's speed and asserted she could outrun any other ship afloat. I hoped he was correct, though I remembered the rebels had some fast ships as well. I certainly didn't want to be captured and sent to the Connecticut copper mines, reported to be hellish, though the prison hulks I had visited could hardly be considered more humane.

The weather was cold, and dank, with winds that cut through any cloth, so I sat below in the wardroom, thinking and regretting.

III

America, 1778

1

IN LIMBO

◆

After doing the rounds of the rebels taken prisoner at the Battles of Brandywine Creek and Germantown, I returned to my billet, thoroughly unhappy. My ministrations were appreciated, greatly appreciated, once the prisoners realized I was not there to gloat. More to the point, my efforts were often rewarded with success. However, my mood was darkened when I reflected on the likelihood of success of the Crown's efforts to quell the rebellion and on the justice of our cause.

The front room of my billet was brightened by a fire in the fireplace, warm and cheering. I found I had a letter from David. The other two soldiers, a sergeant and a corporal, were engrossing the fire, so I sat at a table and opened the letter. It was addressed to me in New York but had been sent on.

> *My dear Thomas of New York*
> *I designate you thus as I can manage to spell New*
> *York, as opposed to your native province. Your ship was*

reported safely in harbour so Dora and I assumed you are safely harboured as well.

We hoped you were successful in your aims, in contrast to H.M.'s armies, whose fortunes appear more mixed. Were you able to find your sister's fiancé? Prisoners can be paroled if someone of good character will vouch for them. Since you are newly there, perhaps you can pass for such. Was your lady love married? Was she overjoyed to see you? We are avid for the details.

My practice continues to expand, much more rapidly than the income therefrom, unfortunately, but I am considering adding a newly-minted doctor to my practice. I think this is necessary, though he won't be as good as you were. I do miss you, God knows why.

Dora is well, despite the London air and provisions. She sends her love. I will be more restrained and merely offer you my best wishes and regards,

David of London

As I stared at this, our hostess appeared with the required meal. As always, she was reserved to the edge of hostility. Her husband was absent, probably serving with the rebels. So our discourse was formal, even frosty, and rare. The two soldiers sat down at the table and the three of us ate. Our hostess did not dine with us. The Army billeted soldiers in the houses of civilians as a common practice. Despite occasional outrages, no doubt reported at great length by the rebel press, the practice worked well. Relations between soldiers and civilians were generally polite, so the billeting continued. But I think all three of us were well aware of her sympathies.

It had been a long and tiring day but I was still too restless to sleep. So I decided to try to answer David's letter. I went to the room the three of us shared, opened my chest and extracted quills, ink and several sheets of paper. I returned to the front room where the sergeant and corporal were once more before the fire and I began to compose my reply, sitting at the table. It took a considerable time and many false starts:

My dear friends

I reached New York shortly after news of Gen'l Bourgoyne's surrender arrived. I was assigned duties which did not take all my time, so began my searches. My sister's swain would be in one of the prison ships, called "hulks." I went to these in turn as soon as I could. He was on the third ship I visited. The state the prisoners were kept in was worse than Newgate Gaol, far worse. Dysentery and scurvy had reduced the numbers of prisoners considerably.

I did find him, or at least his corpse. He had dysentery but I guessed he died of scurvy probably a week or more earlier. He was wearing a locket containing a recognizable likeness of my younger sister, so I was certain it was him. I will try to send it to her.

Finding the Crewes took much longer. I believe New York is the largest or one of the largest cities in the provinces, so I went from street to street knocking on doors and inquiring, as my duties allowed. Finally I encountered her in the street. She had turned to prostitution, as have many formerly respectable young women, to support herself and her family. She had become infected with the Great Pox: her nose was gone as was part of her upper lip. She recognized me as well.

You know how terrified I am of the Great Pox. May God forgive me for I turned from her in fear and horror and ran away. A few days later I had mastered myself sufficiently to try to find her, to offer her marriage, not to lie with her but to protect her and her family. When I found where they were living, I was told by her father that Ann had died the day before, and her body thrown into a great pit for the dead at one end of the city. I went there and I think I saw her body but could not stay for the smell and the flies. So ended my quests.

That night I went to a tavern to get drunk. A Scots

John M. Brewer

surgeon, made quarrelsome by drink, began insulting me and all colonials. I called him out. We met the next morning at dawn. His shot missed, mine didn't, and was mortal. I just pointed the pistol and fired without meaning to harm him, but without thinking. But my regrets are to no avail. I had made one of the greatest mistakes of my life, one I will never forget or forgive myself for. This on top of another greater mistake I made before leaving England has left me low indeed and deservedly so.

I imagine I was sent here to Philadelphia to keep me or others safe, so have been performing the same duties, treating our own wounded and rebel wounded. I am beginning to think Britain will lose this war, lose her North American colonies, and worse yet, we may deserve to do so. I can see that some Government actions are resulting in making our position weaker, not stronger, and I confess I am appalled at the treatment often meted out to rebel prisoners and even sometimes to civilians. But, as I said, I am low so look on the darker side far too often.

I apologize for the news and my state of mind. I would that I had never left England, yet I felt I had to.

My love to you all,
Thomas of Nowhere

I posted this letter. As I did so I thought of Caroline, whom I had so disappointed, and with whom, I realized too late, I had been in love. I went to bed.

Winter passed into spring without greatly changing the military situation. Skirmishes, with honours about even, took place almost daily. I heard that our spies reported the rebel army was growing stronger and better armed and trained. Their commander, a Virginia planter named Washington, was being taken more seriously by our generals and indeed by the rank and file.

2

A RETURN

———◆———

June in Pennsylvania was warmer than summers in New England and much more humid. Thunderstorms gave relief but only for a short time, at the cost of making the air even wetter. Rumours were spreading that we were going to abandon Philadelphia, including all the Loyalists who expected us to protect them, so everyone was on edge.

We were awakened quietly early one morning and told to assemble. We were not told where we were going, perhaps to attack Washington's army. Surprisingly we were ordered into boats, a great many of them, and taken across the river. We were marching to New York.

As the sun rose, it grew hotter and the air stayed wet. We were all sweating, men and horses, well before ten in the morning. Our troops marched alongside our baggage train, a very long one. Army carts mingled with coaches and carts and waggons, many probably seized from the populace. These were piled high with baggage, mostly officers'. Some coaches had civilians in them, probably Loyalists.

We marched long into the night, but I thought we had not

covered much distance as we were slowed by the baggage train. Up betimes while it was still dark, cold rations only for some of us. Perhaps the rebels would be taken by surprise and we would get away without a fight. I think we all hoped so. Yet, why were we running away?

We were nearing the coast of New Jersey when we began to hear cannonading and some musket fire. Still we continued marching, once more "a real steamer" as some of our troops said. Sometimes a man would fall out of ranks or even faint from the heat. I tried to put these men onto carts or even into coaches, but the Loyalist occupants of the coaches fleeing with us refused. I could only lay them onto the tops of the baggage or on top of the coaches and then only by threatening to turn the occupants out at bayonet point and make them walk. Since officers wore no insignia of rank, I found that an authoritative manner was sufficient even though I had no horse or sword. This especially since several private soldiers and serjeants always came to my side to reinforce the threat.

My servant carrying my medical instruments kept a discrete distance during these encounters. For heat stroke I didn't think I had any instruments or specific that would help.

The cannonading and musketry seemed to become more extensive, ebbing and cresting, though still desultory. Now we began to see columns of rebels approaching, but they mainly kept their distance. A big man—he seemed so even at a distance—on a horse arrived along with other rebel officers, and he began shouting at the rebel officers commanding the men, pointing his sword at us.

At this, the rebel columns began stepping out, trying to get closer. But they were tired too, men marching with muskets at all angles, slovenly ranks or no ranks. We kept marching while watching them slowly approaching on a nearly parallel track. Then we heard an order, a drum began to beat a stirring rhythm and a fife began to play.

If I expected any tune, it was "Yankee Doodle," sung by British and Loyalists in contempt and by rebels in defiance. But this was a tune I had never heard, a lilting, pulsing melody that I thought beautiful in spite of myself. Then another drum joined, followed by another fife. The rebels swung their muskets to their right shoulders, their ranks reformed and they began marching faster. After two or three repetitions of the tune, the rebel soldiers began to sing. I couldn't make out the words, but the tune and the song clearly had put new life into them.

Seeing this, the mounted officers in the regiment I was attached to dismounted and gave their horses into the care of their servants. The officers now marched with the rest of us. Now the rebels were close enough for musketry, and halted and faced us. I saw that some rebel soldiers were black men. A cannon pulled by horses drew around their left flank, swung so it pointed at us, and began to be set up. The rebel soldiers, on command, began to load their muskets. There were mutters of "Shit" from our ranks as we were halted, formed ranks and turned to face the enemy. Our officers took their places in line and drew their swords. We loaded our muskets: three shining hedges of steel. The drums of the rebel soldiers began a new beat, insistent, and the rebels, in three lines, advanced on us.

I was behind our third line with my servant, waiting for custom as I was required to do. The baggage train seemed to pick up speed. Now the rebel lines were quite close. They halted, raised their muskets and fired. The trunk of a nearby small tree, little more than a sapling, exploded. I could hear sounds of things passing, snatching at the air. My servant was thrown backwards, his face gone, leaving a bloody mask. Many of our men were down or reeling. I saw my servant was dead, I took my bag of instruments, opened it and went to the nearest wounded, a small knot of men writhing on the ground.

Our first line fired at this point, another great cloud of smoke, vile smelling, I heard screams but some of these were from our own men and some were from wounded horses. I bandaged, tied off limbs where arteries were torn open, tried above all to get the wounded, once they could be moved, onto the baggage carts to be taken to where they could be treated in a proper hospital.

Both sides were firing at each other, volleys at first, then individual muskets as men on both sides loaded and fired as fast as they could. There was so much smoke, no wind, it was hard to see. Our own casualties were heavy, especially the officers. Increasingly

I was relieved to find a man dead—I didn't have to do anything. I worked as fast and hard as I could; trying first to keep men from bleeding to death. No bandages left, I began tearing strips from shirts of dead men then living men. Blood everywhere, its smell rivaling that of the gunpowder.

I hadn't strength now to haul so many wounded to the carts. I needed help. I shouted at the drivers to stop and help but they only whipped up their beasts. The rebel cannon fired canister, cans of lead balls, taking down several men at a time.

Even with my medical duties taking above all my time, I was aware our line was crumbling. A few sergeants tried to keep the men in line; most officers were down, more and more confusion. A big man on a grey horse, an officer, rode up and took command.

"Form a single line!" he roared as he rode up and down the regiment, ignoring musket balls flying about him.

Miraculously, the men did as he bade them.

He then ordered, "Fix your bayonets!" and our men did so. "Now advance!"

The single line moved as one toward the rebel line, no drums beating as our drummers were down as well. Some gaps opened as men fell, struggling and writhing or simply still, still as death. Even so our men gained new spirit; their determination grew as they advanced. The rebels were also hard hit and retreated. They carried off their wounded, a wise action since some of our men began bayoneting the rebel dead until the mounted officer made them stop.

The officer on the grey horse saw the situation with the wounded, drew his sword and a pistol, and stopped the flight of the baggage train. He forced the drivers to pick up our wounded, put them on the carts, and he found more lightly wounded soldiers to sit next to them when they drove off. I realized this was to keep the drivers, once out of sight, from throwing the wounded men off the cart.

The officer asked me, "Where is your surgeon?" He saw my bloodied, torn, disheveled state and took me for my servant.

I told him, "Sir, I am the surgeon. Thank you for your help."

He nodded, turned and assumed command of the battered

regiment I was serving. We were able to continue our course to the coast.

The officer, evidently a cavalryman, rode with us. I could see he was in some discomfort and asked him if he had been wounded.

He shook his head, replied, "An old injury. What is your name, by the way?"

"Thomas Wyeth, sir."

"Are you an American?"

"Yes, sir, from Massachusetts. And your name, if I may ask?"

The officer smiled and said, "I am Lieutenant-Colonel James Montjoy. A French name but an old one, long since English." Then he rode away, leaving me to go from cart to cart, checking on our wounded.

3

A SUGGESTION

◆

I and all the other surgeons were kept busy, tending our wounded. Now with both armies united in New York City, perhaps we could at last go after Washington and his rebels. But I had the feeling we would do no such thing.

I was billeted this time with a man and his wife, Loyalists, in a brick house. My quarters were far more comfortable and without fleas.

Another letter from David appeared. I saw it had been written two or three months ago, sent to Philadelphia just too late before reaching me at last. I opened it with fear, fear to find Caroline married or dead.

> To our unhappy friend
> We were distressed indeed to hear the results of your journey. The death of your sister's sweetheart was mischance, and nothing you could have done else would have saved him. If he had been mortally wounded in battle, the result would be the same.

As for Miss Crewe, she chose her path, admittedly under the most severe compulsion but for unexceptionable motives: preserving her family's existence. As for the result of her choice: again, mischance. You were at length to offer your support to her and her family, a noble gesture, but her end, terrible as it was, would not have been long delayed whatever you did.

Remember, the duel was the result of your opponent's pugnacity as well as your unmerited criticism of your own behavior toward Miss Crewe, again unfortunate, as was the result of your shot. Also remember that the result could have been the contrary, as your opponent was trying his best to kill you. We are certain you will not attempt such a course again.

We agree the Crown has been remiss, greatly so in its treatment of its supporters. Government has perhaps looked too narrowly at the situation in The Colonies, leaving all to the Army, with help from the Navy, and for your lost love, the result was tragedy. Again, you cannot, as a single individual, be expected to be able to compensate for failures at a much higher level.

Miss Vandelys has asked about news of you more than once. A letter from you to her would, we are certain, be exceedingly welcome.

We are well. Dora hints at an addition to our family. If it is a boy, we will name him Thomas, after no-one in particular.

David and Dora

I was certain that some of my friends' reasoning would be condemned as specious if judged by the standards of Moral Philosophy, but I was nonetheless greatly comforted by their letter. Their suggestion that I write to Caroline surprised me, as I felt I had burned my bridges there. Caroline must have learned to despise me, but…would a letter from me do any harm? More speciousness, but, dammit, I missed her.

On my way to the surgical rooms, I fancied that David had shown my letter to Dora and perhaps Dora had shown it to Caroline…never mind, I would write to Caroline regardless. So I resolved, yet my duties engrossed my time and especially my energy. And once I had time, I felt I had to visit the prison "hulk" in which John Fielding, my younger sister's sweetheart, had perished.

As before, I bought a bushel of new potatoes, washed them and carried the basket to the ship. I carried the basket using a cord tied at both ends to the basket and hung around my neck, as I had done before. Even so just as before, I was hard pressed to avoid pitching forward down the ladder. The stench was almost tangible once again, and it took several minutes to master myself so I could hand out the potatoes.

My old nemesis was still alive, though hardly flourishing. Most of the others were also alive, all very glad to get the potatoes. I had enough to give each man one, and told them all I would return with more in a month or so. We parted with tears, from gratitude on their part and pity on mine. Walking back to my quarters, I realized I could not get the miasmic cloud from the hulk out of my nose.

Once more, I felt I had to try to get word to Susan of her sweetheart's fate. Now I was back in New York, I imagined there must be some avenues—no, trails of communication with rebel-held areas. I asked my hostess, asked many other natives of the city and eventually was directed to a tavern where, it was hinted, there was a man who crossed our lines regularly and might carry a letter to my family, given enough money.

This was a low den, though I had seen much lower in London. I asked about, was greeted with suspicion, but had to continue. At length, one fellow acknowledged having heard of such traffic. I finally extracted an admission from him that he himself regularly took messages back and forth. I suspected he was a sort of spy, though perhaps considered useful enough to both sides to be allowed his ventures.

We bargained for a considerable time. To deliver my letter, or rather package as it included the locket, I would give him a pound—a huge sum—for which he promised to take the packet all the way to Shrewsbury. I also required him to obtain a letter from either sister acknowledging my letter, for which I would give him another pound upon his return. I hinted that the reply would go toward ensuring his continued existence, whereat he sneered yet seemed at least willing to credit me with sufficient hostility to cause him overmuch trouble. So I went to write the letter to Susan. This also prompted me to look to other duties, but eventually I forced myself to write:

> *My dear sister*
>
> *The contents of this packet will tell you everything. I took the locket from his corpse, lest some sailor take it before pitching John's body into the Hudson. He had suffered greatly, dying probably of scurvy a week or two before I reached New York. I came as soon as I could, yet too late. The fact that he still had the locket instead of trading it for food to perhaps survive a few more days shows his devotion to your memory. I know you will honour him for that, as well as for his valour.*
>
> *My agreement with the man who delivered this requires a reply from you or Lizzie, in your own hands, so I will know my letter was delivered. Please tell me the news of father, you two and Tabby Too, as I cannot express how much I miss you.*
>
> *Miss Crew is dead of the Great Pox she contracted from prostituting herself to help sustain her family. This course has been the only one many women of good family could adopt and support themselves and their families. This is part of war, as much as battles and banners. Again I was too late to save her.*
>
> *I was able to come to New York only by becoming an Assistant Surgeon to H.M.'s Armies, so in a sense I serve the Crown, yet it is with a divided heart. Still, that heart is wholly, indivisibly yours and will always remain so.*
>
> *Your brother*
> *Thomas*

I took the packet and the money to the fellow, still residing in the tavern. He nodded on receipt of both and somehow I was reassured he would indeed do as he had promised. So I returned to my surgical duties.

Returned, yet I was increasingly vexed by my reluctance to write to Caroline. I found myself composing letter after letter in my head, all uncommitted to paper as I really couldn't marshal my thoughts. Finally, I told myself just to write what I had in my heart, confused and muddled as it was.

> *Dear Caroline*
>
> *I suspect David and Dora showed you the letter I wrote them, telling of what I found when I arrived. I am now back in New York, having performed my offices in a battle, and have been thinking some considerable time about this letter. Probably I should think more as I fear I will express myself but ill, perhaps to your final disapprobation.*
>
> *I miss you. On the voyage here, I spent the time brooding, thinking of you. In Philadelphia, I finally realized what should have been obvious to me, that I was in love with you. And I remain in that state and probably shall continue thus, for the rest of my life.*
>
> *I believe the outcome of the conflict here will be decided not in the Crown's favour by the alliance of the rebels with France. It is impossible to say how long it will take to end this war. Until then I suppose I am almost as much a captive as my fellow countrymen in the prison hulks.*
>
> *I cannot command Fortune. Could I do so, could you command tolerance of my presence, I would kneel at your feet, beseeching your forgiveness for this errant pilgrim.*
>
> *Thomas Wyeth*

I thought my letter a poor one, but probably the best I was capable of. In the event, I posted it then returned to my duties and, since these were insufficient to occupy me fully, to my regrets.

4

A CHALLENGE

———◆———

Returning one fall evening, my thoughts were engrossed by Caroline, inescapable it seemed. I encountered an officer I had seen somewhere before. He at least remembered me, even my name, saying, "Ah. Surgeon Wyeth I believe."

After a moment I remembered the man, the cavalry officer who had taken charge of the regiment I was attached to, yet I couldn't remember his name or rank, so had to content myself with, "Yes, sir." Then I remembered he had what he termed an old injury, and I could add, "Is the injury still troubling you?"

He replied, "Yes, in fact it seems worse." Looking about, he discerned a tavern, and said, "Come join me in a glass or two, Wyeth. The evening promises to be a cold one."

He was right, and I was nothing loath to join him for other reasons, for the diversion of my thoughts, so walked with him into the place. I noticed a hesitation in his walk as though it were painful to do so.

Inside, the place was not crowded, perhaps surprisingly considering the temperature outside. He bought a bottle of rum, secured two glasses, found a table and chairs near the fireplace, and gestured for me to join him. As I sat down his name and rank came to me: Lieutenant-Colonel James Montjoy. This put me at my ease, so I could sip the rum with him and fully enjoy the taste.

At length I asked him, "What is the injury? I can probably do nothing but offer consolation. And buy the second bottle," I added, as the level of the first had dropped precipitously.

My companion took a largish sip and nodded. He said, "A few years ago, after considerable drinking at the house of a neighbor, I wagered I could lift a young calf over my head." Another sip, then he continued, "I won the bet, but felt something in my side tear or give way and a few days later saw a bulge in my lower belly. This has bothered me more and more. I wear a truss, but the bulge is getting more bothersome."

I swallowed some rum and savoured the taste, aroma and the feeling of warmth the drink produced. I commented, "It sounds as though you have a hernia."

Col. Montjoy agreed, said, "It was called an 'in' something…"

"Inguinal," I guessed and he agreed. "What side is it on?" I asked.

"Left side," he replied, pouring the last of the bottle into his glass.

I still had half a glassful, and decided to go and buy the second bottle. I set this on the table after removing the cork.

He continued, "As a cavalry officer, of course I must ride a great deal, something I had always enjoyed, but now I find myself reluctant to ride. And the discomfort, now pain, keeps increasing. I am beginning to fear I will have to resign my commission and return to England. I am a younger son, have no property of my own, my wife and I are on bad terms, so I would much prefer staying in the Army and commanding a regiment of light cavalry."

I poured more rum for myself and asked him, "Does your wife want you out of the Army?"

He smiled grimly and said, "I think she would prefer me out of this world. She has a lover, fellow with an estate and I think wants to marry him. Whether he would marry her is less certain, but there

I am guessing. She had a son, I believe he is mine, but the son and I are on bad terms."

We both drank another glassful or two. At the rate we were going, we would each have drunk a bottle of neat rum before much longer. Admittedly the bottles were small, holding not much more than a pint, but I was beginning to feel light-headed. I couldn't see any effect on him, though I supposed he had a better head for spirits.

Perhaps it was the rum, but that and the sympathy I had for him inspired me to offer, "Let me examine you. Perhaps I can suggest changes in the truss. At least it can do no harm."

He sat staring at the inch or so of rum in his glass, finally nodded, tossed off the rum, corked the second bottle, put it in his pocket and got to his feet with some difficulty. For that matter, my own legs were a little uncertain in their movement. But I followed him to his quarters, each of us steadying the other on occasion.

He was also billeted in a private house but a much larger one than I had been assigned. The owners of the house were also apparently Loyalist in their sympathies as husband and wife greeted him warmly. He responded graciously, introduced me, and we retired to his room after a few more words.

His servant was present, polishing some brass, buttons, regimental nameplates and such. Col. Montjoy explained my purpose there, and the servant hardly blinked an eye while he helped undress the man, including removing the truss.

He was clearly a well-built, strong man, but I saw a protrusion, a bulge on the left side of his lower abdomen, a classic inguinal hernia, yet the extent of the protrusion was greater than I had seen in drawings of this condition. I attempted to push the hernia back, this clearly caused him pain, but I could not do so. This was a hernia that had developed to an extent that I did not know of any truss strong enough to force the intestine back into the abdomen.

I then had Col. Montjoy lie down. This helped, but I still had difficulty forcing the hernia down, and my efforts still caused him pain. This was a serious case, and I told him so.

He nodded, sweating from the pain my efforts had caused, and told me, "From time to time I have talked to doctors and all they could suggest was the truss. My riding makes my condition worse: the truss can't contain the hernia and soon I will be bedridden and wishing for a loaded pistol."

I sat on a chair next his bed and thought. The wall of his abdomen had torn, or rather the muscles in the wall had torn, and his intestine was pushing out through the tear, a condition which was getting worse. I thought of the doctor sewing up my cat's belly, a much more severe wound, and she had survived. I would have to cut Col. Montjoy's side open, open the body cavity, push the protruding intestine back, and then sew the torn muscle and the cut skin together. If I used silk thread, with close stitches…of course, it was risky, very risky, everyone knew that, yet Scheherazade had lived….

I told Col. Montjoy what I was thinking and the risks, the enormous risks, of surgery that I had never done.

He lay listening then quietly said, "Are you telling me I would have no chance?"

I thought, trying to put my thoughts together so they made sense, and began, "In surgery, speed is paramount. This is because patients feel every cut, they scream and struggle. So the faster the better. And some patients actually die from the pain. I would try to think of everything that can happen, to be prepared, but I might make a mistake, in the preparations I mean.

"The Romans, I have read, performed this surgery, sometimes successfully, so it is certainly possible. But the surgery is just the first step. The patient must then recover from the cutting. In hospitals in London, this is actually the most dangerous part. So many die afterwards when the wounds turn septic. I have had good luck with my patients in that respect. I am not sure why, but the things I do to prepare such as wash my hands and all my instruments may help."

He asked, "Are you saying you don't want to try it?"

I struggled with myself. It was daunting, I was afraid of failure, and I liked Col. Montjoy: I wanted to put him back on his horse, riding free, not in his grave….But my Promethean side, as it were, impelled me into the unknown, whispered that at least I would gain experience, even some fame if it worked….

So I said, "Dammit, if you are willing to undergo this ordeal, for ordeal it will be, I will even do my utter damnedest to put you right."

He grinned, stuck out his hand, I took it and shook it and grinned too. At this point, there was a light knock on the door.

Col. Montjoy said, "That will be Emily, my...friend." I looked for something to cover him, for he was quite naked on the bed, but he smiled at my confusion and told me, "Just admit her. She has seen me in this state before."

So I opened the door, expecting to see a bawd, but she was plainly, respectably dressed, a very comely young woman.

She came in and commented, "Why are you not wearing your truss, James?"

The Colonel smiled as she bent to kiss him, and introduced us, "Emily, this is Assistant Surgeon Thomas Wyeth of Massachusetts. Thomas, this is Miss Emily Porter, of Connecticutt. Emily, we were discussing Thomas's performing surgery on me to repair my hernia. He is willing, and I want him to try it. Otherwise my condition will only get worse. But you and I need to discuss matters," he was looking at me, and I understood he wanted to be alone with Miss Porter.

So I prepared to take my leave but told him, "I will make arrangements. I don't think it can be done tomorrow, but let us say the day after in the morning. Until then, I want you to stay in bed. Absolutely no riding or even standing! I may come around tomorrow to tell you what I think must be done for the surgery itself. Goodnight to you both." I bowed to the lady, for I could see she was that, and left.

As I descended the stairs, I looked carefully at them. If I performed the surgery downstairs, I and one or two men would have to carry him back up, for the owners of the house would probably object to their parlour being converted into a hospital room. I was not convinced the stairs would carry the weight, so the cutting would have to be done where he usually slept.

The night was well advanced. Despite this and the rum I had drunk (Did that influence my decision?), I knew I could not sleep yet, so I took my way toward the surgical rooms where several of my patients lay. As I walked, I thought about what I would be doing, step by step, what I would require and how I would perform the surgery.

In the room, I gazed at my patients, all alive, all sleeping. These had bones broken so the ends cut through the skin, wounds my fellow surgeons treated by amputation. I insisted on pushing the bones back so they fit together, using my fingers, after washing the soldiers' skin about their injury using soap and water, then spirits of wine. I washed my hands first the same way. It was difficult because the men screamed and struggled. Then after stitching and splinting, I washed my hands again. I was using spirits of wine as I was not sure of the water, not having rainwater. My fellow surgeons thought me mad, and laughed at my habits. Yet, by gently feeling the foreheads of the men I had treated thus, I found all were recovering, no evidence of sepsis. My assistants were impressed, though bemoaned the misuse, as they deemed it, of good spirits. My fellow surgeons either resented my success or were impressed against their will, for my success was in effect a reproach to them.

Reassured for the moment, I walked back to my quarters, passing patrols of soldiers and individuals, officers and soldiers, going to or returning from whores, even as some had treated Ann….I shook my head; those memories would haunt me all my life. But now I was tired so perhaps would sleep.

The next morning, I again visited my patients: no change, all recovering with their limbs. I had to think some more, then visit Col. Montjoy and tell him what I had planned. For the cutting, I would need a large table…perhaps a door, removed from the hinges, set on his bed. He was a very strong man, so I would lash his arms and legs to posts or axles and have four strong assistants holding him also. The posts or axles would have to be lashed to his bed. I would give him laudanum—opium—dissolved in rum, for he liked rum (as did I).

For the surgery, I would also need a small table, on which I would place my basin of water, a basin of spirits of wine—I wondered if rum would suffice, perhaps that instead as it was much easier to get—my scalpels, needles, at least three, all threaded beforehand with silk thread, and several sponges. I would soak everything in the spirits before using them. And I would need my assistant, who knew my ways.

I reached Col. Montjoy's billet, found the owner and his wife quite atwitter about what I was proposing, yet I could impart little more as I needed to talk to the patient first. I asked them to show me the first floor of their house, explaining that it might be necessary to perform the surgery there. They looked at each other, this seemed outside what billeting usually entailed, but did as I requested.

The largest room on the lower floor was a parlour, still a rather dark and smallish place, with a bed in it. Looking at this, I realized Col. Montjoy had the largest room in the house. So that settled where I would perform the cutting. I thanked his hosts then proceeded up the stairs to tap at his door.

I heard, "Enter," and some sounds that suggested he was not alone, so entered expecting to see Miss Porter again.

I was not disappointed. They lay together, most companionably, and I realized then they were fond of each other, perhaps more than fond.

Col. Montjoy, unshaved of course, told me, "Sit, Thomas, and tell us your plans."

Noting the "us," I told him what I proposed. He blinked at having his arms and legs pinioned, but I assured him he had to be made unable to move or my cutting might sever something essential to life.

I said, "I will give you opium dissolved in rum, which should," I was about to say "deaden" but changed my words to "reduce the pain a great deal. I think this necessary because my cutting and sewing will go on perhaps twenty minutes to a half hour. Once you are sewn up again, you will be freed of restraints. But you will then require moving as little as possible for at least a day and not much for perhaps two weeks after that. If my measures are successful, you will be restored to health." I didn't dwell on the "if" but I saw they both understood me.

Col. Montjoy asked, "When?"

I answered, "Tomorrow morning, early."

Miss Porter said, "I will wait downstairs until the surgery is over, then stay with you, James."

Col. Montjoy gallantly replied, "Nothing would ensure a more rapid and complete recovery, I am sure."

Something occurred to me and I asked, "Is there a smallish table for placing my instruments on, handy I mean?"

The Colonel said, "I think there is a sort of side board in the kitchen. See if that will do. My servant can help bring it up."

So I went downstairs, located the side board, and decided it would suffice. Next I hunted up the Colonel's servant, who helped me clean the table of cobwebs and dust—if cleanliness helped recovery, no point in overlooking such matters. The two of us carried the thing up the stairs, knocked on the door and entered when bidden.

Miss Porter was dressed and shaving the Colonel. We set the sideboard next to the wall and I looked about the room. I conscripted the servant to help me clean the room.

I asked the Colonel, "Are there any strong men in your regiment to help with restraint? And I will need two posts and a door, as wide as possible, to lay you upon."

Colonel Montjoy nodded at his servant, told him, "See to those arrangements, will you?"

So the servant and I left, walked to where the Colonel's regiment was, and together we obtained what I thought would do: two stoutish posts, six feet long and an oaken door that was very heavy but looked about four feet wide and six feet long. The owners of the house where the door came from were willing to let it be used. Or so I was assured. We made arrangements to meet at dawn, tomorrow. Then I went to find my assistant.

I told him what I proposed, and went over my instruments. I decided I needed more needles, at least two, which I would bend like three others of mine into a semicircular shape. I would need these additional needles to finish sewing the torn muscle while at the same time pushing the intestine back. I would need several bottles of rum for soaking needles, thread, lancet, scissors and my hands. I would soak the dressings and sponges in rum as well, then let these dry, so the spirits didn't burn the wound. So a length of cord to hang the dressings on was obtained. I knew where this could be tied.

There was some opium, reserved I thought for the higher ranks, but Col. Montjoy was certainly that. I got enough for a double-strength dose: the Colonel was a big man. Then after looking at my patients, I sat down and concentrated, trying to think of what I would do, what I would need. I had purchased another basin, with a tightly-fitting cover and this would keep the rum for soaking everything in. And the windows of the room would probably need to be opened…. My assistant was back, carrying six bottles of rum. My medical bag was overfilled, but what we couldn't carry in the bag, we would carry in our coat pockets, the rum, that is.

Through the day, I thought and thought, but could see no further measures I had neglected. Unlike cutting for the stone or an amputation at the hip, my surgery would require far more time. I hoped the opium would give us this.

I retired early and was able to sleep the night. It was still dark when I was awakened by my assistant. I shaved by candlelight and nervously washed my hands and once again cleaned under my nails, gathered my bag and coat with the additional bottles of rum and set out. We met the Colonel's men, four of them, two carrying the door and two carrying the posts. We all walked to the Colonel's billet.

At his door, I knocked, heard the Colonel say, "Enter, Thomas" and did so, bidding the others wait.

I had a candle, lit two others in the room, and gave the Colonel the draught of opium. He downed it and I noted the time. I then retired so Miss Porter could dress and, I imagined, exchange words of comfort with her lover, for he was that, I now knew.

We all waited outside until she appeared, then entered with our burdens. More candles were lit; I would need as much light as possible. The sideboard was moved close to the bed, where the Colonel now lay naked upon the door, which also had been washed yesterday I was assured. His arms were lashed to one post, a pillow set between his head and the post. Then his legs were tied to the other post and both posts were lashed to the bed frame. I washed the area I was to cut with soap and water, then with a sponge soaked in rum.

I looked at my needles: still all threaded. These and the lancet and the scissors were placed in the new basin and three bottles of rum poured in. I had two windows opened about a third of the way to keep the rum in the air down enough to let us breathe. I looked at the Colonel: he seemed partly conscious. I nodded to the solders from his regiment. They took good hold of his arms and legs, one man to each limb. I took a breath, now or never.

I cut an incision shaped like a square "C" around the hernia. I heard the Colonel groan but he did not struggle. I used forceps to pull back the flap of skin over the bulge and discovered a transparent film holding the flap down. So I took my lancet and carefully cut the flap free, turned it back and used needle and thread to tie the flap so the area over the hernia remained open. The Colonel was gasping and groaning but stationary.

Now to sew the torn muscle closed. With another threaded needle, I pushed my finger under one side of the torn muscle, put the needle through the muscle nearly half an inch from the torn edge, taking care not to stab myself with the needle, sliding the needle under the other side, then pulling the silk thread so the gap was closed and tied the knot. One done.

I repeated sewing the torn sides together, spacing the ties at about three or four to an inch. The Colonel was beginning to moan and struggle, but the soldiers held him firmly. I was pushing the intestine back, and this I am sure added to his pain. Still the ties were holding. I was more than half done, but the intestine was resisting being pushed back more and more. It was becoming harder, but I kept sewing.

About two inches of tear left. Now the intestine was nearly contained and I began using my other threaded needles to start sewing together the bottom of the tear. Close to the end, I did not knot the ends of the thread. I would put the needles through both sides, so I had the last inch or so unknotted then I knotted all four in succession. This was because I needed an inch of opening, of tear, to be able to put the needle through both sides while still pushing the intestine back. Once all the threads were knotted, the repair was done.

I cut the thread holding the flap of skin, so the flap now covered the stitched muscle.

"Nearly done," I said, but I think the Colonel had fainted. I quickly sewed the flap of skin using one inch interval of stitches.

"Done," I said, the soldiers relaxed their grips while I took the sponges I had placed to catch blood from the cut and put them into the soapy water. A clean sponge, soaked in rum, was used to clean the blood off the Colonel's skin and the door.

The lashings were undone, the posts removed and several of us pulled the Colonel off the door and onto his bed. I applied clean dressings, binding them to his body with strips of clean linen. Only then did I remember to check his pulse to see if he was still alive. His pulse was moderate and strong.

I turned to the Colonel's servant and told him, "Have Miss Porter come up now."

The door and posts were taken back by the Colonel's soldiers. I gave each of them a crown. Miss Porter, pale but composed, went to the Colonel and wiped the sweat off his face. I saw she was carrying a Bible.

The Colonel's eyes opened, he smiled seeing her and said, "Emily. My angel of life."

She kissed him then laid her head on his shoulder. My assistant emptied the basin of soapy water and rinsed out the blood-soaked sponges while I put away the instruments I had used.

I told the Colonel and Miss Porter, "I will return in about six hours and look at the incision. In the meantime, no standing or even sitting up. For food – broth. No spirits."

I then left, carrying my bag. I noticed my assistant had taken the basin of rum. Only after a few minutes did I realize I had not recorded the times of starting or completion. If the surgery was successful (and I was serenely confident it would be), I would not be able to publish what I had done. This vexed me, but I was otherwise relieved, overjoyed, the uncertainty over. If I had to do such again, things would go much faster.

I fear I gave my other surgical patients the most cursory examination. All appeared well. Several of my fellow surgeons had inspected their injuries much more closely, and since they appeared disgruntled, I gathered my patients were all recovering. I overhauled my chest, removed clothing needing washing and took these items to the corps of washer-women that had attached themselves to us. Some of these women appeared to be of good family, formerly employing servants for such tasks.

My clothing went to the woman I usually gave them to, and I was going, before time, to visit Col. Montjoy when one of the other washerwomen took my gaze. She was familiar in more than one sense: I had met her once and she had a look of…Ann about her. It was Ann's mother, Mrs. Crewe. The woman noticed that I was looking at her, so I advanced. I don't think she recognized me. I felt in my pocket, found a guinea coin, and gave this to her. She stared at the coin, then at me.

I forced myself to speak, "Mrs. Crewe, please accept this in, in…" I was about to say "honour," but there was precious little honour in Ann's life, the last of it anyway, so I changed what I nearly said to, "…memory of your daughter, Ann."

There came a look of pain on her face, tears in her eyes, but she asked me, her voice steady enough, "Did you know my daughter?"

From my accent, she guessed I was from Massachusetts, not one of Ann's customers, and I replied, "Yes, in happier days."

Ann's mother said, "Then, thank you, sir."

She curtsied to me and I bowed to her, turned and walked quickly away, my feelings of triumph, of victory, all gone.

As I walked, I reflected that if I had given the guinea or any money to Ann's father, he would have spent it on drink. In the hands of her mother, the guinea would keep them afloat for weeks. I only wished… I hurried on trying to escape my memories of my conduct. I wondered what had been the fate of Ann's younger brother, but shook my head again, as I didn't want to find out.

I passed a market and saw abundant potatoes for sale. So I bought a bushel of them, washed them using a hand pump and changed my course to the prison ships, to check on the captives I had come to consider my charges and hand out the potatoes.

This task consumed several hours and the vile stench of the place did its part in keeping my spirits subdued. The prisoners were still alive, indeed the signs of scurvy were much reduced, and all seemed glad to see me again. They asked me for news, but I had none to give as little of significance was happening. They took this philosophically. At length I escaped, back into breathable air, and took my way to the Colonel's billet.

He was being fed broth by Miss Porter. His appetite was good, and he assured me he was not in great pain. I looked under the dressing and saw none of the signs of sepsis, no reddening or swelling or foul smell, no red streaks and no fever. Of course, not much time had passed, less than eight hours, but I was pleased.

I said, "This looks well. I will return in the morning. Can you sleep, do you think, or should I give you more opium?"

My patient looked at his nurse, then at me and said, "Let us see. I think I can pass a restful night without it. Despite the cutting, I really do feel better."

I nodded and left, very pleased indeed. My spirits were recovering. In fact, I decided to visit a tavern, drink a glass or two, for I really wished to celebrate.

5

CONSEQUENCES

Unfortunately, several of my fellow surgeons were also there. Two of them in particular took exception to my customs of washing my hands before surgeries and soaking my instruments in spirits of wine before I used them on any patient, implying I was violating some Surgical Canon. I drank my rum slowly, kept my temper, explained over and over again that I wasn't sure why I did these things but they seemed to work, at least work better…here I hastily added, to mollify my listeners, better than I had seen in hospitals in London, where most patients died of sepsis and all had contracted it.

By now I was sure one of the other surgeons was trying to provoke me, perhaps get me to call him out. He began insulting me because of my birthplace, which caused mutterings of reproof or caution from some of the others.

So I addressed him thus, "No one chooses to be born or where or how they are born. So scorning them for such matters, things over which they have no control is…" here I made myself smile, and change what I was going to say to, "…tavern talk and a sign your glass is empty. May I buy a bottle to help remedy that condition? For some things, I have an infallible specific."

I signaled the tavern keeper for a bottle, of rum as it turned out, opened the bottle and poured my antagonist and myself each a half-glassful. I raised my glass, said, "The King," and the fellow had to accompany me.

This quieted things, but I resolved to stay clear of the fellow in the future, at least in taverns. Returning to our billets, I thought he was looking at me in a sullen, hostile fashion and decided to stay clear of him at all times, if I could.

The next day, I arose early and visited the Colonel. I was told Miss Porter was with her parents but would return in the evening. Once more, I saw no sign of sepsis, though there was a small irritation about some of the stitches, and indeed the Colonel admitted he was up and walking more than he should. I insisted he spend more time prone and he said that when Miss Porter arrived, he would do exactly that, which was not what was required. Still, the results were so far superior to what I feared that I couldn't be adamant, just told him to pay attention to the stitches: pain or discomfort should be taken seriously. He smiled and said he would do so. We shook hands and I went to a market for some more potatoes.

I distributed these in the hulk, examined all the surviving prisoners and was pleased at the disappearance of the scurvy. Even the stench seemed less, or perhaps I was just more accustomed to it now.

Back on land, I visited the surgical room. Nearly all my patients had been returned to duty, a condition that caused the senior surgeon to look askance at me. I feared he would begin assigning me difficult cases, probably other surgeons' mistakes, which would either sink my reputation or cause the other surgeons to dislike me even more. I began to wish myself back in England, Caroline or no.

Walking about the city consumed the remainder of the day. I overhauled my kit then retired. I would simply try to stay as much out of sight as possible for as long as possible.

A few days later, I was indeed assigned a difficult case: a wounded arm had become red, swollen and hot, despite the bullet entry apparently healing. The bullet had been removed. The soldier was feverish, and was clearly not going to live unless something was done. Feeling the arm, I fancied I felt something foreign in it. I knew bullets sometimes carried bits of cloth into wounds and… and if the cloth was dirty, could this not cause sepsis? If I was right, I would have to cut the arm open from the far side of the wound and probe and probe until I found whatever felt anomalous in the soldier's arm.

I told the head surgeon what I thought was causing the swelling and fever and how I thought I would have to deal with the situation. The head surgeon was skeptical, but since he had asked me to look at the soldier, felt constrained to let me proceed.

I once again gave the soldier opium in rum, only half as much since the soldier was a much smaller man than the Colonel, had the man's arms and legs secured, and opened his arm from the side opposite to the bullet entry. The soldier shrieked and jerked nearly free then evidently fainted. So I was able to cut into the muscle until I did indeed find several pieces of torn cloth carried into the wound by the ball but not removed. When I pulled the bits of cloth out a great deal of pus followed, not of the "laudable" kind. I allowed the wound to drain then bleed a few ounces, and sewed it up and dressed it. When I finished, I saw several of the other surgeons watching me. No one said anything. I did not know what that meant.

But now some good fortune ensued. Col. Montjoy's recovery was so rapid that I removed the stitches, the outer ones, within two weeks of the surgery. He began riding again with an exuberant happiness apparently without ill effects, for he loved to ride. And the soldier whose arm I had lanced and drained, who seemed near death, also recovered rapidly and was restored to duty within ten days. Best of all was the transfer to Gen. Cornwallis's force of the surgeon who seemed to be trying to provoke me. As a result tavern meetings with my fellow surgeons became actually convivial.

At one of these meetings, one fellow surgeon asked me why I had bled the soldier after the cutting: "Do you recommend bleeding patients after surgery, Thomas?"

I sat thinking and staring at the rum in my glass trying to

answer his question. At length, I responded, "No, not always. In fact, almost never. You see…"

Here I moved closer to the man. Three other fellow surgeons also moved closer.

"You see," I repeated, "I think sepsis comes from dirt, filth, or some part of it, and I bled the man to allow the clean blood to wash out the sepsis from the bits of cloth, perhaps some dirt from them as well."

Here I took another sip of rum.

"If the blood itself was septic, the patient would die. So…" I thought some more, "I try to keep everything that will be in contact inside the skin of the patient clean, as clean as I can possibly contrive. As I said before, explanations are not as important as the result."

Everyone took a sip of their glasses as I thought more.

I added, "Perhaps any explanations must derive from the results, facts, rather than theories."

"You are an empiricist, then, eh, Wyeth?" asked one of my companions.

I replied, "I am a doctor. My desire, my duty, is to cure. I do not care how. Call that what you like. But, dammit, my desire now is for more rum," waving to the tavern keeper.

My colleagues smiled and joined me in another glass or two.

Returning to my billet, I found a visitor: the man I had paid a pound to deliver my letter and the locket to my younger sister. He had a letter for me. From the hand, I saw it was from Lizzie, my older sister. I went to my room, secured another pound and gave it to the messenger, as we had agreed. He left me with the letter, which I opened and read:

> *Dear brother*
> *I write this reply because Susan is too distressed to. I think she knew John was dead but seeing the locket has left her incapable of speech. Only a single tear, but John's death, now confirmed, has hurt her beyond measure. I fear she will not recover from this loss.*
> *Father was very happy to hear from you, though*

*of course he feels for Susan. With the withdrawal of
the Crown forces, some measure of order has returned
to our province, so Father now has much more work.
This has eased the concerns of Susan and mine about
his state of mind.*

*I am well. Daniel and I correspond, though letters
are but a poor substitute for being together. If he can
get leave, we will wed as soon as he gets here. He sends
you his regards and respects, for your treatment of our
prisoners, your kindness and good will.*

*Tabby Too (or is it Two?) is well, perhaps too
well, as he insists on assisting me—I believe that is his
motive—with this composition. I do not hesitate in
blaming him for any blots, as well as misspellings or
obscurities, so he truly is a friend in that respect.*

Your sister
Lizzie

Looking at her letter, I could indeed see what appeared to be paw
prints here and there, and was once more reduced to tears. Odd how
the doings of a dumb beast did affect one so; that and Susan's sorrow.

The next day brought a note from Col. Montjoy, inviting me to
dine with him at the tavern where our conversation led to his surgery.
His servant brought the note, and I wrote an answer, accepting his
invitation. In truth, at the moment, I had few duties, but I was happy
to meet him in convivial surroundings. In fact, I was beginning to
regard him as a friend.

Seeing him, I was struck by his energy and his cheer. He
appeared renewed, transformed. So though the fare was indifferent
at best, it was a most enjoyable meeting. I told him of my surgery on
the soldier with the septic arm and my thoughts on the precautions
needed for surgery.

He looked interested as well he might, for he had benefitted from
those same precautions. He took another sip of rum—that at least
was decent—and said, "Thomas, I feel better than I have in years.
No pain and no constipation either. I think my indifferent health

led to my regiment's being passed over for service with Cornwallis. I do regret that, for the riding, the cavalry action over hundreds of miles is something I long for. The only thing better would be the hunts riding around my family's estate."

He took some more rum. I asked him, "Where is that?"

He replied, "West of London, in the Chilterns about ten miles north of High Wycombe. The village is called Chilterndale. I still dream of the place. Perhaps I will see it again some day."

I said, "Surely you can get leave?"

He shook his head, saying, "My older brother and I were never on good terms, so I wouldn't be welcome. My wife and I are estranged: I think she has felt increasingly humiliated at being the wife of a younger son—so I suppose my home is my regiment."

We both drank then he reflected, "No. No. I am beginning to see my home is…is here, I mean… I mean my home is with Emily Porter."

Silence while he thought, before he resumed, "If I were unmarried and Emily and I were in England, I would marry her. If. Oh, God."

I could see he was now distressed. I must have looked the sympathy I felt.

He leaned forward and confided, "Emily has told me she is with child. Thomas, I am sore perplexed. I feel I should marry her, give her my name, give her some protection, not just money, for, dammit, I love her and I think she loves me."

I asked, "Have you told her this? Does she know you have a wife in England?"

He leaned back, signaled the tavern keeper for another bottle of rum and answered my questions, "Yes, of course. She has told me she considers me her husband before God. Emily is a very religious girl. I like her for that, for everything."

Silence while we both drank, then he said, "I will go through a ceremony of marriage with her. Whatever happens, that cannot hurt, can it?"

I shook my head, partly to clear it.

Then he resumed, "Thomas, we would both appreciate it if you would stand up for me, as best man, I mean."

I stared at him, then reached across the table and shook his hand, saying, "I am honoured beyond measure, certainly beyond my deserts, but, yes, yes indeed. Just tell me where and when."

We both drank to his nuptials, irregular and questionable from a tickle legal view as they were.

He said, "As to where and when, I will have to speak to Emily about that."

From this I knew they were indeed in love, and was emboldened to ask, "So if the Crown wins, you will stay in America?"

He sighed, shrugged and told me, "Given continuance of my salary, yes."

A pause ensued before he leaned forward and said, "But I doubt His Majesty's Government will prevail. We must win all our battles, the major ones I mean, simply to remain. And if we lose one or two more major battles, I fear Government will throw in the towel."

I nodded understanding, indeed agreement, and we sipped our drinks in silence.

Out of curiosity I asked him, "Have you any other brothers or sisters?"

He stared at his glass in silence then roused himself to answer my question.

"Three of us survived. My brother is ten years older and was Father's favourite. Father and my brother had little use for me. Our sister was two years older than I, and also was somewhat overlooked, so we were each other's companion and playmate. My sister also liked to ride, so we went about the countryside together, fair weather or foul. We had no secrets from each other."

"What happened to her? I assume she married," I said.

He was again staring at his glass, finally telling me, "She was married to a merchant who wanted to enter the ranks of the aristocracy. Not a bad fellow, I found. I think he was fond of her, but she died in childbed. Child died too. Come to think on it, my mother went the same way when I was born. Perhaps that had something to do with my father's treatment of me."

He drank a small mouthful then asked me, "Thomas, have you attended women in childbirth?"

I said, "Yes, now above two dozen."

"How many of these died?"

I shook my head and replied, "None, at least none in childbirth."

"How were you able to prevent that?"

I in turn stared at my glass, putting what I hoped was an understandable reply into sentences, before I said, "I am not certain that what I am saying is true, but the belief has been growing stronger in my mind that sepsis results from introducing dirt or some part of dirt inside the skin of a human being. In practice that means keeping any wound clean by any means, soap and water or spirits seem to work. Childbirth is followed by the release of the placenta, in effect opening a wound inside a woman. So I try very hard not to get dirt in the birth canal. So far perhaps by good fortune, the women have survived the childbirth. As I told some of my surgical colleagues, if my methods work, it does not matter why."

He listened to me then commented, "I owe my recovery to your methods, so cannot gainsay them." A pause, and he said, "Dirt."

"Or something in it," I remarked, "Though we can only guess at what that agent of sepsis might be." I leaned forward and told him, "I think our skin is the barrier, the most important, first barrier against sepsis. There may be others." I was recalling that some patients with sepsis recovered.

I bought the next bottle as the last (the last three actually) was empty or nearly so. I was curious about the Colonel's—James's—wife and had drunk enough to ask, "How did you meet your wife, the one in England, I mean?"

James took no offense, and said, "Her father was another merchant, a fishmonger actually, who also wanted connections with the gentry. I don't know if money changed hands, our estate is not a rich one, but I had just received a cornetcy of light horse, which of course my father purchased for me, and was told that in return I was to marry this girl he had selected.

"So I went to their house, in uniform, to pay my respects. The girl, my future wife, was presented. I brought her a small bouquet and we sat and talked. The girl's mother was there, too, of course. Agnes—my intended—looked all right, no surplus of heads or anything like that. She seemed agreeable, biddable really, and was very interested in our estate, the house and grounds, the size of the estate. I realize now she was very disappointed that I was a younger son, had no prospects beyond the Army, and those likely to be slow of achievement. But, just like the Army, I was ordered to marriage and married the girl.

"I will say this for her: she produced a son less than ten months after the wedding. I am fairly certain I am his father, but soon realized she didn't care for me, preferred I stay away. I suspect she would not have been sorry if I were killed or died. Selfish. That I think sums her up. Cold-hearted. And the son is very like the mother. So I was perfectly willing to come to America to fight and came with her blessing."

We each sipped our drinks. I was beginning to understand why he enjoyed riding so much: on a horse, he was in control, could get away from what sounded a thoroughly unhappy home and was being paid by the Crown to do so.

"Does she have money?" That might, often did, oil otherwise unhappy marriages.

But he answered, "Not as much as my father was led to believe. She gets enough to keep herself in fashionable company. Our son went to Oxford a year or two but is basically idle and dissatisfied. Like his mother."

We each sipped some more.

James asked me, "And what about you, Thomas? Have you a sweetheart? Here? In England?"

I smiled wryly and told James, "Before I went to Edinburgh, I was in love with a girl in Boston. The reason I came here was that I was told she was here in New York and might need my help as her family had lost everything. There was another reason as well, so I mounted my steed and sallied forth, only to discover she had had to turn whore to keep her family alive. She took the Great Pox and died of it shortly after we met....

"In England, I left behind a girl I now realize I was in love with. So my venture into knight-errantry has proved doubly, damnably expensive."

James asked, "Does she know you are in love with her?"

"I wrote her a letter saying so—friends told me she wanted to hear from me—but no reply so far."

James reminded me, "Winter is approaching, the close season, so any letters will be delayed."

He stopped, stared into his glass, then looked up at me and asked, "Does drinking port wine produce gout?"

I in turn stared into my glass, nearly empty but I decided to keep it so, as I was feeling some muzzy-headedness.

After thinking, I replied, "I don't know. That is, I can't be certain, but…yes, I suppose it is possible. Why do you ask?"

James leaned back and reflected, "My father was a 'three-bottle-a-day-man' and proud of it. But he became gouty, so couldn't walk about much. He bought a sort of wheeled chair. Then he became dropsical and that finished him.

"My brother drinks port too, now has gout, and our steward told me became dropsical as well. I never liked the taste of port, took whiskey and water instead. And save for the hernia, have never had an ill day."

I was staring off at the far wall of the tavern, and felt connections being made in my mind, connections between gout and dropsy, port wine and movement.

I leaned toward James and said, "If port does cause gout, then the patient will walk about less, and… and perhaps that in turn promotes dropsy, the accumulation of water in the patient's tissues."

Silence before I qualified myself. "Of course, I am speculating."

Another pause before the enthusiasm of my idea impelled me to add, "But, yes, it is possible. It does fit." I sighed, and remarked as if to my glass, "Perhaps too well."

James laughed and raised his glass to me. We both finished our glasses and noted the rum bottle—our fourth—was empty. Still we walked together with fair steadiness until we separated, bidding each other a good night.

The next day, feeling rusty from the rum, I once more told myself to restrict my consumption in future, and went to my shop. There I was greeted by a spate of soldiers, one corporal and seven privates, all with what was termed a "great dose": they could not piss, evidently because of the Lesser Pox. I got out my catheters, washed and oiled these, washed my hands and began opening the obstructions. Partly to divert the men from the pain, I asked each the name of the woman they had lain with. All named the same woman, and I told them to avoid her in the future and to warn their comrades not to purchase her services either.

This provoked objections, that the woman, "lass" they called her, had to make a living after all....

I had washed my hands between each man, and sat afterwards trying not to think of Ann. Instead I wondered whether the soldiers generally should be warned away from the woman, whether to the detriment of her livelihood or no. Then my thoughts drifted to the question of how men on a wage in hand of fourpence a day could afford the services of even the cheapest whore. I decided they must be working for wages outside the Army, as so many did.

I rose to my feet and walked about, looking at sick soldiers but venturing no comment to the other surgeons as any such comment would be taken ill. I sighed to myself, for I could see treatments being meted out that I was sure would do more harm than good, and wandered outside back to my billet. Perhaps I could persuade the lady of the house to prepare me some breakfast. Or lunch. As I walked, it occurred to me that it was likely that one reason for my unpopularity was that I had a MD, not a licentiate in surgery though I had never mentioned this to anyone. So in a sense I was both unqualified yet was imagining myself to be above them, at least socially. That was probably why the eight enlisted men fell to my lot. And there was little I could do about any of this.

6

AN UNDERSTANDING

In the house, the lady and her husband were just sitting down to table. They kindly invited me to partake and I thanked them, accepting their invitation.

The lady told me, as I was sitting down, "Doctor Wyeth, there is a letter for you, just arrived, I think, from England. I left it on your bed."

Probably I should have feigned unconcern, but I rose, excused myself, and went to my room and seized the letter. The hand was unfamiliar, but a lady's and the return was C. Vanderlys! My heart gave a great bound, though I told myself she might be giving me my quittance. I took it down to the table, as I was hungry, and excusing myself to the others, opened it. It was indeed from Caroline. In it she said,

> *Dear Thomas*
> *I must confess your very welcome letter put me in such a state I have been hard-pressed to reply. But reply I must, so must trust my feelings outweigh any infelicities of expression.*

I hope you are well, hope you may be able to return when spring brings better weather so we may meet again. I do not know if you can resign your commission or if you are indeed the Crown's captive. Perhaps you can be reassigned to England. Wherever it is, I will join you.

Dearest Thomas, I am in love with you as well, and once together, there is nothing to impede our union. So do return, but return safely, that above all.

David and Dora did indeed show me your letter to them as they fancied, correctly, that part of it concerned me. While I ache for your sister's lost sweetheart and for the woman you once loved, I rejoice in your affection. Believe it to be fully returned by

your Caroline

My hosts remarked my grin and commented, "Good news is always welcome."

I laughed, shook my head, and replied, "The best possible news, at least once I am able to return to England. Thank you," to them both.

I ate, not really tasting anything. I had shared my rations, salt beef or pork, with them so I daresay the meal was superior to those on countless other tables in the city. Still, my head, my heart and my soul were overfilled with joy. At the meal's end, I rose, thanked them both again, and walked outside wishing I could dance instead.

I was going to tell James, there was no friend else at hand to share such news, but he would be out with his men on reconnaissance or to capture a prisoner. The sky became cloudy, so I walked or rather skipped back to my place of business. It did begin to rain. I cared not: my armour of happiness was invulnerable.

This feeling persisted, despite two officers with hernias asking me to repair them as well. My successful cutting on Col. Montjoy was now increasingly common knowledge, which in a way flattered me, yet was certain to provoke more hostility from my fellow surgeons. Could I repeat my success? Almost certainly, but that "almost"...

I examined both officers. Both wore trusses, and this allowed them to perform their duties. While their conditions were not as severe as James', both were despondent and talking of having to sell their commissions and return home. My Promethean itch was taking possession of me. So all I could do was explain the surgery, what it entailed and the risks. I concluded by asking them to think matters over, then if they felt they would undertake the surgery, I would do it.

After they left, I wandered about again, my mind elsewhere, doubly distracted, and I decided to reply to Caroline's letter. So once again quill in hand I sat before sheets of blank paper trying to marshal my thoughts. Finally I produced:

My dearest Caroline

Your letter gave me more happiness than any event save our marriage could. I will ask a friend and former patient, Lt.-Col. James Montjoy, about whether I can escape H.M.'s service without danger of gaol or firing squad. I suspect I can, but must keep tight reign on such suspicions untill if they can be converted to fact.

By fits and starts, I am gaining experience, so feel my tenure as military doctor is not a waste, but I do so wish you were a part of my life, a constant part.

My older sister responded to my letter. My younger sister had suspected the worst, but was hard hit by the reality. I hope she can recover but suspect she will never marry. My younger sister has very deeply held feelings, but I suppose that is true of the rest of us, including my father.

I will end this letter now in order to try to get it to you as soon as possible. I do love you.

Your Thomas

The letter was added to the collection accumulating, to be sent by dispatch boat whenever the General commanding us decided.

CUSTOM

There was another officer waiting on me, also with a hernia or so he thought. However on examining him, I concluded he had only a strain in an abdominal muscle, so counseled him.

"Avoid as much as possible any activity that involved that muscle. Two weeks of an easier regimen should help," I told him.

He agreed to return in two weeks.

With James away, I was left with two possible patients for hernia repair. I had little to do but think over what I would have to do if one or both officers decided to risk the surgery. I would require more opium, more silk thread and about a dozen bottles of rum. So I set forth to obtain these, as I didn't think my servant sufficiently capable, saving for the rum. My errands took the entire day, as I was sent from shop to shop, and when I returned to my billet, found both officers willing and waiting to tell me so.

I apologized to them for their loss of time, and then sat down and once again went over what I proposed to do. We fixed on a place, a time and an order. The first would be the day after tomorrow, the second the day following. They agreed to this, looked somewhat askance at the rum, but left. I ate dinner and then to bed.

On the morrow, I recruited four strong holders and obtained two stout wooden posts, rope, and the loan of a door. I told the holders what I proposed and showed them where I proposed to do it. Then I returned to the apothecary shop I had employed before and prepared the opium drinks. I had to guess at the doses but decided too much was better than too little. The rest of the day was spent worrying and the night tossing.

The first patient had evidently as little sleep as I. At any rate, the opium drink rendered him unconscious. So I proceeded with the cutting. He groaned but did not struggle. The tear in the muscle was shorter and narrower. This made the sewing more difficult and I had to be very careful not to pierce the intestine. His hernia was on the right side and I caught a glimpse of his appendix. I saw no sign it was inflamed. And this time, I had my servant record my start and finish.

We moved the still unconscious man to a bed after his wound was dressed, and I recovered the unused rum, much to everyone's disappointment. However if I was paying for these things out of my pocket (and I was), I wanted to keep my expenditures as low as possible.

The rest of the day was consumed by preparation for the morrow's surgery and incessant checking on today's patient. He was slow to awaken, complained of pain when he did, but there was no early sign of sepsis. At his request, I gave him another dose of opium, a much reduced dose, which eased the pain.

Late that day, I was presented with another patient, a private with clear signs of the Great Pox. I prescribed the usual treatment, a dose of mercury, not that I imagined it would do much good, and sent him to the house where men with such diseases were collected. I washed my hands several times after. Then, being worn out, I returned to my billet, wondering if that soldier had infected Ann or she him.

My servant got me up with difficulty, and I hoped I would be alert enough for what I was to do. I gave the opium drink to my second patient, had him tied to the posts and while the opium was taking effect, examined the first patient. He was once more in pain but otherwise all was well. I prescribed a light diet of mostly broth with some rice then returned to the second patient.

He was still conscious, so there was work for the restrainers. I guessed that nearly the same dose of opium must have different effects on different patients. Consequently, this man screamed and writhed, making my cutting much more difficult. In exasperation, I thought of clubbing the man, but instead persevered, finally sewing the tear in the muscle closed. At this point, the man fainted.

"Good enough at last," I thought, as I sewed the flap of tissue closed. This surgery took longer, nearly eight minutes. But it was done.

The rest of the day was much like yesterday after the surgery save I had two patients to watch. Otherwise, instead of a private with the Great Pox, I had a major with a bad case of piles. Examining him was of course very unpleasant, but I had to decide what to do. I could cut off the hemorrhoids, but how to prevent sepsis? I wondered about using cautery to seal the wounds. That would be intensely painful, but if it worked….

I told the major what I was thinking: I would cut off the worst of the hemorrhoids, cauterizing the wound and see if the man recovered.

But the major wanted them all—there were four—removed, and he was prepared for the cautery.

So I told him I would make my arrangements and would perform the cutting three days hence, on a Monday.

He agreed and left.

I began a search for cauterizing irons, a room with a fireplace or stove and anyone with experience cauterizing wounds. I knew cautery was once the procedure employed after amputations until it was found that gentler methods worked better (except for sepsis). What I was proposing would cause raised eyebrows among the other surgeons, who, I thought, considered sepsis unavoidable, perhaps even necessary: generation of "laudable pus" was supposedly the road to a cure. Since my patients seemed to recover without this, I was skeptical, but kept my doubts to myself. Aside from the cautery, the surgery was simple. I practiced heating the irons and touching them to a piece of ration beef. The smell was pleasant, in fact made me and my servant hungry.

After our meal, which was disappointing, I continued practicing. I wanted to sear the smallest possible surface of skin, so needed small irons. And having the tip flattened would be helpful, especially if the flattened tip was set at an angle to the iron rod. I sought out an Army blacksmith, and told him what I wanted. He obliged me and I returned to my quarters with three irons fashioned as I wished.

There was a message awaiting me from James: he and Emily were to marry tomorrow, Saturday, at 10 of the morning in the below named church and would I honour the occasion with my attendance? I wrote a reply saying I was the one who was honoured, otherwise, yes. I sent this to James's billet by my servant, while I began searching for a flower for my lapel.

Winter was nearing, so I feared my search would be fruitless or rather flowerless, yet after asking everyone in sight, I was directed to a wooden building with a hothouse concealed behind fences and bushes. There I was able to purchase, for half a crown, a perfect-appearing rose. Considering the price, the thing should have been exceptional. I brought the rose to my billet and placed it in a glass of water, after cutting off the end of the stem, as my hosts told me was necessary.

I bathed in honour of the occasion and set out my better uniform for the morrow. I had obtained a second, as my original was mended and worn. Then I went to bed rather early, because I was tired.

The morning was cold but bright. After I dressed, I used one of my semicircular needles to secure the rose to my lapel. A straight needle would have been better, but I couldn't find any. I dined, explained my garb to my hosts to their approval, and set out. I asked several civilians for the direction of the church, but reached there in good time.

A great many officers were present. Judging from the badges, all were from James' regiment. There was a couple in civilian clothes; from the resemblance to Emily, I guessed these were her parents. They were sufficiently in favour or at least resigned to the proceedings to be there. There were no bridesmaids or other family of hers.

James arrived, immaculately turned out, with his servant. We all shook hands, then the clergyman and a woman who would play the organ appeared, and everyone else sat down save James and I. The woman began playing the organ, the church doors opened, and Emily, veiled and dressed in what I took to be silk, walked in accompanied by James's hostess. The guests all stood as Emily advanced to James's side. They plighted their troth to each other, pledges that I imagined both regarded seriously. James put a ring on her finger; they embraced and kissed to loud cheers from James's fellow officers. I signed the certificate, "Thomas Holmes Wyeth, MD, of Massachusetts." We all went to James's billet for cake and rum. Emily was taken by my rose, and I gave this to her with my best bow. Her condition was not obvious yet.

Despite my reiterated pledges to myself to keep my consumption of rum moderate, I had to be assisted back to my billet by James's servant. I alternated reproaches, vows of better behavior, and excuses to myself, managed to undress, then slept the rest of the day and on until next morning, Sunday.

Sunday was spent thinking about the surgery I was to perform Monday but in great part recovering from the celebration of the previous day. I concluded I would live but had to do my best so my patient would as well.

Monday early was cold and snowing. I was awakened by my assistant very early it seemed, yet when we got to the room I was to perform the surgery in, everyone else was awaiting me.

The room was cold, so I had the fire built up. I needed to heat the cauterizing irons and wanted some warm water, as I guessed the officer's arse would require washing. He would be tied to a table, with his knees on cushioned chairs so as to better present his backside to me. I gave him the opium in rum to drink.

I had the officer doff his garments then lie on the table. I had his arms and legs secured, then began washing his arse. This was unpleasant but necessary. I washed the area twice, in fact. I looked at the man: he seemed unconscious. I asked him twice what his name was, got no response and decided to start.

The men I had recruited to hold his arms and legs grasped these.

My scalpels were soaking in a glass of rum; the irons were glowing red at their tips. I took the first freshly sharpened scalpel and began cutting. The officer tried to move but to no avail. Two hemorrhoids cut off. A third was harder to get at so it took longer to remove. The officer was now groaning loudly and struggling but the last pile came off with a flick of my scalpel.

The rum-soaked, then dried sponges were used by my assistant to wipe the bleeding wounds as I grasped one of the irons with a woolen cloth. I quickly and briefly applied it to a small wound. A sizzling sound, accompanied by more groans and struggles, then a second iron to the largest wound. By now, the holders were becoming hard pressed. I forced myself to remain calm. Too much haste could result in very serious burns.

The irons were red-hot again and I applied one, then the other to the remaining two wounds. Then I stepped back, realizing I was shaking and sweating. At this point, I wondered again whether sewing the wounds might not be better but I once more decided that cauterizing them would seal the surface better, so the patient's shit would be less likely to produce sepsis. But now I and the patient were going to find out if my ideas were correct.

The man was laid on his stomach on a bed then covered with a blanket. I ordered a second blanket laid upon the first, as this was a cold day indeed. Then I thanked the restrainers, gave them each six pence, and watched my assistant put my instruments away. The irons were allowed to cool before quenching them in water. Only then did I go for breakfast.

8

A BRIGHTER DAY

◆

Owing to the greater diversion of surgeons to Cornwallis's force, I found myself busier than before. In addition, my successes at treating hernias and piles attracted custom from the entire New York garrison, including the Loyalist forces. This was flattering but the work increasingly left me exhausted. Several of my officer patients rewarded me with five or even ten guineas. These payments were very helpful as I was otherwise sustaining the charges for the surgeries I was performing, for rum for example, myself. Being paid in guineas suggested my possession of a MD instead of a licentiate of surgery was generally known but how? My only diversions, aside from taking potatoes to the men in the hulk, came from occasional evenings with James, and of course letters to and from Caroline, all too rare. So the winter passed into spring.

Emily's pregnancy proceeded quite unremarkably. James and Emily both wanted me in attendance when the child appeared, probably late May or June. Emily had been presiding over James's regiment's mess to high approval from the officers though they must have been aware James had a wife in England. I gathered such arrangements were common in the British Army, both for officers and men. It seemed rather hard on the women and particularly the children of such unions; not that officers and men had a particularly easy time of things either.

By mid-spring I had received two more letters from Caroline, and I had sent two. It was awkward sustaining such a correspondence, with months passing between sending and receipt. At one point Caroline told me she would join me wherever I would practice; but if I had a choice, she would rather live in the country, away from London. My reply promised I would try to obtain such a position, but Caroline wouldn't have received that yet.

James and I had established a custom of meeting at the same tavern Friday evenings. I struggled to keep my consumption of rum below two bottles, preferably a pint and a gill, with indifferent success. The last Friday in April, James had news: his son had married. James's English wife had sent him a short letter, more like a note, to that effect. I sat staring at him, not sure how this news was to be regarded.

James took a sip of his drink, leaned back in his chair and remarked, "Came right out of the blue. Of course, Agnes and I don't correspond, but I suppose I should have been told…" here he took another sip, "but I will write to George with my congratulations, congratulations he actually secured a living bride, no, I won't say that, but…" another sip, then, "I suppose I am being too hard on the boy, no, he is a man now, twenty two or three, personable enough… perhaps having a wife instead of that mother will improve him. I hope so."

We both drank some more rum, and I asked, "What is the girl like, does…" I was about to say "your wife," but changed that to, "Agnes say?"

James shrugged, replied, "The usual things: pretty, accomplished, sweet disposition, good family, no mention of a tail or a dearth of eyes. I don't really envy the girl, though if it be a good match, I don't envy either. The fact that he is next in line for Chilterndale assuredly was mentioned more than once."

Another pause for the usual reason, then James commented, "Emily says we can only hope and pray for their happiness."

I nodded, noting that James was quite open with Emily about this part of his life, and our conversation drifted in other directions.

Emily's confinement was perhaps a week or two away, when James gave me another piece of news. This time, it was on a black-bordered sheet of paper. Reading it, I saw that James's older brother had died. James was addressed as "My Lord Chilterndale." Looking at James, I realized he was very upset, and I knew this was because of the choice forced upon him. So I said, "Have you decided what you will do?"

James turned in his seat and gestured to the tavern-keeper for another bottle. Once this was brought, opened and poured, James took a longish sip and told me, "I showed this to Emily, of course. She told me she wanted me to stay until our child was born and a few weeks after, but she knows how much Chilterndale means to me. She said she knew that our marriage here on earth wouldn't last forever, but we would be together for all time after."

There was a pause while James wiped his cheeks.

He went on, "The woman is a saint, an absolute saint. I don't deserve her, I really don't. But I will do all in my power to keep her and her child...*our* child comfortable."

Here he stopped, overcome. I sat, not saying a word.

He resumed, "If I give up my commission, I am sure of a buyer. That money will go to Emily. I could stay until this war ends but we might be ordered to join Cornwallis... And I do want to see the place again, I do indeed, and put some things right that are needful... but I cannot bring Emily with me, not across the Atlantic with a baby or even a small child, so we will be separated, probably for years, perhaps for the rest of our lives..."

He sat shaking his head.

I said, "Right now your duty is to Emily and the child. In the mean time, make arrangements for selling your commission. And remember, you have a friend at need here, at this table."

I raised my glass to him and sipped. He began to smile, raised his glass to me.

"To my wife and child," and we both drank. We were both silent.

"Thomas, you want to return to England, don't you?"

I nodded and replied, "I've been busy with repairs as I call them, not casualties, and of course I will see Emily through her delivery. Then, if I can, I will leave."

"Since I am succeeding to a title, I can help you resign your commission. But, once you marry your Caroline, I want you to join me at Chilterndale. I don't believe we have a doctor in the village, so you could practice there. Or, if there is, you could become my steward, factotum, what you will. I will certainly need a friendly face and an ally there. What do you think?"

I thought. Caroline wanted to live in the country and James was offering me the possibility, no the certainty, of doing just that. Even if a doctor was in the village, James could simply insist that his servants and tenants come to me. I did want to be of service to him, as otherwise he would be surrounded by his estranged wife, lumpish son and a daughter-in-law of unknown qualities. Further, his patronage, if that was the right word, would help in allowing me to leave the Army.

So I said, "Yes," and we shook hands.

9

FINISHING

James was able to sell his commission to a major without difficulty. However, he wanted the money in hand to give to Emily. This required a voyage across the Atlantic and back at the very least. Wisely, James made the actual transfer of the rank conditional on receipt of the money. In the meantime, I attended Emily and assisted in the delivery of a son named James Porter Montjoy. Wet nurses in New York were regarded with suspicion by Emily, who as a result nursed their son herself. I know this was common practice in other countries and other times, so paid close attention to the child. So far as I could tell, he had inherited his father's robust good health and appeared to thrive.

James was also able to foster my resignation as Assistant Surgeon. Perhaps my unusual treatments, particularly their successful outcomes, promoted this result. Whatever its origins, I was very happy to be allowed to leave. My happiness was allayed only by the fact that I would no longer be delivering fresh provisions to my fellow countrymen imprisoned in the hulk. And I would once more be cut off from news of my family. I did send another letter to them, with my plans and hopes. This time I had to take the messenger on faith as I would be gone before he could return.

I wrote to Caroline and to David and Dora, telling them of my intentions to return. The letters were sent by dispatch vessel. I would follow in a larger and no doubt slower ship. This was carrying crippled or sick soldiers for the hospital in Chelsea they had all been paying for with one of the stoppages from their wages. A few officers who were resigning their commissions, as I was, were also passengers.

Alas, the dispatch vessel returned, "put back" into New York Harbour, after a rebel privateer nearly captured it, so I realized my letters and I would arrive in England simultaneously. Worse, as an experienced doctor with extensive surgical experience [I could not find out who told the ship's officers this] I would be expected to treat all the sick soldiers on the voyage. I had so hoped for a respite from medicine, but it was not to be.

My chest was as heavy as before; my medical bag was enlarged by additional instruments. I added some drugs and several pints of rum, so the bag had gained considerable weight. But if I was to serve as doctor to sick soldiers—without pay be it noted—I would need these. Otherwise, I collected my pay, what was left after all the stoppages, from the Paymaster's Office and was carrying it in my money belt. I had a trifle over £30, not far from the amounts I had carried to Scotland, to England and to America. Ann's comment that I would never be rich, but would always have enough and more for my needs came to mind, saddening me anew.

I tried to shake these feelings off. I was returning to claim a bride and establish a country practice under very favourable circumstances. Our ship was actually a small frigate of 24 guns. Assuming we didn't fall victim to Lord Sandwich's neglect in failing to provide sound masts and spars to the Navy, we should reach England despite rebel privateers.

In consequence, I stood on the quarterdeck as we set sail feeling hopeful and excited. The wind was nearly astern, brisk but not excessively so, and our ship appeared a fast sailor. I hoped and prayed we would persist and finish as we had begun.

IV

In Cytherea, 1779

1

ADVANCE TO YOUR PARTNER

—◆—

The sailing went well, nearly as well as my voyage to Scotland only six years ago (though the elapsed time seemed longer). My fears as to being conscripted or rather press-ganged into caring for the discharged soldiers proved prescient, but it transpired our ship carried no doctor or surgeon, so my duties expanded many-fold. Many of the soldiers were healthy enough, merely crippled through loss of arms or legs, but some had venereal complaints which I had to steel myself to treat. Add that my treatments were not particularly efficacious, not that I knew of any that were, and this alone made for an unhappy journey.

Some of the sailors too had such symptoms, an additional source of repugnance. Otherwise there were some broken bones, more sprains, and one or two hernias which I could not correct surgically as I felt I could not do so in the quarters provided without the near certainty of sepsis. So I was kept very busy indeed, yet without being able to produce many cures. Fortunately, the expectations of the captain, crew and soldiers were so easy I could have done much less and been much less effective without cavil. This made me think very ill of naval surgeons and physicians, perhaps unjustly.

We were London-bound, of course, but an appearance by a French squadron caused us to make for Bristol; the French Navy seemed much more active than in the Seven Years War. We reached Bristol at sunset. The dispatches (and my letters) would go post. The officers would stay aboard, unless any were free of the Army. Those, as civilians, could leave if they chose and some did so choose. I decided I would leave as well. I really didn't think my efforts could possibly make much difference in a voyage about the south of England to the Thames, but the captain seemed to regard my presence as almost a kind of talisman, as, I gathered, did the crew. So there was a prolonged argument but I stood my ground. I was in fact a civilian and had done vastly more than I could possibly be considered required to do. More than all, I wanted to reach Caroline as quickly as I could, and was certain travelling overland to London was faster than continuing by sea, even if the French ships had all run aground and sunk.

This meant I finally got ashore the next midmorning with my chest and bag. By the time I reached the coach for London, it was about to leave, so I had to ride atop with the driver, with my bag in my lap and my chest unsecured at my back, occasionally sliding into me when we were going downhill. At least the weather was fine, and I was prepared to endure the rest for the sake of the object of my journey.

We stopped at an inn near Avebury, for a coincidence. Though leagues superior to the places I had endured in Scotland, this one provided passing indifferent food and beds I fancied were certain to provide me with a cargo of lice as well as fleas. So, once again, I slept curled upon my chest, my medical bag and tricorne for a pillow and my cloak for a blanket. I slept badly but cared only that I would continue my journey tomorrow.

Our road was more uphill than down, rough enough so we lurched often. I gazed at the countryside, which appeared stony and not particularly fertile. We rolled around a turn marked by a huge boulder, and found two men on horseback nearly blocking our path.

For an instant I thought them possible passengers then realized that both were armed and wearing handkerchiefs across their faces. They were highwaymen.

Both flourished pistols and demanded we stop and "deliver," hand over our valuables. They seemed ferociously in earnest and the driver of our coach obediently came to a halt. The passengers were ordered out and emerged, with looks a mixture of fear, resignation and anger. The shorter of the two thieves gestured at me with his pistol to step down. I caught the whiff of spirits and guessed one, perhaps both, had been drinking.

At this moment I was overpowered by anger. The little monies I was carrying had been hard earned and were for my wedding, and I was damned if I was going to allow these ill-washed, drunken louts to carry it away for taverns and whores. My right arm was grasping the strap of my chest. With all my strength, I hauled it up and hurled it at the shorter highwayman.

He was not expecting resistance, certainly not resistance such as I provided. My chest, still quite heavy, caught the man full in the head and body. He went over, off his horse, his pistol, fully cocked, escaping his hand. The chest landed atop the man, pinning him to a boulder. His startled horse dashed past the second highwayman, nearly knocking over the six inside passengers on foot beside the coach. The second highwayman's horse also turned, forcing the second highwayman to concentrate on keeping his seat.

I threw my medical bag at him, hitting his horse and causing the animal to try to bolt. I jumped to the ground and dove for the pistol, still cocked, that the first highwayman had dropped. For a miracle, it had landed upright on some furze, so I hoped and prayed the priming hadn't fallen out of the pan. I snatched it up and pointed it at the still mounted highwayman who was swinging his pistol toward me.

His pistol fired as I was turning toward him and I felt his ball tear at my left upper arm. I steadied my aim, saw the still mounted highwayman drop his discharged piece and reach for another in his belt, and I pulled the trigger. There was a blessed flash, a moment's pause and my pistol fired. Its ball caught the ruffian full in the upper chest. He also went backwards off his horse which escaped. He lay stunned then began coughing up blood, and I knew his end would be soon.

I stood, disbelieving what had happened, then felt the tear in my arm begin to hurt in earnest. I looked at the wound, the outer muscle was torn and I was bleeding. I searched for my handkerchief, I knew it was clean, and began trying to tie it around my arm. Here I was assisted by a stoutish, well-dressed woman. There was also a stoutish, well-dressed man I somehow took to be her husband who collected the undischarged pistols of the two thieves. A tall passenger, a clergyman by his dress, walked over to the two horses and secured them.

The coachman walked over to the two corpses, for that is what my efforts had rendered them, and pulled the handkerchiefs from their faces. Both were badly shaved and not very impressive looking.

I asked, "Does anyone know these two?"

No one did. I pulled my chest, fallen over onto the ground and struggled to put it back on top of the coach. I had to accept the assistance of the coachman as I now felt weak, wanting to sit down. One of the other passengers brought me my medical bag, which also seemed very heavy.

The stoutish, well-dressed man claimed to be a magistrate of a town near Reading and asked us to lay the two dead highwaymen across their horses and tie them there. Looking at the two dead men, I judged that the first had died of a fractured skull when he had landed on a boulder under my chest. The second had choked to death on his blood. The horses were tied to the coach. I managed to mount the coach, resuming my seat by the coachman and we set off again. I thought the other passengers were too surprised and shaken by what had happened to say much to me.

The lurching and bumping of the coach was causing me pain, try as I might to keep my left arm free of contact with anything. When I got to London, I would have David treat my wound, but the journey now seemed interminable. Keeping my chest as stationary as I could was most wearing.

Passing through villages or past isolated country people, I could see how interesting a procession we were, food for many hours of gossip and speculation. I suppose I should have preened, played the hero, but I felt sickish and utterly tired. At times I was afraid I would fall off the coach. I hoped my wound wouldn't become septic; I certainly didn't want to lose the arm. A bridegroom should be fully armed I thought then realized I was becoming feverish.

The day stretched out ahead of us. We stopped to change our horses, an occasion for the coachman and passengers retelling our adventures to an avid crowd. I could see them staring at me, in fact they followed me to the jakes where I went to piss. I bought some beer, drank it, but felt no better. Looking at the horses and furniture the two men had, it appeared they had been prospering at their trade, for all looked expensive. I supposed the Crown would profit from selling it.

Mounted once more on the coach, I endured another stage then another. Now the sun was declining and the road was more downhill as well as being smoother. There was still one more stage and further changes of passengers. The two corpses and their mounts had been removed a stage or two back. The magistrate had gotten my name and destination and told me he would deal with the legal issues. This was acceptable to me, I only wanted to finish my journey and sleep in a proper bed. I still had to ride outside, there were so many passengers.

It was night when we got to Windsor. I booked another stage to take me to London. This time I could ride inside, but though I tried to doze, I couldn't sleep for the pain in my arm. We were on cobblestones, so the ride was noisier, another annoyance. Some of the passengers insisted on talking to each other, not to me, as they saw I had nothing I wanted to say.

Our coach crossed the Thames at Westminster Bridge, which meant we were in effect in London. We stopped at an inn. I got out and waited while my chest and medical bag were handed down. I definitely felt feverish. Being injured was novel for me, and I tried to prescribe for myself, but other than rest and cheerful surroundings I could think of nothing.

A man with a handbarrow asked to carry my chest and bag. I eventually nodded; I was certainly slow this morning. I gave him Caroline's location, a longish journey for him (and me), but he seemed glad of the custom.

We set out, I following. I realized the eastern sky was lightening, no "rosy-fingered dawn" just metal-looking, slowly less and less grey. I didn't bother looking at my watch. As we walked, we encountered more and more people, not bauds or thieves, just men and a few women going to work, all walking quickly, their shadowy figures growing steadily more distinct. Seeing my medical bag shifting about on top of my chest, I wondered for the first time how my instruments such as my apothecary's scale and the bottles inside had fared. I had thrown the bag hard. This worried me, until I reminded myself that everything could be replaced, and I did have money, some money, should such be necessary.

Now we were in familiar territory. The man had to stop and puff and wipe his brow and I stopped as well and looked about. The light was much stronger, dawn was not far away and the crowds of hurrying folk thicker. I would arrive at Avebury Apothecary near its opening. I hoped Caroline was well; I wished I were.

We were close—perhaps a street or two away, when I stumbled, nearly fell, righted myself, and realized I was near my end. The man carrying my things was going on, not paying attention to me, and I tried to rally, to force myself to follow, to keep up. I kept stumbling—drawing amused glances from passers-by who I supposed thought me drunk.

At this point, the barrowman turned and seeing me, said, "'ere you awright?"

I shook my head, replied, "No. I have a wounded arm. But I will try to keep up."

I coughed, the smoky London air now affecting me. A familiar corner greeted me.

The barrowman said, "Not far now."

My legs were heavy. I was hard put to swing them before me in time to prevent my falling. But here, at last, was Avebury's. I leaned against the doorframe to steady myself and the door opened. It was opened by a tall, flaxen-haired woman. It was Caroline.

She saw me, exclaimed, "Thomas! What is the matter?"

I tried to say something, tried to straighten my legs...

2

NUPTUALS

———◆———

My eyes opened to a smallish room with a window by me. I was in a bed, immersed in softness and warmth. I was wearing a nightshirt, one I recognized as my own, made by my mother and sisters a decade or more ago. My chest and medical bag were crowded next to a dresser, a table with basin and ewer moved to provide room.

I needed to piss. There should be a night-jar under the bed. There was, and I was able to arise to use it. I saw the window looked out on a back alley. It was a clear day.

I inspected my arm under the new dressings and saw the arm was better: red about the wound but not much swollen and without the stink of sepsis. I lay back down in the bed, certainly Caroline's, and reminded myself I now had the specifics for recovery: rest and cheerful surroundings.

I dozed until I heard steps, Caroline's steps, outside. The door opened and she entered. She was wearing the bluish shop dress and dark brown apron she always wore when working. My face exploded in a great smile and her face lit up as well. She bent over to kiss me. Her scent was familiar somehow, the scent of... of lavender, that was it. I remembered giving her the bouquet, how many years ago? I was able to use both my arms to embrace her. At length, she pulled a chair over and sat down and took my hands in hers.

"Thomas, I paid the barrowman a crown for bringing your things here. How do you feel? What happened?"

I was still smiling, no doubt idiotically, at her; but, after another exchange of kisses, I was able to answer her questions.

"Thank you. He brought my things a goodly distance, so a crown is reasonable, though for bringing me here to see you again, I would have given every penny I have."

We embraced and kissed once more.

"I feel much better. I am sure I will recover, given my nurse."

We smiled beatifically at each other until I remembered I had not answered her last question.

"My coach was stopped by two highwaymen, not far from Avebury in fact. One of them shot me."

Caroline looked puzzled, and objected, "But your money belt does not appear to have been touched. Did they overlook it? And why did one of them shoot you?"

I daresay I was prolonging the conversation to keep her in my arms but had to confess.

"I threw my chest at one of them, which cracked his head against a boulder and I threw my medical bag at the other. He shot me but his horse was moving and I got the unfired pistol of the first man and shot the second with it, killing him as well."

Caroline stared at me, shook her head and commented, "Thomas, you insist you are only a healer, a man of peace, yet you seem to attract brawls. It appears I must marry you if only to steady you and to protect others."

I shook my head, replying, "I am only a simple pilgrim, seeking…"

"Your Celestial City?" asked Caroline, smiling.

And I responded, "…Cytherea. Home. A refuge, a center, a place of peace if you like. That is why I fell in love with you, why I returned."

This pleased her greatly and we exchanged many kisses then lay in each other's arms. Caroline spoke into one of my ears.

"I talked to the minister of this parish. Our banns will be read this Sunday and two Sundays hence. We will wed on the last Sunday. David will stand up for you. Is that soon enough?"

I replied, "I would prefer an immediate marriage, but it shall be as my lady wishes. Will there be any objections to our union, do you think? Must I call a host of unhappy suitors out?"

Caroline was silent, partly because we were kissing and fondling each other, before she told me, "There is a pothecary two streets over who made my father an offer for me, but I heard his mistreatment of his first wife hastened her death, and I told my father I would leave here if he insisted."

"Did he beat her?"

"Yes, I think so."

"Then he is a damned scoundrel," I said angrily. Caroline kissed me, and I asked her, "Where are you sleeping? For some reason that question entered my mind."

Caroline archly replied, "I am not sure I should tell you, lest it prompt a midnight visitation."

"More than one, surely," I answered with like archness.

She continued, "I sleep on a couch. It is comfortable enough but too small for two."

I shook my head in denial and she laughed. Caroline got up off the bed, kissed me again.

"David said you needed to rest and rest you shall have. I will tell Father and my stepmother you shouldn't eat at the table for a day or two. I will bring your meals and dine with you."

I nodded, we kissed again and she left giving me a glance as she did so that guaranteed I would not be able to sleep for some time. Still, lying in Caroline's bed, smiling at the ceiling, I gradually began first to doze then to sleep. My arm indeed felt better, I felt such a relief from all my worries, my depths. I was at last away from so many things that had oppressed my spirits over the years. I was in truth at home and soon to be in Cytherea.

3

ARRANGEMENTS AND
UNDERSTANDINGS

───────◆───────

The first Sunday our banns were read I was able to dress, shave and accompany Caroline to the church. We went arm in arm, attracting notice, Caroline from her appearance, which was best described as "radiant," and me, from the fact that my exploit in killing the two highwaymen had been described in various newspapers. The latter embarrassed me, as my profession was to save, to prolong lives, not take them and I shrank from being portrayed as a bully-boy or a ruffian myself. Still, I was so happy to be sitting with Caroline that I was able to endure the entire service with hardly a wince.

After, we dined with her family, her father seeming a trifle in awe of his prospective son-in-law, and her stepmother obviously joyful at losing a stepdaughter. The half-brother and half-sister were interested only in the meal, as was I.

Caroline's stepmother asked me, "What are your plans for practicing medicine, Thomas?"

I glanced at Caroline and told my fellow diners, "I have an offer of a country practice in the village of Chilterndale, west of London. The offer was made by the recently succeeded Lord Chilterndale, so," looking again at Caroline, "if Caroline is agreeable, then there we shall go."

Caroline smiled at me, the father and stepmother seemed impressed, and supper ended cheerfully. I very much wanted to walk out with Caroline to apprise her more fully of the situation, yet feared becoming a target for ruffians. Caroline seemed to understand this and suggested I rest until the evening meal. So we went to her room.

There I removed my coat and waistcoat and boots and lay down on Caroline's bed. She again sat on the chair next to the bed and took my hands, whether from affection or to keep them from venturing onto her person, or perhaps both reasons.

We kissed and I told her, "What I am going to tell you must remain a secret between us."

Caroline took this without great surprise, and agreed, "I shall tell no one without your leave, dear."

I said, "James Montjoy—now Lord Chilterndale—is my friend, and wants me by his side when he returns. He has a wife here in England. She is now Lady Chilterndale, but James has long been estranged from her. They have a son, the next heir, who is also not close to James. In America, New York, James met a young woman, daughter of Loyalists who lost their property and fled to New York. They fell in love. I have seen them together many times, and love is the correct description of their feelings for each other. He got her with child and married her in New York, a lawful marriage there. I stood up for him."

Caroline interrupted, "Does she know of the English wife?"

"Yes. She feels she and James are married in the eyes of God. James sold his commission but had to wait until he could get the money to New York so he could leave it for her and their child. Their child is a healthy son, named James Montjoy. But he has to come here to succeed, and knows his English wife and son will insist on joining him at Chilterndale, the name of the estate. Hence the invitation to me—and to you."

Caroline remarked, "A pretty plot for a romance, or rather a tragedy. Couldn't he stay in America? I suppose not."

"The war will end, we will probably lose, and he would have to return anyway. And he loves the place. He does not want it in the hands of his English son; at least he wants to keep it out of his hands as long as possible."

Caroline asked, "What is the reason for the estrangement?"

Here I had to content myself with kissing her hand before answering, "She was the daughter of a fishmonger with social aspirations—I suppose disappointed ones. Separations because of his service, perhaps a disappointing settlement contributed."

Caroline commented, "Love would overcome those obstacles."

I nodded, "And that is, I suspect, the crux of the problem. But while I recover, I also await a letter from James, requesting my—our—presence at Chilterndale Park. He told me of a dower house that we could live in if we wished."

"So he knows of me?"

"He does indeed. Your letter made me so happy I had to share that happiness with someone."

Here Caroline's resistance melted and she once again lay beside me on the bed while we embraced and fondled and kissed. We had to stop to recover our breath.

Caroline remarked, "Stepmother has been asking where I would go after we married, that is to say, she wants me out of this house. And I certainly want out as well. Understand, I love my relations but it is past time I had my own household."

Here we fell silent.

Caroline resumed, "Perhaps I could help your practice as a pothecary."

This struck me as so novel I momentarily stayed my hands.

"You seem to know the trade." I said. "Yes, I think you will be a great assistance."

We kissed to seal the agreement, perhaps for other reasons as well. At that point, we heard Caroline's stepmother calling for her, as there were customers waiting. So we parted for the nonce.

Now our marriage was settled upon, my hands were permitted

vastly greater liberty, caressing Caroline's bottoms through her dress, petticoat and shift, her bosoms as well, exercises that left both of us breathless, yet wanting to continue. We agreed it was well that our marriage was soon, and drawing ever closer.

4

AN INVITATION

———◆———

Our marriage was two days away and Caroline and I were to dine with David and Dora when James's letter was delivered. After paying for it, and noting it was sent from Chilterndale Manor, Caroline and I set out arm-in-arm. I broke the seal as we walked, and held it so Caroline could read it as well. It said:

> *My dear Thomas*
>
> *As you see, I am installed at Chilterndale. Unfortunately Agnes, our son and his wife had preceded me, and I have had to make a number of changes after my arrival. So you can guess I very much desire your presence, along with, I hope, your lady wife, as soon as may be.*
>
> *I have had the dower house cleaned and aired, I hope to your satisfaction. There is no doctor in the village, so you may imagine you are needed and will be welcomed here by more than*   *James*
> *Lord Chilterndale*

I told Caroline, "I will reply directly, in your name as well as mine, I trust?" She was pleased. She nodded, smiled and pressed closer to me as we walked.

David and Dora welcomed us. I was presented to my namesake, healthy and talking, and viewed their daughter Dora, also named according to David after no-one in particular. Caroline and I were served wine in their parlour, in which a bright fire gave warmth that was welcome, as the day was cool.

David asked me, "Are you prepared for your great day, your last as a bachelor? Remember, I shall be there at your back."

I rejoined, "To assist me or keep me on the path? What if I bolt for the door?"

David: "It will be locked and barred against such a possibility."

Glancing at Caroline, I sighed theatrically, and said, "Then I daresay I have no choice."

The others, with one voice, replied, "None."

After our laughter ebbed, Dora asked me, "And where will you practice, Thomas?"

I withdrew James's letter and told my hosts, "I am invited to practice at the village of Chilterndale and in the Manor of Chilterndale by the new Lord Chilterndale. The dower house is for our use, and Caroline has volunteered, I will not say under what compulsion, to be my pothecary."

This was received by amusement; then we were called to dine. We returned to the parlour after the meal, to sip our wine and talk. The war in America became our topic.

The capture of Charleston was mentioned by David, who asked, "Does this victory not lead you to a more favourable view of the Crown's fortunes?"

I shook my head and commented, "From time to time, we have captured the larger towns in America, only to have to abandon them eventually. The larger towns are but a small part of America, and the rebels, to an increasing extent I fear, have the rest. For the rebels, losing a battle means only having to fight another. For us, a major defeat—I mean, another major defeat—would mean the end. With our Navy, we can hold towns on the coast as long as we will, but to what end?"

Everyone was silent at this point until Dora commented, "I still think of the young women turning whore to keep their families from starving. And you say the Crown did nothing for these people, who had lost everything because of their loyalty?"

I sat thinking, thinking of Ann's fate, of the Loyalist regiments armed and trained, yet not paid. They were expected to support themselves by plundering their once neighbors. I understood then what the Crown and its Army should have done....

But Dora's question required an answer and I replied. "No. Nothing."

I could have said more, but Dora forestalled me by remarking as if to herself, "Then perhaps it is only just we should lose."

At this, Caroline and I noted the time and the advancing evening. We rose, thanked our host and hostess sincerely, pledged another meeting two days hence, and took our leave. We were silent on our journey back, but it was a contented silence. We were together in person and in heart and would soon be together, one in law and body.

5

PREPARATIONS

◆

We returned to Avebury's and despite occasional demands on Caroline's attention to a customer or to the new 'prentice who was to replace Caroline, we began collecting what we would take.

The following morning I wrote a reply to James, warning him we were likely to present ourselves at Chilterndale Manor in two to three weeks.

Our wedding was tomorrow, but Caroline's father had promised to present her with everything she would need as my pothecary. These would take some time to collect. There was, however, the matter of the pothecary scales in my medical bag: was it intact or would Caroline's father have to purchase another?

I told Caroline, "In the encounter with the highwaymen, I threw the chest at one and the medical bag at the other. I have been loath to look into the bag because I feared what might have happened, to the pothecary's scales, for example. And there were four bottles of rum. They were wrapped in paper and I have seen no sign of leaking, but…"

Caroline shrugged and told me, "Let us have a look." So we did.

I opened the bag for the first time in nearly three weeks and smelled the contents. "No rum," I observed, and began taking the rum bottles out. Each appeared without damage; the papers had kept all from harm. The box with the pothecary scales was removed and I handed it to Caroline. She carefully opened it and assembled the scales and tested them with the weights.

"There appears to be no damage, Thomas," said Caroline, to my great relief. Those scales were very expensive, yet necessary to us. We replaced all in my bag, my mood in particular much elated.

My chest also would go, of course. We overhauled it. In the end we decided to take all its contents, including my notes from Edinburgh and London for I might need to refer to these.

That done, I fancied myself at leisure to fondle Caroline and generally take liberties with her person but here I was informed by Caroline and her stepmother that a bride required certain preparations in terms of clothing, a "trousseau." Caroline had already cleaned and repaired my shirt and red coat that were torn by the second highwayman's bullet, so I was very much in the way. My fiancée made amends to an extent sending me to purchase certain items, cloth, stockings and a pair of shoes. This effected, I returned to Caroline's bedroom after dinner to nap as I had naught else to occupy me save carnal thoughts.

It was as well that the wedding was so near, I was thinking, when the door opened and Caroline appeared. She knelt by the bed, we embraced and kissed.

Then she told me, "Only a few hours, my love. Thank you, thank you for being so patient. I know the wait has been hard on you; be assured it has been hard on me as well."

Her words overthrew my urges to be the reverse of patient and take her immediately, though I had the impression she would not have resisted such a course.

I said, "Yes, dearest, only a few hours until I can carry you over this threshold and any others we fancy."

She replied, "Perhaps at the dower house as well, my sweet."

Then she kissed me again, noted my obvious readiness to complete our union, smiled and blew a kiss at me as she left. I lay, wondering if I could possibly sleep after such a leave-taking.

I was startled awake by a knocking at the door.

"Who is it?" I asked and the door opened to reveal the 'prentice.

"Tis six o' the clock, sir, and the ladies bid you rise, dress and go to the church."

After a moment, I remembered the custom or superstition that I was not to lay eyes on my bride until the ceremony, so I did as I was bidden, with especial care as to my toilet and dress. Yesterday I had managed to buy a surreptitious sprig of lavender, which I pinned to my lapel. Then I took my way to the church, bells sounding everywhere as if in honour of Caroline's and my union.

My place was near the front. As I walked there, I noticed a man, stout and grizzled, who was glaring at me. I guessed he was Caroline's rejected suitor. I wondered if he had come armed then reminded myself that David's function was to guard my back from such. As though my thoughts had transported him hence, David with Dora on his arm and young Thomas held by the hand walked through the door. We grinned at each other, though I was feeling the beginnings of nervousness. Dora and young Thomas sat down in a pew near me and David took his place by my side.

I spoke to him: "Ring?"

David affected surprise, clutched his brow as though only just remembering the subject. The excessively theatrical gesture reassured me he had not forgotten the ring Caroline and I had decided upon ten days or so ago, but my nervousness continued to increase. More and more parishioners appeared, chatted and sat.

The doors opened again and Caroline's father entered with a heavily-veiled woman on his arm. I gazed a moment before recognizing her height, her willowy figure and her step. Caroline was dressed in white silk. This must have cost a great deal. I reflected, though, if we should have a daughter, the dress could be used again. For the nonce, she looked like a princess, my princess. I heard sounds of admiration from the parishioners; I imagined the rejected suitor was much less favourable to the spectacle. She was carrying a bouquet of lavender, naturally.

The service was fairly short. The clergyman read the service, Caroline and I both assented, I placed the ring on Caroline's finger, raised her veil—she was so beautiful—and kissed her. So we were wed. David signed, as did Caroline's father and we walked up the aisle, out the door to universal cheers, and returned to Avebury's. On the way, she touched the sprig of lavender on my coat and we exchanged smiles.

6

CHILTERNDALE

Caroline and I had decided to rent a coach-and-four to take us to Chilterndale Park. We were able to affect this for what always seemed a great deal of money. The coach was to appear at Avebury's at five in the morning. We were assured this would deposit us at our destination by early afternoon, as the distance was but 35 miles or so, though in part uphill.

On the morning set for our departure, we were just able to complete our packing when the coach driver hammered at the door.

We sat in the gently lurching coach, her head on my shoulder and my arm about her. Despite the motion of the coach, we were dozing, perhaps from the early rising but probably more from our frequent matrimonial exercises. We were aware that Caroline's father and stepmother and, probably, the 'prentice and the servants were vastly amused at our behavior. Late risings, frequent adjournments to Caroline's bedroom, early retirements marked, indeed hallmarked, our status.

Since we were both novices at the rites of Venus, we agreed that frequent practice was the only course, a course we held to the limit of my capacity. We became better and better partners for each other, making our union complete.

Now and again, one or the other of us would awaken and gaze out one of the windows of the coach. Our road rose as we entered the Chilterns. The harvest was past its height. Even so we were encountering many carts, empty and laden, which slowed us, yet unlike the coachman, we were content.

It was well past noon when we reached Chilterndale village. Though the houses were brick-built, in size it resembled Shrewsbury. The colour of the bricks was a brighter red than we were accustomed to in London where the smoke of so many coal fires had darkened the brickwork. There was a parish church and an alehouse. I wondered if James had the "living." I decided his family almost certainly did.

Now we were going through a gated entrance, though the gates were open. To either side, we could see vistas, hills, patches of woods, dales, all most picturesque. I now understood why James loved the place. To our left was a cottage of a single story built we guessed of limestone, grey-brown. We bade the coachman stop. We would put our baggage in the dower house, as this was obviously what it was, before calling on James at the Manor, clearly visible a few hundred yards along the road.

There were two servants, a man and a woman, in attendance. On being assured we were indeed Dr. and Mrs. Wyeth, they helped us shift our baggage to the house. Caroline supervised its bestowal as I dealt with the coachman. Whilst paying him, I noticed the money I had brought from America was notably lessened, but I was now in my practice, so I needn't worry about money. Going inside our cottage, I assisted with setting our things where Caroline felt they should go. She and I refreshed ourselves, dusted and adjusted our clothing. I re-shaved. Then we walked together to the Manor.

As we set forth, I asked Caroline, "Does the cottage please you?"

She took my arm, arresting my movement, and kissed me before saying, "Very, very much. I shall enjoy every minute we have here."

We resumed our walk and Caroline added, "I gave no orders for meals, as I expect we will be invited to dine at the Manor."

The Manor now lay square before us. It was built of the same grey-brown limestone, but was of two stories, two wings either side of a central hall. The stables and other outbuildings were behind the Manor, out of sight. The lawn, a lush green, appeared unkempt, the men who would keep it cut probably at work assisting with the harvest. The house was complemented by scattered oaks, very large and old, whose downed branches were unremoved so far, likely for the same reason as the unkempt appearance of the lawn.

We pulled at the bell, heard it ring, and waited.

A man of large dignity, yet rather shabby, opened the door, looked at us and asked, "Dr. and Mrs. Wyeth, I believe?"

We nodded, and the head butler, for so we judged him to be, said, "Lord Chilterndale is expecting you. Please follow me."

He led us through the hall. There were some trophies along the walls, arms and armour, as well as a few pictures. Lighter coloured rectangles here and there on the walls suggested to me that some paintings were missing, probably sold. It appeared the estate was struggling, though the village appeared prosperous. The head butler walked to a door in a dark paneled wall closing off the far end of the hall, knocked briefly, opened the door and announced us. Then he stood aside and gestured us through.

The room was lined with bookshelves, though not overmany books. James sat at a desk. A slender woman of middle height, a trifle overly fashionably dressed, stood near the desk. She looked annoyed at our entrance, which I somehow understood was superposed on annoyance at Lord Chilterndale about something. James rose as we approached his desk and extended his hand to me, which I took.

He said to Lady Chilterndale, for so I guessed her to be, "This is Dr. Thomas Wyeth and his wife—Caroline is it?"

Caroline and I both nodded.

"Thomas is to set up practice here, as we currently lack a doctor. He was eager to return to England, and I can see why."

He bowed to Caroline, who curtsied in response.

"Pray allow me to talk alone with Dr. Wyeth, as there are several pressing matters we need to discuss."

This was addressed to Lady Chilterndale, who bridled but turned and stalked out, closing the office door overfirmly.

Politeness would seem to require Lady Chilterndale to offer to show Caroline about the Manor, but it was really better if Caroline remained. James, looking at me, raised his eyebrows.

I replied to the unasked question, "I have no secrets from Caroline."

James looked at Caroline, smiled and turned back to me.

"Lady Chilterndale came here expecting a well-appointed manor and instead found shabbiness and penury. She also expected to be able to wear my mother's jewelry, but that appears to have been sold, along with a few pictures."

I asked, "Your brother—was he a man of extravagant tastes?"

James shook his head and told us, "Not particularly, and in his last few years was bedridden." James paused then told us, "We have a factor, an agent, who collects the rents. I have spoken with him and he assures me that harvests have been poor and the rents reduced as a result. He showed me the figures; they are well below what I remember, but…"

I spoke, "But these are just numbers on paper. What is the name of this factor?"

James replied, "Pips. Samuel Pips. He was the assistant to the previous agent and succeeded when the man died."

There was silence until James resumed, "I gave the money from selling my commission to…" looking at me. I nodded, and James said, "Emily. I also had some pay owed me by the Crown and brought that here. Emily told me I would almost certainly need some money and she was right." James sighed and continued, "When I got here, I found the servants' wages in arrears and several tradesmen's bills unpaid. I was able to deal with those, but I cannot believe rents have declined that much. The estate, aside from the Manor, looks as prosperous as I can recall which leaves only one explanation."

I sat and thought. I asked, "With you here, Pips may decide to bolt carrying what he has stolen. Is rent due to be paid soon?"

James nodded and told us, "Within the next few days. Much of the harvest has been gathered and sold. What do you have in mind?"

I leaned forward and said, "If he has been embezzling on such a scale, that is a hanging offense. On the other hand, he is probably consumed by greed, so will at least wait to collect the rents before absconding. As the new doctor, I will go around talking to your tenants and casually find out how much they are paying. Then I will call on Pips. If he has stolen that much he will have a hiding place. I will try to find it and also try to see when I can get at it. Are you a magistrate?"

James shook his head.

So I said, "Otherwise we will have to keep our eyes on him, day and night, and take him when we think he is trying to escape."

James frowned and shook his head, remarking, "If I had some decent horses..." Then he sighed again, "I remember our stables when my sister and I were young. Now: just three worn out hacks. The rest died or sold, I suppose. But," looking at us, "that will make taking him almost impossible."

I said, "Then I will begin by spying the situation. I will pay a call on our factor, a purely professional call, after talking to all the tenants, also purely professional. Can you give me a list of your tenants and their approximate locations?"

James looked at me, a wry smile on his face, and reached for a sheet of paper. He began writing while commenting, "You were invited here as a doctor, not a thief-taker, though I have heard about your exploits. Just be cautious: if Pips is the villain we believe he is, he won't hesitate to try to put a ball in your brain if he thinks you have discovered him."

I sighed in turn, glancing at Caroline, and replied, "I am a man of peace, just trying to practice my profession and live happily with my bride."

James handed me the paper, with six names on it along with a sketch of where they dwelt and said, "Aside from what we just discussed, I have the pleasure of inviting you both to dine with me tonight. I should warn you my son and his wife will probably also be here, so I shall be very happy to have some congenial company."

I looked at Caroline, who nodded, so I replied, "We are honoured and accept your kind invitation with pleasure. When?"

James smiled and told us, "Let us say seven o'clock."

Caroline and I nodded, rose and we left. On our way to the

door, we saw Lady Chilterndale peering at us from the banisters ringing the upper half of the hall. I was relieved she apparently was not listening at the door.

As we walked back to the dower cottage, I told Caroline, "We have to put our things away or perhaps nap before dinner. Tomorrow I will go round to the tenants. If that factor has been embezzling, he must be stopped. I am sure James wants to make great changes. For that matter, I have an idea that will cost money, but I think is a good one."

Caroline, on my arm, looked at me and asked, "What is this idea, Thomas?"

I walked in silence a few steps to marshal my thoughts before replying, "I want James to pay me a *salarium*, say £50 per *annum*, in return for which I would treat James, his household, his tenants, everyone of the estate without charging, at least directly. But of course, the estate must be able to sustain that charge."

Caroline nodded and asked me, "Where will you meet the patients?"

Consideration of Caroline's question left me shaking my head. I was actually considering using the cottage, but I didn't know how my wife would take that.

But she had to be told, so I said, "I was thinking of the cottage because of its location, so handy to everyone. But what think you?"

We were approaching the cottage as I said this. Caroline's brow was knitted as we walked through the door. The place at least looked clean and cheerful.

Caroline finally nodded, telling me, "We can try it, Thomas. This room will do," I nodded and she went on, "and I can put my pothecary things in this small room next to it."

I was vastly pleased we were in agreement and, I saw, so was she. We celebrated with a nap, after indulging ourselves with each other.

The dinner was not nearly so pleasant. We ate in the hall, at a great table capable of seating thirty or so. As there were but six of us, we all sat at the head of the table with James and Lady Chilterndale. Unfortunately, the son, George, was also with us, as was his wife. I was prepared to endure Lady Chilterndale, but George, who was the same height as James though lumpish, was disposed to be critical of everything, including, we felt, James's choice of dinner guests.

The conversation consisted of queries from George as to whether there would be anything for him to inherit, complaints, echoed by Lady Chilterndale, as to the tableware (pewter instead of silver), unhappiness as to the lack of diversions, and suggestions, probably welcomed by James, that he (the son) was disposed to return forthwith to his customary pursuits in London. During all this, George's wife, who I guessed was six or seven months along her pregnancy, sat silent. She was a thin young woman of middle height, in those respects resembling Lady Chilterndale.

At one point, Lady Chilterndale, who had made a point of asking me where I had qualified, and who was slightly taken aback at hearing it was a respectable place, informed me that for her daughter-in-law's delivery, she and her son had engaged a doctor in London. This was said with a sneer, which I was beginning to think was one of her customary expressions.

James was roused to my defense: "Thomas has successfully delivered dozens of children, without the loss of the mothers."

I knew he was thinking of Emily's delivery, and we exchanged glances. Turning my gaze to Caroline's, I saw she was struggling to keep her temper. We were seated next to each other, and I reached over to press her hand. She smiled at me in response.

While George had much to say about the meal, nothing was complimentary, though Caroline and I thought it quite palatable. Perhaps the tableware prompted these criticisms: after the meal and wine (port), I learned from James that the family silverware had gone the way of some of the portraits and presumably his mother's jewelry. Lady Chilterndale, Caroline and George's wife had retired leaving James and me before one of the portraits, a pleasant-looking young woman, fashionably dressed and surrounded by Life: birds and flowers.

"My brother's wife," said James. "That is one portrait he would never sell. He never got over her loss and that of the babe as well. Living here now, I feel sorry for him. Nothing left in his life but port."

I told James, "Tomorrow I will meet your six tenants and visit this Pips as well. Just to introduce myself. When are the rents collected?"

The ladies were approaching. James turned to me and said in a low voice, "Three days from today."

I nodded, Caroline took my arm, we took our farewells and left.

When we were well away from the Manor, Caroline commented, "What an awful pair, the wife and the son! I don't envy James. I wonder why he returned."

"This is his ancestral home, his heritage and responsibility. He has fond memories of hunts and rides here in his youth. He certainly has a great deal to repair if he can. How did you find George's wife?"

Caroline replied, "She is rather quiet, but I was able to get her to talk about the child she is carrying. How soon would her delivery occur, do you think?"

"From a distance, I guessed two or three months."

Caroline shook her head: "Eleanor—that is her name—thought two or three weeks."

"My estimation is rather off, then. If delivery is that near, having her travel to London might bring on a premature one. But I misdoubt my advice would be taken seriously."

We were at our cottage, and I once more opened the door, swept my wife up in my arms and carried her across the threshold. This was as well received as my previous essays, so we both went to sleep in each other's arms, content.

7

AN INVESTIGATION

———◆———

I left early, after breakfast. The estate was over 1,700 acres, but the six tenant houses were all within a mile of each other and the Manor. I went to each in turn, introduced myself as a doctor hoping to establish a practice. All six tenants were favourable to having a doctor in residence, some very much so, and all promised me their families' and servants' custom. I then remarked on the harvest, was told it was a good one—though not the best—and I proceeded to try to indirectly, obliquely bring up the subject of rent. But each tenant was very forthcoming: the rent would be collected two days hence and each was quick to tell me how much each paid. They seemed proud of the amounts. I affected being impressed, and after leaving noted the amounts on James's paper, I hoped inconspicuously.

After talking to the sixth tenant, I added the claimed rents and saw the amounts paid to James's brother and prospectively to James by the factor were less than half the total the tenants claimed they paid. Someone was lying and it was most unlikely that it was the tenants. I decided to pay a call on the factor Pips.

James had told me Pips lived rent *gratis* in a house owned by the estate and received £50 per *annum* as well as the services of a maidservant and a groom. The latter was because Pips had been allowed use of a trap, drawn by one horse, in which he journeyed about the estate as well as to and from London. I hoped he wasn't gambling away his takings or investing these in the four percents or something like that. If he was that greedy, it seemed most likely that he had cached his loot, probably where he lived, but here I was speculating.

The house itself was small, a single story. I walked slowly toward it until I saw a slight, spare man leave to visit the jakes. Once he was inside, I picked up my pace, knocked on the door when I got there, and was admitted by a rather slatternly-looking maidservant.

She asked, "Wots yer bisness, sir?"

"I am here to speak to Mr. Pips."

She opened her mouth to say something then changed what she was going to say to, "Well, 'e's out. Just fer now."

I edged past her into the house and told the woman, or rather girl, "I'll wait for him."

She gave way. Inside were a kitchen-scullery, a closet with door ajar, some ratty looking cabinets and a bedroom, also dark with decrepit furniture. The room I was standing in was larger, with a substantial brick fireplace. The floor was stones, squared and cemented, but a large patch near the fireplace was covered with a good-sized hearth rug. Looking about, I could see no place to hide gold coins. There was no cellar that I could see evidence of, no way to get into the eaves. Of course the money, if it was here, would have to be effectively concealed from the maidservant and from the groom as well.

It was far more likely if Pips were as greedy a scoundrel as I guessed he was that he kept his gains near his person. I paced slowly back and forth on the hearth rug, but could not be sure if any of the stones under the rug moved. Looking carefully at the fireplace, I did see one of the bricks was loose. At this point the rear door opened and Pips, or so I guessed he was, came in.

He seemed surprised to see me and was clearly displeased. He turned angrily to the maidservant, probably to upbraid her, when I advanced to intervene.

"Mr. Pips, I believe?" I asked in my blandest manner.

"It's Peepeez, sir. And just who are you?"

"My name is Thomas Wyeth. I am a doctor, sir."

Here I bowed, forcing him to do the same.

I continued, "I am setting up a practice here in Chilterndale. I am calling on the principal men in the parish," here I bowed again, and I think this mollified him some, "to acquaint them of my existence and my plans."

"I am in perfect health, sir," he said.

I smiled and returned, "I rejoice to hear it, but if your servants or other acquaintances are not so blessed, I hope you will remember there is now a doctor in residence here. I thank you for your attention, sir."

Bowing once more, I turned toward the front door, which a now rather anxious-appearing maidservant opened for me. I walked away in as stately a manner as I could.

If he learned of my connection with the new Lord Chilterndale, he might run. I wondered about asking James to send a servant to keep an eye on Pips but decided that was useless: James had no horses to chase the fellow if he fled. We would have to rely on his greed.

An idea for forcing the issue came to my mind. I knew how much James was supposed to get, from what the tenants told me they paid. If I, James and two servants, preferably all armed, waited at Pips' house and insisted Pips turn over the rents he had collected, then Pips was fairly snared. Embezzlement of even smaller sums was a hanging offense. Pips could be forced to reveal where his loot was in return for being allowed to go free, perhaps to fasten onto some other gullible soul. Well, my duty was to James.

By now it was well past noon and I was hungry. I glanced casually after me to be certain I was not followed by Pips or the groom, but I saw no one. Even so, I changed my course several times before arriving at the cottage. Caroline was concerned at my absence; she was beginning to realize I was engaged in an adventure that could be dangerous. I kissed her, sat down to the meal, and after eating, I suggested we walk to the Manor. She agreed as she understood I wanted to tell her what the situation was, without the servants hearing.

On our way, I told Caroline, "I asked each of the six tenants what they were paying. It totaled over £400. From what James was saying, his brother was getting less than £200. Pips is a thief. Now that a healthy and active Lord Chilterndale has succeeded, James and I think Pips will collect this year's rents and probably try to flee."

Caroline asked, "What are you going to do?"

"It is for James to decide, but we are going to insist Pips turn over the rent money. That will show who is lying, and if it is Pips, that is enough to get him hanged. I will suggest James force Pips to disgorge, assuming it is secreted in the house he lives in, this in return for not taking Pips to a magistrate."

"Do you think the stolen money is somewhere in his house?"

I shrugged and told my wife, "That seems most likely. I think Pips is so greedy he would keep his gains near him, concealed of course."

Here we were at the Manor. We were admitted by the butler, who was as shabby as before, but vastly more cheerful, and walked to the study where James received us.

I told James, "I talked to each of your six tenants and what they say they pay comes to over £400 per *annum*. Pips will collect the rents in two days. I suggest you, I and two manservants, all armed, wait for him to return, ask him how much you will get, and you insist he turn over the rent money then and there. If, as I strongly suspect, there is a major discrepancy, you threaten to take him to a magistrate for what is a hanging offense.

"I believe he has a cache of money, probably hidden in that house, so if he turns that over, you will let him go. If he has other valuables hidden perhaps in London, insist he will not be allowed to go free until these are in your hands. If, as I judge, he collects the rents and then tries to flee, we should be able to take him and force him to disgorge."

James's face had darkened when I told him how much his tenants said they paid then showed no further change in expression while I described my plan.

He thought and finally said, "We will do it as you say, Thomas.

Your stratagem should work. Did you visit his house? Are there any possible hiding places that caught your eye?"

I returned, "I did visit. He has a maidservant who lives with him and is not retained for her housekeeping skills. I doubt she is party to this, so he has to keep any cache hidden from her as well. So the hiding place is one that is easy to get to and conceal after. I have a thought as to its general location: under a hearth rug in front of the fireplace."

James began to smile, leaned back and commented, "The trap he drives actually belongs to the estate. But he is likely to return after collecting the rents to get the rest of his gains. We will be waiting for him. I will send the groom, who is also one of my servants, to our stables to help the head groomsman, so Pips will not be warned. In fact, I will send the maidservant with him to help our cook. So he will hopefully walk into our trap."

I nodded, then Caroline asked, "Will he resist? Will he be armed?" Glancing at me, my wife went on, "I don't want Thomas hurt."

James replied, "There will be four of us, all on the *qui vive*. I have no idea of the fellow's metal. Thomas?"

I shook my head; Pips was almost certainly a damnable scoundrel and thief, but only the event would prove his manhood. So having agreed on my plan, Caroline and I left the Manor, returning very thoughtful.

At one point she asked, "Will you be carrying a pistol?"

I answered, "If James gives me one. I don't have one of my own. Remember, I am a man of peace…"

Here Caroline, smiling but with tears in her eyes, turned to me and kissed me. We then continued to the cottage.

8

EXECUTION

---◆---

The next day passed quietly though I was increasingly uneasy. James decided to improve the odds slightly by conscripting Pips' groom for service at the Manor today as well, so Pips would be less likely to flee before collecting the rents. Three townspeople appeared, having heard a doctor was at hand, and where I resided. I asked them and found they had heard this from a servant at the Manor. I hoped Pips hadn't heard of my location and become suspicious, but there was nothing I could do save treat my first patients. I collected a shilling from each, Caroline assisting me, in part by putting the patients at ease. Our marital relations that night seemed more urgent as we were both nervous.

We were awakened near dawn by a loud knock at our door. We dressed, kissed and I walked out of the cottage to find James and two servants, these of middle years but stout enough. The servants were carrying fowling pieces and James had a pistol in his belt. He didn't have one for me, he told me apologetically, but I said I thought our force sufficient. We walked to Pip's house to find Pips and the trap had just left, according to the groom. James ordered the groom back to the Manor, knocked on the door until the maidservant opened it.

James told her, "Go to the Manor to help the cook. She requires your assistance this morning."

I thought the girl was going to object but James's manner forestalled this.

James told her, "Leave me the key to the house. I was told there were some changes your master wanted made, and I will look into the matter."

The girl reluctantly handed James the key and set out for the Manor. I saw the groom look back at her and she picked up her pace to join him. I fancied she was shared by Pips and the groom, though probably Pips didn't know this.

We went inside. To our great relief, we saw two bags set on the floor next to Pips' bed. They were not unduly heavy, so any gold was elsewhere. We posted one of the servants as sentry and I pulled up the hearth rug. It was very dirty beneath, I thought excessively so. I looked at the stones until I thought I found one that was not cemented like the others, only dirtied in as it lay with loose dirt used to fill around the stone. I pointed this out to James, who tried to shift the stone with his fingers. It would not move.

I remembered the loose brick in the fireplace, looked until I found it and pulled at it. It came out. I looked inside and saw the shine of metal. I reached in and just managed to pull it out. It was iron, a stout C-shaped piece. I showed this to James who immediately understood that it was for lifting the square stone.

He pushed it down the crack on one side with the bottom of the C parallel to one edge. Then he tried to turn it so the bottom of the C was under the stone. He had to push the tool farther down twice before it caught the stone. Then he lifted. The stone rose from its edging of dirt. I and the other servant grasped the edges and we pulled it away from its bed.

There was a hole in the dirt underneath, and in the hole were four leather bags. I reached down and pulled them out one by one. All were heavy, three especially so. These clinked pleasantly as they were shifted. James opened one, poured a handful of gold coins into his hand, and nodded to the other two of us. The lighter bag, on opening it, was found to contain many pieces of jewelry. James took this bag to a table near the fireplace and carefully removed several pieces.

"My mother's jewelry," he told us.

James and I each put two bags into our greatcoat pockets then we set the stone back, brushed dirt over it and recovered all with the hearth rug. We returned the tool to its nest in the fireplace.

By now, Pips had been gone above an hour and might be expected to appear at any moment. James checked with his sentry then searched Pips' bags for arms. He found none. We continued to wait, James and I pacing, the servant who was with us stoic.

Then the door opened and our sentry entered, saying, "Trap coming, sir."

Now our waiting was nearly over. We heard the trap arrive then heard Pips angrily calling for the groom. Shortly, he entered, calling for the maidservant, but stopping frozen on seeing us. Our sentry alertly stepped behind Pips and closed the door, remaining between Pips and the door with his hands on his fowling piece.

Pips looked at him, looked at us then tried to muster a show of indignation, saying, "Now what's all this, My Lord? A man's home is his castle in England. Where are my servants? This is an outrage."

James replied, coldly, "The groom and maidservant belong to the Manor and were needed there this morning. My friend and my servants are out looking for game, and it appears we have our bag. You have been collecting the rents, I believe. Put the money on the table and let us see how much there is."

Pips was standing near the middle of the room. James was on the edge of the hearthrug and I was closer to the fireplace. Pips' face turned red, then white. His mouth opened but no sound came out. Then he grimaced and his face filled with anger and hatred.

I realized I should have been watching his hands, as he suddenly reached for something in his belt, a pistol which he yanked out and turned toward James. I came awake of a sudden, reached back and grasped the fire iron and swung it over and forward, thrusting its tip at the barrel of Pips' pistol. I saw the primer flash as I thrust the end of the fire iron into the barrel as hard as I could lunge. Pips screamed with rage at James. My right arm was jolted out of its socket as Pips' pistol exploded. James pointed his pistol at Pips. The primer flashed, James's pistol fired and Pips' curses were cut short as Pips was thrown back onto the floor.

Moving my right arm to try to reinsert it, I moved to Pips and confirmed he was dead. James' shot had hit him in his open mouth. The powder smoke in the room shifted slowly. James's two servants had brought their fowling pieces to bear but there was now no need. I pulled the fire iron from the barrel of the exploded pistol and saw the lead ball impaled on the tip. I showed this to James, who shook his head, smiled and clapped me on my shoulder, my right shoulder. Though the shoulder felt the same, I felt much better.

"That's twice now, Thomas," he said.

James again took charge, telling his servants, "This man assured me that rents had fallen to £200 a year because of bad harvests. That is why your wages fell in arrears. Now let us see how much he actually collected."

James reached into Pips' greatcoat pocket and pulled another leathern bag out. He walked over to the table, opened the bag and poured the money, all coin, mostly gold but some silver, onto the table top. We all gathered around as James counted the rent money. It came to £403/6. The servants were impressed by the money and by how much Pips was stealing.

"My brother trusted this creature," gesturing to Pips' corpse, "and my brother's trust was betrayed."

James walked to the bedroom door and pointed to the two bags. Clearly Pips was planning to flee with the money.

James told one of his servants, "Take the trap and go to the magistrate. Tell him what has happened. There must be an inquest and you both may have to tell what you saw."

Both servants nodded.

James turned to the other servant and said, "Bolt one of the doors and stand guard at the other. Don't allow anyone in until the magistrate gets here. Thomas, we must tell everyone at the Manor what happened."

So James and I set out for the Manor, our pockets filled with gold and jewels, gold and jewels that must be hidden before the Crown stepped in and seized everything. While James could probably recover most, it would require a suit at law and only God could tell when the money and jewels would return to their rightful owner.

I asked James, "Have you a hiding place?"

"I will tell Lady Chilterndale I found Mother's jewelry. I won't say where, but she will be happy—for a while."

James sounded sour. We were silent; then he resumed, "As to the money, I have a place, two places in fact. The rents I shall use to reestablish my stables, and… we had a custom here in my youth, of inviting the tenants and their families to the Manor for a feast, a harvest feast. I will do that as well. Let us say a fortnight, I think that will be notice enough. You and your wife are invited as well, of course."

We were at the cottage. I could see Caroline at the door. I waved, using my left hand and smiled. In fact, I grinned. We were returning in triumph, our pockets filled with booty, the villain killed…. No, that was not a memory I wanted to revisit.

James's thoughts were in a similar vein, for he said, "The fellow died cursing me! He hated me, though we had met only recently. Why, Thomas?"

I thought about this before essaying a reply. "Well, he realized he was likely to hang, that you had foiled his scheme…. No, I think there was more to it. You had everything he lacked: a title, an estate, the deference and respect of all, simply because of who your father and mother were. He would do you all the harm he could, merely because of that."

James asked, "Is that what the war in America is about, do you think?"

I shook my head and answered, "Only in part. Many of the people in America went there because they wanted to work for themselves and their families and not some noble. Perhaps those who stayed were more accepting, though Pips was not.

"In America, there are no formal gentry, that is, with titles, but people with money, land," here I thought of the Crewes, "think well of themselves, fancy themselves above their poorer neighbors. This angers some, and this resentment fuels some of the rebellion, though most don't take the pretensions of the well-off that seriously. No, I think the main reason for the rebellion is that the rebels *want to be left alone,* to strive to their uttermost, to better themselves and their families so they or their children may join the upper ranks of the populace."

We went through the front door of the Manor. Lady Chilterndale, George and his wife were sitting down to table. I pulled my watch out, my shoulder still felt painful, and I saw it was nearly noon. James nodded to them and we both went into James's study. He locked the door, set the bag with the rents on his desk and we pulled the bags of loot out of our pockets. The bags of money were heavy and my shoulder resented the effort I had to make.

"How much, do you think?" I asked James.

He lifted the money bags then told me, "Say two thousand pounds, perhaps more. Do you want to lunch with us, or will your shoulder hinder that?" He had noticed my discomfort.

I replied, "I will go back to Caroline and tell her what happened. And I may have patients. But I thank you."

James had set the bags in a place I could not see, I heard a key turn, he straightened up and said, "Let us join the others."

So we went out into the high-ceilinged hall.

James told the others, "You will hear of this shortly. Pips was stealing the rent money. When I told him to produce what he collected today, he drew a pistol and tried to shoot me. Thomas here saved my life, once again. In future, I will act as my own factor so this does not recur. I told Thomas I want to hold a Harvest Dinner in two weeks, with Thomas, his wife and the tenants and their families all invited. As we once did."

James nodded to me. I bowed to Lady Chilterndale and walked out the door to Caroline and our cottage.

9

SEE THE CONQUERING HERO COMES

———◆———

Caroline threw herself into my arms or rather arm. She noticed my discomfort and asked, "Are you wounded?"

I kissed her and shook my head before saying, "A shoulder dislocation, not too serious, just uncomfortable. Pips drew a pistol and tried to shoot James, but James shot and killed the factor. Pips was stealing all right, we think several thousand pounds and James's mother's jewelry. All recovered," here I glanced around, "but it is best not to talk of that. James wants to hold a Harvest Dinner for the tenants and their families once again. We are invited. I am hungry."

Caroline laughed and drew me into the room where we ate. There was a steaming tureen of soup. The servant was setting out bread.

Caroline asked, "Will you be able to eat?"

I assumed an air of gallantry and said, "Given the victuals and the service," smiling at the servant, "and most particularly the company," smiling at my wife, "I will manage."

And indeed I was able to.

After the meal, I remembered my profession and asked Caroline, "Any patients?"

She said, "One woman came in midmorning. I told her you were with Lord Chilterndale and I didn't know when you would return. She said she would return this afternoon. I think she was put out that you weren't here. Thomas, how did you come to dislocate your shoulder? You didn't tell me that."

I leaned forward and told my wife, "I thrust a fireplace poker into the barrel of Pips' pistol when he fired it. The jolt was considerable. James thinks I saved his life, but if anyone comments, you just tell them that I had James as a patient once and didn't want to do so again."

Caroline clapped her hands and laughed.

The woman did return shortly thereafter, and four more patients. I fancied some merely wanted to set eyes on a man of notoriety, as James was off limits. But I think the woman was mollified at being treated by a celebrity as it were, so I collected shillings and sixpences, dispensed advice and Caroline dispensed a drug, her first at Chilterndale. I gathered Pips was not a popular man, being considered harsh and unpleasant save of course to his employer, to whom he was considered excessively deferential. My regrets at having a hand in his death receded.

The next day I had a round dozen of patients. Aside from advice and several more drugs, I lanced an abscess, removed a wart and bandaged a mild sprain. My shoulder was still troublesome but I felt it was getting better. The following day, I walked round to each of the tenants' houses and found several people with injuries or diseases I endeavoured to treat. These I did not charge, explaining that Lord Chilterndale was paying me to treat his servants and tenants gratis. This news was very well received. And on my return, I found a roomful of patients from the village.

The next morning brought further custom, gratifying but I began to wish for some leisure, for walks with Caroline especially, as there were many paths, each with pleasant vistas. Caroline herself became more and more useful, talking to patients, calming them and cheering them into the bargain. This was in addition to compounding drugs and making up pills, so I was beginning to wonder how I could possibly function without her.

The early afternoon brought a servant from the Manor: George's wife was going into labour. This was a great surprise, unless the child was to be premature, in which case its survival was doubtful. But I picked up my medical bag, my shoulder indeed noticeably better, and walked quickly to the Manor. Lady Chilterndale's London specialist was going to lose this fee.

In the woman's bedroom, I barely had time to wash my hands and forearms before the child arrived. All I did was catch the infant, a girl. The baby began to breathe almost immediately, appeared fully formed so, as far as I could tell, was full-term. No wet-nurse had been engaged, so unexpected was the babe, so I told the mother to suckle her daughter herself. Lady Chilterndale, who was present unfortunately, demurred but I stared her down.

Once the mother was comfortable and nursing her child, I asked her how she could have been out on her delivery time.

She told me, "I just couldn't be certain. My menses are irregular, and I think that caused the confusion. Why did you wash your hands, Doctor?"

I replied, "I am not sure, but I believe cleanliness generally prevents sepsis, in this case, childbirth fever."

"Are you an empiricist, then, Doctor?"

I looked at George's wife, surprised, but answered her: "I daresay I am. If a drug or procedure works, I will employ it."

Silence, then I admitted, "I think theory should be based on facts, on results, not the other way about. We pretend we know so much, yet the reality is quite different. Is your father a physician?"

The woman smiled, "My father and his brother are both doctors. I can remember them arguing about just that point."

"Have you brothers who are doctors?" I asked.

She shifted her daughter to her other breast. Lady Chilterndale, I was happy to observe, had left. A maidservant wiped the new mother's forehead.

"Father and Mother had just three girls. I am the youngest. I was always interested in medicine but of course women can't be doctors."

I sat silent. Of course what she said was true, though there were examples of women doctors. And there was Caroline.

So I told George's wife, "I am certain my wife could be an excellent doctor. Though she cannot obtain the license because of her sex, she is a first-rate apothecary and a great help to me."

We both smiled at each other and I took my leave, telling her I would return that evening and again tomorrow morning.

I left the Manor without talking to James or George. Lady Chilterndale had undoubtedly informed them of the sex of the new arrival. Since George had not made an appearance, I guessed he was not happy at having a daughter. There were several patients waiting when I got back to the cottage, which I realized had become recognized as my surgery. That evening, in bed with Caroline, I told her about what had happened and how impressed I was with George's wife.

"I hope the fellow realizes how lucky he is, but I expect he doesn't."

Caroline only kissed me and we fell asleep together in each other's arms. George's wife and child were still healthy.

This remained true the following morning, but George's wife complained George had not yet been in to see her or their child.

I though George needed a kick up his arse, but merely told her, "I will speak to him."

Instead, I went to talk to James, as stronger compulsion than mere words from me was required. James was with Lady Chilterndale, a little surprising, but looking at them I saw Lady Chilterndale simpering and James appearing a trifle tired and more than a trifle embarrassed. I guessed they had resumed marital relations.

But perhaps together they could effect changes in George's behavior, so I told them, "George is ignoring his wife and child, both of whom continue in good health. What is he doing?"

I noted Lady Chilterndale was wearing some jewelry that almost certainly had belonged to James's mother. She seemed to object to my tone.

James answered: "Drinking port in the gunroom."

I offered, "I will warn him about port, but he needs to pay much more attention to his own family."

James told me, "Sit down, Thomas."

I did so, though Lady Chilterndale looked less pleased, apparently deciding to ignore my presence.

She told James, "I wish you would have that great wheeled chair of your brother's removed. It is unsightly."

James looked at her, then at me and said, "I will have it moved… moved so George can wheel his wife and babe about the grounds. That's it, there are several pleasant paths, all level enough, and that chair takes a fairly strong man to move it and… I will tell George all our manservants are at other tasks. It is a fine day as well."

James got up and went to have the chair shifted.

I addressed Lady Chilterndale, "My Lady, if you would, speak to your daughter-in-law about the proposed excursion, suggest she malinger a bit"—for George's wife was up and walking about at my suggestion much more than Lady Chilterndale thought appropriate—"and have her dress attractively for out of doors, this would help. I will go speak to your son."

Becoming a part of a stratagem seemed to appeal to her, as I guessed it might, and we separated for our respective roles.

I had to ask one of the servants where the gunroom was then went there and found George with a glass and a bottle that I guessed was port. I couldn't see how much was in the bottle but the day was yet little advanced.

I addressed him without preamble, "Your Uncle Charles' great wheeled chair is being brought downstairs. Your wife would greatly benefit if you would push her about in it. It takes a strong man and Lord Chilterndale told me he requires the manservants for other tasks."

George looked resentful but got to his feet. I picked up the bottle and looked at the label. It was indeed port.

I told George, "Sir, as a doctor serving this household, it is my duty to remind you that your uncle and grandfather both developed gout, which is produced by drinking port."

Here I was guessing but if I had to put money behind my guess, I would have wagered a substantial sum.

Seeing I had captured his attention, I continued, "And the gout, besides making their lives a misery, made them bedridden, which helped bring on the dropsy and that killed them."

He stared at me, half unwilling to believe me but at least I had warned him.

Outside, near the door to the Hall, stood a very large chair mounted on four, big, iron hooped, wooden wheels. It certainly looked heavy enough to require two men pushing or one strong one. I guessed this would appeal to George's vanity.

Lady Chilterndale appeared at the balustrade that circled the Hall and spoke to her son, who was trying the chair, to see how easily it could be moved, "George, come up and carry your wife down. I don't want her walking down stairs."

Lady Chilterndale glanced at me and I could almost swear she winked; clearly she had entered into the spirit of the enterprise.

I went through the servants' quarters seeking custom, but aside from minor symptoms, all appeared well. Then I emerged into what was indeed a fine day. Ahead I saw George's backside as he pushed the chair along. The chair seemed to roll easily. I walked up alongside, nodded to George, who was not perspiring much and bowed to his lady, who smiled at me.

George's wife was not especially pretty, but was dressed in clothes that certainly flattered her. She was clearly enjoying the outing.

As I passed them, I heard her say, "Oh, George, let us try that path, if you will."

And George changed the direction of the chair without a grumble or word of complaint. On I walked, thinking that George stood little chance against Lord and Lady Chilterndale and George's own wife, aside from me as well. Having James and Lady Chilterndale working together to help bring George and his wife closer should promote greater amity in that household. I reflected that a doctor's function was not confined to pills and nostrums.

I canvassed two of the tenants' families and servants over the remainder of the morning. Two of the labourers' wives were due in another month. I was stunned at their quarters: having their babies in a stable would be safer. On returning, I thought about bringing the women to our cottage to birth their children, but that required consulting Caroline.

Over lunch, once the servants had retired, I related the intrigue I had been a part of this morning. Caroline was amused.

"George has no chance," she agreed.

I also told her about the two labourers' wives near their term and the conditions during their delivery.

I asked, "Have we room for them to give birth here? Looking about when I came back, I confess I have my doubts."

Caroline shook her head, said, "There really is no room here, not for that. What about that house the factor lived in?"

I tried to imagine Pips' house put to that use. I eventually decided it would hold just two mothers, but that might be enough....

I said, "I will ask James."

On returning from visits to the remaining four tenants, I found three patients awaiting me at the cottage. Caroline and I dealt with them all, enjoyed a late dinner then retired to enjoy each other.

After, Caroline told me, "This is what I have dreamt about: my own place, my own family. By that I mean I am living and working for us, us alone and our future together. If we have children, I cannot imagine heaven being better."

I replied, "If I have made you happy, I am more than content." So the day ended.

The next day, patients appearing throughout the day kept us about the cottage. We did reach a decision respecting drink: Caroline had lived her life in London drinking beer and ale while I had grown fond, perhaps, as I confessed to her, too fond of rum. So we decided to drink rum-and-water or "grog" as the sailors called it. We mixed one part rum to three parts water and sipped that.

Three days later, James called on us with news and a souvenir. The coroner's jury ruled that James had acted in self-defense, so Pips was buried in an unmarked grave and no further action was taken. I had expected to be called as witness but only James testified. He told us this, and showed Caroline the poker I had thrust into Pips' pistol barrel with the pistol ball impaled on the tip of the poker.

James told us, "This will go over the mantle of the great fireplace."

He grinned at us and was turning to leave—he was driving Pips' trap—when I remembered the intrigue and asked him, "How are George and his wife getting on? Calling on her, we didn't discuss that."

James turned back to us and said, "George has been wheeling her about two or three hours a day. They both seem to enjoy the exercise. And I have gotten George to drink, and I think enjoy, rum-and-water. Oh, and George was persuaded to hold his daughter, so I think matters have improved considerably there."

Once more James turned to go, and once more turned back, "Upon my soul, I am becoming forgetful. I am driving to London early tomorrow to look at some horses. If you have letters or requests for things to buy, let me have them." Finally, with a wave, he left.

James reappeared the next morning in such very good time our cook had to awaken us. We hastily dressed—I had not time to shave—and we gave James Caroline's letter to her father and stepmother and one for Dora, along with my letter to David and Dora. We also had a list of medical items along with the shops where they could be purchased. I offered James money to pay for these, but he waved that away, saying it would be extracted from my *salarium*. Then he drove off in the trap, evidently overjoyed to be leaving Lady Chilterndale and George behind. Perhaps he also had a letter to post of his own, as I told Caroline. I did not know what arrangements he had made for corresponding with Emily and of course would not ask.

Despite the hour, there were three patients waiting. I went to shave and finished dressing while Caroline talked to them. Two more appeared by the time I did, and I guessed this would be a busy day.

Patients who came to the cottage were mostly townspeople. Tenants, their servants and their families were beginning to wait on my weekly visitations, unless someone had things to discuss of a private nature or else someone who required urgent treatment.

Townspeople we charged usually a few pence, on occasion as much as a shilling. Though our fees were modest, the pennies and odd silver mounted up, and Caroline and I were becoming increasingly confident we would clear over £50 a year in addition to the £50 James had agreed to pay me. With no rent and two servants also paid by James, we felt we would lack for nothing.

Some of the rush of custom derived from the absence of any doctor in the village these three years or more. I was beginning to realize the last, late doctor was not highly regarded. In fact, I was coming to view him in the same light. He was one of those men who relied heavily, nay almost exclusively, on cupping and bleeding. I had come to the conclusion that while bleeding was a useful treatment for apoplexy, it had no beneficial effect, and that was at best, on any other condition. My patients were surprised at this, but were for the most part accepting of my views. Of course, they had little alternative.

James was away three days, essentially on holiday I told Caroline. When he drove the trap to our door late that afternoon, he had two horses attached on behind, a very big, strong-looking grey and a glossy black pony. Though I saw he was pleased by his purchases, I felt he was happy for another reason, probably of a correspondence character. This he confirmed to me, handing me a letter apiece for Caroline and for myself along with our medical requests.

"Emily sends her regards. She and our son are well."

"Pray send her mine and Caroline's in your next," I replied, for I knew he would write to his American wife and soon. He nodded, climbed back into the trap and drove to his stables. I went inside, speculating that James had some discreet agent, probably a lawyer, in London to serve as intermediary for letters.

"James is trapped between the romantic and the real," I remarked to Caroline that night as we lay together in bed.

"You don't believe romance is real?" protested Caroline.

I thought, and finally amended my thoughts to, "Romance is a striving for, and of course a belief in, the ideal, the perfect, and reality is by its nature imperfect, irregular at times. James is, as I told you, trapped between two loves, for Chilterndale and his position and responsibilities and the other is his love for his Emily. I think if he had more confidence in his heir, he might just resign Chilterndale to George and return to America."

I lay silent at this point, thinking how George, by his behavior, was keeping his chances at such early inheritance of Chilterndale close to nil.

Caroline remarked, "Perhaps George's wife might improve George's behavior."

I replied, "In time she might. I will speak to James about Pips' cottage and our plans. I will also see if relations between George and his wife are improving, in the sense that George is starting to listen to her."

James agreed readily to our plans for Pips' cottage and further agreed to provide two servants, a scullery-maid and an upper servant who would live in the cottage and serve as a sort of nurse in residence. This disposed of, James took from around his neck a locket which he gave me to open and look at. It contained a very creditable likeness of Emily.

I handed it back to James, with the remark, "A very good likeness."

James returned it to its former place and told me, "Thomas, when I die, I want to be buried with this. My will charges you to assure that is done."

I was going to protest he had many years yet, but held my tongue and nodded.

As to George, I saw no evidence of miracles, but some of his greater attention to his wife, though this probably was because he wished to be lying with her once more. Still, that could be the basis for a better understanding between them. So I left the Manor that afternoon, after speaking to all the inhabitants save Lady Chilterndale, fractionally more optimistic.

The Harvest Feast was to be held on a night with a full moon, allowing everyone a better opportunity to return home safely, clouds permitting. This was to begin late afternoon. I had dealt with the day's patients; Caroline and I had bathed in the large tin tub and dressed in our finest liveries as we termed our garb. Caroline held my arm as we walked to the Manor. She held it very closely to her person, in fact, and I thought of suggesting we return to the cottage.

She said, "There will be tonight, my dear." So we continued.

In the Hall, all the tenants with their elder children were standing about, gazing at the weapons, portraits remaining and the Hall itself, as none of the children and not all of their parents had seen a Harvest Feast. There were twenty eight guests in all, including Caroline and myself, as there were but thirty two places at table. Drink was served on side tables: some rum, a deal of port—I thought James was trying to rid his cellars of as much as possible—and cider from this year's harvest. Caroline had a glass of port and I took one of cider, most aromatic and refreshing.

James was talking to a knot of tenants and Lady Chilterndale was very much the grand dame of the gathering, presiding over the ladies, perhaps overgracious and detectably condescending. George was talking overloudly to some of the other tenants and their older sons, giving his opinions on whatever crossed his mind, though he occasionally glanced at his lady. She was sitting on a sofa before the fire, talking to two of the wives.

Caroline and I were standing apart, occasionally sipping our drinks, when we noticed the other guests glancing at us and talking to each other, clearly about me. I heard the phrases "killed his man" and "downed two highwaymen" and "saved Lord James's life" with frequent looks at the poker and its leaden tip mounted above the mantle as James had promised. This made me feel uncomfortable, the more so because I saw it depriving George of much of his audience. The heir to the estate was becoming my enemy.

We were called to table and seated: James and Lady Chilterndale at the head, George and his wife next, facing each other, Caroline and I at the foot of the table. We were served: great masses of beef and pork, game pies (the season had started), apple and cherry tarts, greatly more than our company could possibly consume even over two days, but we all paid our respects to the meal.

There was no music, so no dancing, though James, called to speak, said he would try to arrange for that at next year's Feast. This was met by sounds of approval from the sons and daughters of the tenants. James further promised that next fall venison would be part of everyone's fare. This prompted considerably more enthusiasm, boding ill for the deer on the estate. Finally, the senior tenant rose and proposed a toast to Lord Chilterndale and his lady. This was drunk with cheers.

So we left under a bright moon in a cloudless sky to light our way. I began to wonder why Caroline seemed so happy and asked her, "Have you had some good news? You are in such good spirits."

Caroline leaned her head on my shoulder and told me, "I believe I am with child, our first child."

I stopped and embraced and kissed her. I could say nothing, my heart was so full. Then we continued our walk back to the cottage.

10

ET IN ARCADIA NOS

◆

Caroline and I stood on the foredeck of the ship, our arms about each other, steadying each other as we had done to counter the pitches and rolls of the Ship of Time as it carried the two of us together on our lives' journey. We were in sight of land, the coast of Massachusetts growing steadily more distinct and accented. Our children stood near us to see their new home.

In memory, our eighteen years at Chilterndale living in Lavender Cottage now seemed serene, unmarred by unhappiness. This though I could readily call to mind what the generality of human beings would term unhappy occasions or incidents, but our life together so softened such experiences that "Arcadia" was the only way we could describe that place. We were saddened by our loss, yet were still together so could look forward to returning together to my native province with near equanimity.

Our first child, a son named David after no-one in particular, arrived after several hours of labour, but otherwise seemed healthy and very alert. The delivery was in Pips' cottage, as we still called it. Prior to Caroline's lying in, it had seen some fifteen arrivals safe for both mother and child. I found dealing with my own wife and child was frightening, but there was no one else I could employ. And the aftermath found me exhausted, but I had to carry on.

There were two midwives in the village, and some preferred to employ them. By the time our second child arrived (a daughter which we named Susan after my bereaved younger sister), everyone in the village and estate were aware that my patients almost always survived, in contrast to those of the midwives. These women were sensible and experienced; so I recruited them to assist me and trained them in my ways. This greatly reduced any hostilities due to competition and improved maternal health in the region.

Because Caroline was three years older than I, these two children were all we had; but because they were both healthy, active children, we were content. George's wife produced three more children, two sons and another daughter, over our first seven years at the Manor. I attended all three occasions, the last threatening a breach delivery but I managed to turn the babe before he emerged. George's wife told me she had insisted I attend. This was to the unhappiness of Lady Chilterndale, who felt my services were insufficiently prestigious, and to George's somewhat more mixed feelings. George accepted my abilities but I think desired me to be more deferential, as he was of course the heir.

James was remotely pleased at his daughter-in-law's production. Otherwise, he was out on horseback in even faintly passable weather, often merely riding about visiting his tenants, or on hunts on the Chilterndale estate or abroad on hunts invited by his neighbors. He was universally acclaimed as a fearless rider and most determined huntsman. All admired his character.

As a master, he was revered for his good humour and open-handedness, the exact opposite of his brother. It was as though the estate was suddenly bathed in sunlight after a long night of reclusiveness by Lord Charles Chilterndale, though James and I (and Caroline) knew the real story was more complex. Villagers and tenants were much more reserved about George and more reserved still about Lady Chilterndale. George's only tolerably well-regarded habit was visiting the ale-house and talking to the other habitués, mostly about himself. He was otherwise being more attentive to his wife, who seemed to be extending her influence at the expense of Lady Chilterndale's.

George at one point had been interested in standing for Parliament, which ambition, I, James, Lady Chilterndale and George's wife all favoured for divers reasons. But James concluded a successful campaign would simply cost too much. At this news, George sulked a considerable time, but James showed his calculations to George and me. It was not a matter of wholesale bribery, though that was a factor. There were too many electors for James's purse. If there had been some popular cause that George could espouse, his chances would improve and James's expenditures would drop, but this was not the case. Of course as a peer, James could take his seat in the House of Lords whenever he wished, but had no interest whatever in politics. He confided to me, however, that if impeachment of certain ministers of H. M.'s Government were to be decided, he would certainly add his vote.

We were able to exchange yearly or twice-yearly visits with David and Dora, once Caroline's and my children were old enough. David, as a younger son, and Dora, also coming from a landed family, were acceptable to Lady Chilterndale for lodging at the Manor. This was necessary as Lavender Cottage was simply too small, now that David and Dora's brood had grown to four. With the children of George and Eleanor Montjoy being about the same age, David and Dora's visits to Chilterndale Manor were occasions for sustained uproar, whereat James smiled. Lady Chilterndale and her son were less pleased; Eleanor was tolerant.

Our visits to London had to be briefer, as my services might be required, instanter as the expression was. Still, our hosts extended themselves in every possible way to make our visits entertaining—though at times restful would have been preferable. We were able to call on Caroline's family as well, one which continued to grow despite death of some of Caroline's stepmother's children. As I remarked to Caroline, living in London was especially hard on children, but I did not know why. I was able to take Caroline to some plays and operas, along with David and Dora and the older children.

As our children appeared and grew, Caroline and I began to use Pips' cottage for all my practice, as we didn't want to expose our children to whatever our patients had. This was actually closer to the town, which pleased the townspeople, and also Lady Chilterndale, who had not been happy at having so many of the "lower orders" on the grounds of the Manor.

We were the only other "gentle" family always about: a curate gave the services at the parish church. [James told me the living had been sold, but there was nothing he could do about that.] Hence, our children and George's children were together a great deal. As was customary with James, he paid for the governess and tutor for our two and George's four children. Our children were extremely clever, George's four not so much so, yet Caroline's and my children were willing to help with the instruction of the others. All very amiable, but our children noticed a subtle division separating them from George's.

This came to a head when our Susan was made aware, I did not know how, that she and Charles Montjoy, George's older son, would not marry: our Susan had no money. Instead, there was talk of Charles marrying the daughter of a man who owned an adjoining estate. Our Susan was despondent. Our David, we suspected, had experienced a similar disappointment with respect to one of George's daughters, we were never made privy as to which. Otherwise, our David was not greatly interested in medicine but talked of reading law. David and Dora Withrow and Caroline and I had talked of matches between our children, but my children's attachments to the Montjoy children forestalled anything beyond talk.

Caroline and I were always aware of how fortunate we were: being together, our two children healthy and clever, living on a beautiful estate, with good friends here and in London to help sustain us. We hoped this would continue all our lives.

Only I was fully privy to James's profound regrets at his separation, probably forever, from Emily. When Lady Chilterndale persuaded James to pay for each to sit for portraits, James secretly had a miniature of himself painted as well. This was sent to Emily, along with occasional amounts of money. They exchanged letters every two or three months. After the war ended, Emily, their son and her mother and father were able to return to Connecticutt: her parents' holdings, some of them at any rate, were restored. I rather thought that James's frequent sojourns were partly an escape from his unhappiness. But I could not criticize his decision, especially as I was a major benefactor in a sense.

I remembered one bright morning. Caroline and I had come from Pips' cottage to our home to eat, when James rode up. He was just from London, the picture of a Cavalier, and in high good spirits.

"Hear are your letters and the medicines you had requested."

"How much do I owe you for these? I would fain retrieve it inside."

He waved me off. "The monies will come from your *salarium*."

Since he had yet to do any such thing, Caroline and I smiled. I guessed he had received a letter from Emily and he rode off, smiling himself. I turned to Caroline, who was watching his departure with a quizzical smile on her face.

She turned to me, put her arm through mine, and commented, "I quite prefer a man with both feet on the ground."

We went inside and dined with our children.

Correspondence had resumed between my Massachusetts family and myself. Lizzie had married her Daniel and had given life to four children, one named Thomas. Susan kept house for Father; she would not marry, though she had several offers. Father now had apprentices himself, so his business was prospering. They seemed to accept that I had chosen to be an Englishman.

It all ended suddenly. One of the labourers found James's horse loose but nuzzling at something and that something was James. He had been thrown, had fallen off, or struck his head on a limb; a mortal blow that had also broken his neck. The man ran all the way to Lavender Cottage where I was eating supper. He was crying, for James was loved by all. I went immediately but to no avail. The labourer ran on to the Manor to gain more assistance, and James's body was borne back to the Manor by his servants, in some state, and with mourning.

James had appointed me to be in charge of his funeral, his will stated that. George, now Lord Chilterndale, could not gainsay the will. I knew that James wanted to be buried with Emily's miniature. He also wanted me to secure Emily's letters and return them to her. She would get some money. I was to see to this, but keep it secret; the last of Pips' loot was to go to her. I had to write to her, a heavy task:

> *My dear Mrs. Montjoy*
>
> *I am writing to you, for James cannot. He died of a fall from a horse. I believe he felt no pain so died as he would wish, riding full tilt of a fresh-scented summer morning on his beloved estate, his day's duties done. Yet I know his grief over his separation from you and his son darkened his every living hour.*
>
> *He charged me to send you your letters, to join with his to you, for your son to perhaps read someday. He was buried with your miniature about his neck, so in yet another sense you are joined to him for all time.*
>
> *He was my friend, and I shall always miss him, though of course you have been missing him these eighteen years.*
>
> *He also left you some money, about £400, which will be sent you and James Jr.*
>
> *Please accept these few words of condolence, as they are all I can muster.*
>
> *Thomas Wyeth*

The grief felt at his funeral was universal, even by the now dowager Lady Chilterndale and George the new Lord Chilterndale. Though hardly was it over, and James buried, before George—I could not think of him in the same light as James—informed Caroline and I that the dowager Lady Chilterndale was to remove to Lavender Cottage, so Caroline, our children and I would have to leave. I had the impression the new Lady Chilterndale very much wanted George's mother out of what was now her house. And the cottage was built for just that purpose.

Only in our bed could Caroline and I talk, without having our children, our servants or our patients overhearing.

I told Caroline, "I could probably persuade George Montjoy to permit us to stay in the village could we find a dwelling we could rent, to be my patron in other words. But while James was my patron, he was my friend, that above all. And I lack the stomach to seek a new patron, be it George or anyone else. I realize I am simply too much a provincial, no, too much an *American,* to seek or tolerate patronage."

Caroline asked, "What about your patients?"

There was silence as I shifted in bed before replying, "That is the only consideration keeping me here, a most puissant consideration to be sure, and I daresay I would miss this place as well. But everything else is drawing me back to Massachusetts. But give me your thoughts, pray."

Caroline was silent in her turn before telling me, "As long as we are together, our location is not as important. I would miss David and Dora, miss them greatly, as I am sure you would as well."

"Indeed," I said, ashamed of having forgotten them, "but we have to think, it seems to me, of our children, them above all. In America their lack of a personal fortune would be much less important. And our David can establish himself in the law without cost to us, while our Susan can certainly attract suitors who can support her and their children."

"Susan can teach school if needs be," remarked Caroline.

"That is true," I agreed. And so our decision to quit England was made.

Letters from both Lizzie and Susan had told me that Father would like to set eyes on his son and two grandchildren by me at least once before he died, as did my sisters. And if David wished to read law, what better place than with his grandfather? Further, getting our Susan (and David) away from being constantly reminded of their failed romances could only help them recover. So I told George that Caroline and I would leave to return to America, giving up the practice I had here for eighteen years. I think George was pleased, but I also thought the rest of the souls here in Chilterndale would not be, so I foresaw a long period of unhappiness in this parish.

We removed from Lavender Cottage to London, where we stayed with David and Dora while we obtained passage on a ship to Boston. Our farewells from our friends of over twenty years were sad indeed, though David and Dora both agreed with our reasoning. Their own children would either have to find heirs or heiresses to marry or struggle many years, even as their parents had.

Over the years as Caroline and I worked together, we were not accumulating a fortune—whatever we had saved went for our children's educations, our David at Eton while our Susan attended a good, female academy in London, staying with David and Dora. Yet, we had all we needed otherwise, and as I observed one evening to Caroline, that was wealth indeed. She kissed me in response, which I took for agreement.

V

Massachusetts, 1797

1

FULL CIRCLE

———◆———

Boston Harbour appeared more crowded than I recalled from my departure nearly a quarter-century ago; I fancied there were more buildings as well. A light east wind took us past a great warship flying American colours at anchor. "Constitution," a fellow passenger told us, "48." That meant it was only a frigate, though its size was nearly that of a ship of the line.

We were able to tie up to a quay and walk ashore. Everything was busy, like London but without the smoke, pickpockets or whores. I inquired until I found the location of a coach to take us to Shrewsbury. Unfortunately that was not until tomorrow morning. Until then, we would rent quarters at the inn the coach started from, as my Uncle Holmes had died this last winter. We dined at the inn as well. David and Susan thought the meals aboard the ship were better, whereat I thought them addled, or, on reflection, simply unhappy at leaving Lavender Cottage.

We arrived in Shrewsbury about mid-afternoon after an extraordinarily early start. I knew where we were, though the town had grown and become much more bricked than when I had left. I knew where we were to go. So, with bags and parcels festooning us, we walked the half mile in weather that was warmer than Caroline or our children were accustomed to, arriving at my family's house sweating, tired, and, in the case of the children, thoroughly out of sorts.

Father and Susan were there, along with a boy about David's age. Father, whom I left tall and robust, was now grey and stooped. Well, I was greying too, as was Caroline. Susan looked much the same save for her eyes, in which I could see sadness, despite the years. The boy was Thomas Mechin, Lizzie's son and so David's cousin. He was also to read law with his grandfather. We were told that Lizzie and Daniel lived in a new brick house about a mile away.

For New England, our greetings were boisterous, though David and Susan were not yet accustomed to New England reserve. I could see that Father was delighted at having two grandsons to read law with him. My younger sister was pleased at having a namesake. She praised the beauty and height of mother and daughter, compliments which I could see garnered a mixed response from the younger Susan. Father insisted we stay with them, though this made for cramped quarters. And we were tired, tired of traveling.

The meal was abundant in quantity, though Caroline, David and Susan were not yet used to New England cuisine. I related our travel experiences. Father and Susan told me the town very much needed another doctor, and one with my qualifications and experience would be a Godsend. My Loyalist sympathies and even service in the British Army now might even be considered in my favour. We did need to start to work, as we had brought less than £60 from England; just about the amounts I had crossed the Atlantic with on four occasions now. Ann's remark on our parting had been prescient.

David, Susan and Thomas went out to meet their Aunt Lizzie and Uncle Daniel. I was happy to see my nephew friendly with his cousins. Tomorrow Caroline and I would visit my sister's home. For now, we were tired and would sleep in my old bed, hopefully without the fleas, for I saw no cat.

As we rose to retire, Father said, "We are very glad you are come home, Thomas."

I smiled, shook my head, exchanged a glance with Caroline, and replied, "No, sir, I brought my home with me," and my wife and I, arms across each other's shoulders, went to bed.

JOURNEY'S END